ROSE-TINTED

HARTMAN SISTERS
BOOK ONE

A.N. LEE

First Edition: April 2026

ISBN: 979-8-9944304-2-2 [digital]

979-8-9944304-0-8 [paperback]

Editing: Amy Pritt

Cover Design: A.N. Lee

A.N. Lee

Visit the author's website at www.authoranlee.com

CONTENTS

AUTHOR'S NOTE

Rose-Tinted contains several explicit sexual scenes, explicit language, and scenes dealing with past trauma (car accident). *Rose-Tinted* is not suitable for young readers. Happy reading!

CHAPTER ONE

DIEGO

"Whatever you do, you better pray for a miracle or you'll be bankrupt by next season." I overhear the accountant tell my dad and grandfather.

I knew the winery was slower than usual, but I didn't realize it was nearing bankruptcy. We opened a small shop in the city that offered wine tastings, in hopes to bring more publicity to our brand. But that was a few years back, I guess it hasn't had the desired effect.

"Diego?" Mom's voice startles me.

Turning around, I see she spotted me on her way into the office. "Mom!"

She looks around, suspicious given her furrowed eyebrows. "Everything alright?"

Oh hell, no reason to beat around the bush with this one. "Is the winery going bankrupt?"

"Who said that?" She feigns confusion, but I can always see past her acts.

"I just heard Hugo say that to Dad and Grandpa." Mom bites her lip, eyeing the door Dad and Grandpa are currently occupying. I scoff at her blatant attempt to hide the truth. "So, it *is* true then. Why didn't you say anything to Mia or me?"

"And you could do what? No, this is our problem, not you kids'." She palms my cheek, looking up at me. "You and Mia are too young to worry about it."

"Too young? Hate to break it to you Mom, but I'm thirty-two and Mia's no kid either."

"Yeah, but you're still not as old as your dear *mamà*." She winks then shoos me away. "Now go back to what you do best. That's all the help we need right now." I nod and give her a soft smile before walking out of the office, down the stairs to the stock room.

Some days I take living out here for granted. I'm surrounded by architecture that has withstood over one hundred and fifty years. When I was a young boy, I would call this building a castle. And looking at it now as an adult, I'd say that assessment was pretty accurate.

Its fortress-like stone walls build up the foundation to the house itself. Well, the old house that is. Grandpa converted the space to include a public tasting room and office space in the late 1970s, and it's seen several renovations since.

Our family's house is across the stone path from the office. It's built in a similar manner, stone walls with a castle-like feel, with plenty of bedrooms for our multi-generational family.

In the more recent years, we bought a property in the city, using it as a small wine shop, providing a place for tourists to sample and buy our products. In the beginning, I was the one running it. It made more sense at the time for me to buy an apartment in the city, but I don't use it all too much now. It's mostly lent out to my sister when she needs a break from living here with Mom and Dad, or if the shop stays open late.

It takes a little over an hour to get from the vineyard to our shop in Barcelona, and driving when it's dark can get dangerous, especially with how Mia drives. I love my baby sister, but her driving is some of the worst I've ever seen. It's just better for Mia, and safer for all of Spain, for her to stay the night in the city, then drive back to the winery the following day.

I start my morning off by heading to the stock room below the office and putting together a few orders for Mia to bring with her into the city. Most orders include our family's classic Grenache.

It's a wine we've used for generations and we don't dare to touch that bottle's process. We do, however, each take our own liberties with the seasonal labels, including some of our revolving GSM blends. Though finding the winning ratio of Grenache, Syrah, and Mourvèdre is an art form all in and of itself.

If you lean heavier on the Grenache, the wine will taste lighter and a bit fruitier. Most times you'll pick up on the spice notes with a Syrah heavy recipe. And the more Mourvèdre you have, the bolder and more structured the profile becomes, most times giving notes of dark fruit and smokiness. Which basically equates to a wide variety of flavor profiles with this red blend.

While I do favor experimenting with the GSM, my personal favorite is our Syrah. I enjoy the heaviness as well as the peppery aftertaste. There are a few bars in Barcelona that carry it, thanks to me putting a little pressure on their owners. But the orders keep coming in, and those guys don't like me *that* much to just give me pity orders. If they're ordering it, it's because the wine's getting asked for.

"Diego!" Mia comes strutting in the cellar. "You almost got those orders ready? I'm leaving in ten."

"Relax, Mia. I'm finishing up the last one now. Help me load them?" I ask, putting the last two bottles in their boxes.

"Fine." She huffs, reluctantly walking over to grab a box. "Dad's in a mood this morning."

I scoff. No surprise there, after what I overheard earlier. "Yeah? What happened?"

"He just gave me shit about not taking my role here seriously. How I'm always dodging the hard work and spending too much time at the shop in the city, not helping out enough over here."

While the statement does hold merit, he shouldn't be dumping all his anger out on Mia. "You know, the usual stuff for his *favorite* daughter." The word favorite drips in sarcasm.

"I'll talk to him, sis." I promise as we head back and grab more boxes. I stopped allowing Dad to talk to me like that years ago, but unfortunately, the same can't be said about Mia. I do my best speaking up whenever I hear about it, but as we've gotten older, Mia just internalizes it.

"Don't worry about it." She attempts to shrug it off, but I know her better. "It's true anyway."

"Hey." I step in front of her, demanding her attention. "Don't do that to yourself. And if you're not happy here, we can figure something out, okay?" Lowering myself to her eye level, I continue. "There's no reason you should feel obligated to stay here, Mia. You deserve to be happy, and if this isn't making you happy, let's find something that will."

Mia pats my shoulder as we walk back over to load more orders. "Thanks, Diego. You know the same goes for you too, right, big brother?"

"We're not talking about me."

She just rolls her eyes and playfully shoves my shoulder. "That's right. The dragon *loves* his lair." I shove her shoulder right back, and she rolls her eyes. We finish loading the rest of the boxes before she drives out for the day.

I attempt to talk to Dad about the conversation I overheard as well as what he said to Mia, but he's not in the office. For all I know, he might have gone into town with Mom. He does that whenever he's stressed about the winery. His own little version of escapism.

Dad wasn't really given a choice of this life either. It's just been expected as a member of this family, that you pour all of your energy into this winery. Everything else comes second and I mean everything.

He's always tried to be present when he can, but ever since I can remember, he's been busy with the winery. Over the last five or so years, Grandpa has slowed down drastically, causing Dad to take over as head of the business.

During that time, I've waited for him to give me more responsibility, but nothing has changed. Dad instead doubled his work load. I always knew something had to give, I just never thought he'd let it get this bad before asking for help.

Technically, he still hasn't asked for help, but hopefully that'll change after this last conversation with the accountant.

I walk out to one of the vineyards. Inspecting the leaves and grapes as I stroll the grounds. It's quiet here, which makes it easy to get lost in your own thoughts. Once you get a few rows deep, you start to lose cell service which is why we're supposed to keep a walkie on us while traversing out here. It's a damn shame I'm so forgetful, most times it conveniently slips my mind to grab one.

I lose track of wandering the endless rows, soaking in the sun and thinking about ways to save the winery from closing or even selling. It's been in our family for over a century and though I may not be opposed to selling it, I know it would devastate the rest of the family.

"There you are!" I hear Mom before I see her. "We've been calling you for what feels like an hour." She pauses, taking in the sight of me. "You forgot the walkie again, didn't you?" she asks with a knowing glare in her eyes.

She hates it when I do this. Something about being irresponsible since there's no cell service out here.

"I'm sorry, Mom. Is it time for lunch already?" I ask as we start to head back to the house.

"I know this morning was a little chaotic but—"

"Why haven't you told us how serious this is?" I scold.

"Your dad didn't want you worrying about it until you needed to."

"Well, I guess it's time to start worrying, huh?" I take a calming breath. Mom doesn't deserve me taking my frustration out on her.

"You and Dad keep forgetting Mia and I are grown adults." I

put my hand on her back, softening my tone as I continue. "You don't need to shelter us. This is our future, too. It affects *all* of us. Had I known how serious the situation was, I could've done something sooner." She nods as we reach the edge of the vines. "From what I heard, we have less than a year to turn this around before the decision to sell is made for us."

Mom remains quiet for the remainder of the walk back. We continue that silence through lunch until Dad and Grandpa enter the dining room. I figure I don't have anything else to lose, so fuck it.

"Dad, I overheard you talking about finances this morning with Hugo." He drops his fork and looks up from his plate across the table. "I'd like to help save the family business."

CHAPTER TWO

EMMA

"We should be landing in Barcelona in the next fifteen minutes. We know you have several options to choose from when flying and we thank you for choosing us for your flight today." I hear over the loudspeaker of the plane.

Man, that flight went by super quick. After an eventful past couple of weeks, I'm excited to start my time in Spain. I've worked my ass off this past year after getting my MBA, and it didn't go unnoticed. When this overseas position opened up, I was the first to apply.

Surprisingly, there weren't too many people who were interested in the position, most wanting to stay in Raleigh and not liking the idea of uprooting their life to Spain. But I, for one, am excited for the change of scenery and the opportunity it will bring for my future with the company.

I was born and raised in North Carolina, never even left the state. Up until now that is. I did all my college education and internships in town. Moving out of my parents' house and into my college dorm was one of the biggest changes in my life, followed up by my move from my dorm to my apartment. I rent a cute little studio by my office. Close enough that I can walk almost everywhere I need to.

When I got the overseas promotion, I decided it would be easier to keep my apartment and just pack a few of the necessities for the month and a half I'd be there. There's no reason to end my lease when I'll be back in a few weeks. Plus, I'm not having to pay rent in Spain, since the firm owns a few apartments in the blocks surrounding the office, lending them out to their temporary associates. Which I guess is me now.

The only bummer is, since I'm *not* paying for it, the firm decides on which apartment I receive. But lucky for me, I won the jackpot in terms of apartments. I've seen a couple pictures of the place I'll call home while in Barcelona, it's definitely Pinterest worthy and very spacious. Much more than the five-hundred-square feet-studio I have in Raleigh.

In fact, there's so much room that my three sisters could easily visit whenever they want to. Now, whether or not they make the flight over is a different story. I know my oldest sister, Tory, is always trying to find ways to save money, so I don't expect her to make the trip over. But Taylor and Lindsay, the twins, are both in a spot in their lives where they could take a short trip over the Atlantic.

Lindsay has so much unused vacation time saved up, she could probably take six months off and still have days to spare. While Taylor doesn't work in the conventional sense, she does a lot of work with nonprofits, making her calendar a little more flexible. But now that we all have passports, maybe a little trip overseas is warranted.

We did a sister-date at the post office a few weeks ago, in the hopes I'd get this promotion. Well, that and Taylor has a honeymoon in Italy later this year. But it looks like the positive vibes paid off.

Leaving the plane, I'm quick to pass through customs and collect my bag at baggage claim. My firm has a car service that they use to pick employees and clients up at the airport and to use around the city, which I will definitely be taking full advantage of.

I'm not a fan of driving. Correction, I'm not a fan of being in a car altogether. The thing is, I'm afraid of cars, and the damage people can do with them. Metal death traps on wheels.

When I was younger, I was involved in a car crash with my mom and sisters. Ever since then, I've never felt comfortable riding in a vehicle, let alone even *attempting* to drive. Because of that, I always try to walk whenever I have the option.

Thankfully, most places are in close proximity to me back home, and when I checked out my new neighborhood, the same can be said for Barcelona. I just have to get there without having a panic attack on the car ride into town first.

I'm greeted by a man in a black suit with one of those signs you see in movies that reads "Miss Hartman." He insists on taking my bags for me while we walk to the sedan parked in the passenger pickup zone outside, a driver already waiting inside. I confirm the address when I slide into the leather seat in the back, quickly buckling my seatbelt, and we leave shortly after.

I took Spanish back in high school, but needed a little bit of practice before I flew over. It was only after I felt confident enough for the trip, that a co-worker let me know there's another language used in Barcelona—Catalan. Lucky for me, most people speak both in Barcelona, so I shouldn't have too much of an issue.

The drive was quick, thankfully filled with a bunch of beautiful sites to see out the window to distract me.

Pulling out my phone, I text my family.

EMMA:

Made it safe and sound! Love you all and I'll
text soon.

It's still early morning for them, so I'm not surprised when my phone doesn't chime for the remainder of the drive.

Focusing on all the sights surrounding me instead of the tornado of emotions swirling within, I set my eyes on the calming shoreline to the east, enjoying how the view changes the more we drive.

I busy myself watching all the people walk around the city streets, admiring the architecture as we get deeper into the city. I even spotted some castles a couple miles back, some of which I'm sure are centuries old.

When I researched the neighborhood's walkability, I came across a plethora of shops, bars, and even some upscale restaurants. I don't believe I could have chosen a better location for my stay myself. My building is only a five minute walk away from my office, and the most popular market is within a few minutes walk down the other direction.

It's midday when I get to the apartment, and the streets are busy with people. Some are walking, some riding their bikes, and others are driving to get to their next destination.

The sun hides between a few clouds, keeping the temperature cool and enjoyable. There's a light breeze in the air when I step out of the car, just enough to lightly tangle my long wavy hair. I was, and still am, teased by my older sisters on how "the kitchen must've run out of ginger when I was made," leaving me with strawberry blonde hair instead of the coppery hue of my sisters'.

My temporary apartment building has a very lively look to it, windows on almost every floor are open, fabric from the curtains blowing in and out of the framed squares.

There's a busy tapas bar on the ground level, currently buzzing with activity inside, as well as having every table outside filled. I can definitely see myself enjoying multiple meals here.

Leading the driver through the door, I attempt to tip him but he shakes it off, only accepting my thanks after he brings the last of my bags up.

My welcome email from my new branch manager said they'd leave everything I need at the front desk. I do a quick scan of the room and find a gentleman who's currently on the phone. I walk up to the desk and wait to be helped. After he hangs up, he smiles. "*Bona tarda.*"

That's not Spanish. I'm having to make an educated guess on what he's saying, maybe good afternoon, given how close it sounds to *buenas tardes*.

"*Hola!*" I greet. "My name is Emma Hartman. Javier said you would have a key waiting for me?"

"Ah, yes, Emma. Do you have your passport so I can verify your identity?"

"Yes," I rifle through my purse to grab my passport as quickly as possible. "Shit." I mumble under my breath when I can't find my passport immediately.

While rummaging through my purse, a few things spill out, including a boarding ticket, a snack I bought on the flight, and the book I read on the plane. And of course, it's the book where the main character is dating almost half the hockey team, the steamy cover art not helping one bit to hide the content inside.

You know what, it's fine. I'm sure this fine gentleman might enjoy a spicy book rec. Who knows? Maybe in two weeks, we'll be grabbing coffee and talking about our favorite reverse harems.

Reaching to the deepest depths of my bag, I finally run my fingers on what feels like the cover of my passport. Pulling it out, I hand the little blue book over to the gentleman behind the desk, the gentleman who *definitely* just did a double take of my book cover. "Here you go." I smile, picking everything up and stuffing it back into my tote bag.

He flips it open, does a quick glance at my information, then closes it, handing the book back to me in a matter of seconds. "Perfect. Everything is good. Here are your keys." He hands me a set of what looks to be antique keys. "The smaller one is for the top lock and the larger one is for the main lock. The elevator is out of service right now, and honestly, I'm not sure when it's going to be fixed." He peeks over the counter and looks at my stack of suitcases. "Would you like some assistance with your bags?"

I wave my hand like it's no big deal. "Oh no, but thank you. The walk will be nice after all that time cramped on the airplane."

But fuck, I'm definitely going to be getting my work out with bringing them all the way up to . . . wait what floor is it again?

"Are you sure? You're at the top. That's four flights of stairs," concern and doubt clear in his voice.

I try, and fail, to resist the help after hearing how many steps I have in my future. "You know what? I would appreciate some help, if you don't mind."

"Oh, absolutely! You take what you can. I'll be right behind you."

"Thanks so much." I grab one of the larger bags and my small roller, leaving the other large roller for him. I'm beyond excited to see what this place looks like.

I take each flight of stairs slowly and carefully, all while my anticipation builds, sweat running down my back for the extra sixty pounds or so I'm hauling up the steps. It's not very hot out, since it's still early April, but I'm working up a sweat hauling the bags up these steps. At least I won't need to workout after doing this.

Who am I kidding? Me? Working out? Never.

While catching my breath between floors, I look down and really take in how beautiful the stairs are. The steps are made from some type of smooth stone and give a warm feeling with its creamy undertones. Each floor feels light and airy making everything seem cozy and inviting.

We finally reach the fifth floor, and I get the first look of the wooden door that leads to my apartment. I use the keys to unlock the door and am welcomed by ethereal natural light shining from the outdoor balcony into the living room and kitchen.

The front door opens right into the open concept living area. The gentleman drops off my remaining bag and I give him my thanks again. "Oh, wait," I shout from inside the apartment. "What was your name?"

He stops at my threshold, turning around and smiling. "Manuel, Miss Hartman."

Extending my hand out to shake, I smile. "A pleasure to meet you, Manuel. I'm sure we'll be seeing a lot of each other. Have a great day and thank you so much for the help with my bags." I make a mental note that while I'm out tomorrow, I need to pick up something special to thank him for his assistance.

Immediately locking the door when I'm alone, I do a more thorough inspection of the place, even though it already looks like paradise.

A bottle of wine is waiting for me on the kitchen bar counter. I open the card attached to it and see it's a gift from the branch manager, Javier, welcoming me to the city.

The bartop doubles as the dining area, while the living room is just left of it. The patio doors leading outside take up almost the entire back wall near the couch, allowing plenty of sunshine to brighten up the space, the view of the patio tempting me to explore the outside space before the rest of the apartment.

I step outside and can immediately tell that someone put a lot of time and effort into this space. The floor is covered in wood tiles and the furniture is all teak, very contemporary and chic-*teak* furniture.

An eight person table sits on one side, while a couch and chair set is on the other. There are an abundance of potted plants around the space, with string lights reaching from one corner to the opposite. A net covers the space, protecting it from birds, at least, that's what I assume it's for. The rail surrounding the edge is just tall enough to let me peek down to the street, but still keeping the balcony super secluded, making me feel like I'm in my own private oasis. I'll definitely be spending most of my time out here, at least when I'm not at the office or enjoying that tapas bar downstairs that is.

I reluctantly walk back inside, deciding to explore the rest of the apartment. There's a skinny little hallway, just off of the kitchen, that leads to all three bedrooms and two bathrooms, one of which is an ensuite. Though the bedroom with the ensuite is probably the primary bedroom, I decide to make the one at the end of the hallway mine for the next few weeks.

It has the largest space, and the biggest bed. Plus the view outside to the street below is my favorite out of all of the rooms. The only downside is that the bathroom isn't connected, but it's just outside of my door. And really, the only time I plan on having people over is when, and *if*, my sisters visit, so it's no big deal to be walking around naked from my bathroom to my bedroom. Hell, I could even cook naked if I wanted to.

Returning back to the entry, I grab my bags and roll them to their new room. What a perfect start to this new season of life.

CHAPTER THREE

DIEGO

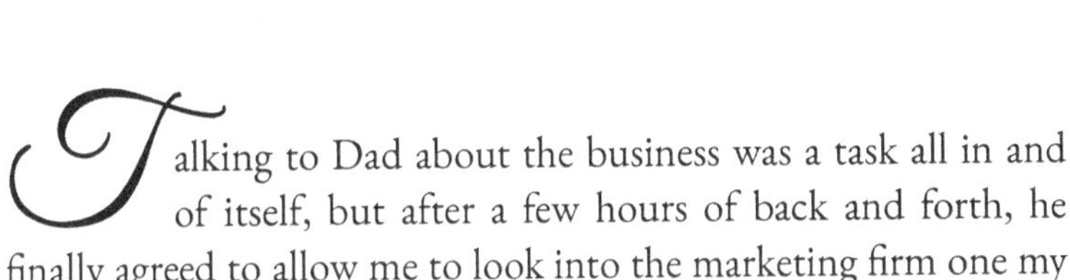

Talking to Dad about the business was a task all in and of itself, but after a few hours of back and forth, he finally agreed to allow me to look into the marketing firm one my friends, Lorenzo, used.

About two years ago, Lorenzo worked with the firm to help grow his business. Now, he has over five thriving locations, and last time we talked, he was looking to expand even more.

Surprisingly, Dad is allowing me to take the lead on this. After promising to call the firm in the next couple of days, I say my goodnights, heading to my room for the remainder of the night.

I hear a knock on my door a little later. Pulling it open, I find it's Mia, but her eyes are red and swollen. She's definitely been crying.

"What happened? Did Dad say something again?" I motion her to come into my room.

Mia grabs one of my pillows and sits at the edge of the bed, hugging the pillow tight up against her. "I got my license revoked." She cries out before covering her face with the pillow.

"What? How did that happen?" I mean, I know she can be a

reckless driver, but she hasn't gotten any tickets before to cause it getting taken away, at least none that I know of.

In Spain, the average person has twelve points on their license, though some have eight and others, up to fifteen. For every violation, there's a corresponding point deduction, three point deduction being the lowest. You can get this for not wearing a seatbelt, helmet, or using your phone while driving. Six points is the highest, but that's normally for reckless driving, like being caught going double the speed limit or driving under the influence. Which leads me to my original question, what the fuck did Mia do?

"Well that's the thing," her eyes peek out at me over the edge of the pillow, still hiding the majority of her face. "I may or may not have had a few tickets over the last year . . . " She trails off, clearly not wanting to talk about this.

"Okay," I exhale out, "but that means you had to have gotten a lot of tickets. Or you got caught driving recklessly." I nod to myself. "Which I guess isn't *all* too surprising." I thought I said the last part under my breath, but given Mia's reaction, I failed.

"Hey!" Mia throws the pillow she was holding right at me. "That's not true!"

As I catch the pillow, I quickly retort, "You're the one without the license." Keeping the pillow, I walk over and take a seat next to her on my bed.

"Ugh!" She falls back on my mattress. "What am I going to do? Now I'm stuck here until I do stupid driving school and retake the test."

"Why didn't you take a course to make up for the points after your first few tickets?" That's what you're *supposed* to do after getting a ticket.

Raising herself back into a sitting position, she smiles sheepishly. "Because I forgot." I drop my head, shaking it because of course she forgot. How very Mia of her. "What?" She shrugs. "I've been really busy, and it just . . . slipped my mind I guess."

I turn my head, facing her again. "Have you told Mom yet?"

"No, but I'm not sure I need to." She adjusts herself so she's facing me. "I might be able to fix it without her knowing, if I have your help that is." Ah, there it is. The true reason she's here. "I would just need you to take me to my testing appointment when the time comes."

"I can do that—"

Mia cuts me off. "And maybe do all the deliveries." I nod along in acceptance. "*And* take over the shop in the city for the foreseeable future."

"Mia!"

"What?" She shrugs like it's no big deal what she just asked me to do. "It's just until I can get my license back." She's so full of shit. I know it takes a minimum of six months to earn back your license. "Plus it'll be good for you to spend some time away from the winery. Trust me, the shop is much more entertaining than spending all your time up here." She does have a point there. "Come on, Diego. Please? Don't you get lonely being up here? You might even find someone who will *finally* agree to date you."

"You're not exactly making me want to help you." I lower my head but perk back up when the last part of what she says registers. "And for the record, I have no problem getting dates."

"Oh please." She scoffs and crosses her arms. "You're so grouchy and alone up here. Like a dragon guarding his treasure. Only your treasure comes in green bottles."

"Fine." Rolling my eyes, I point at her. "But you have to pick up my slack here at the winery."

"Deal!" Mia jumps up and gives me a big squeeze. "Oh you really are my favorite brother, you know that?"

"I'm your *only* brother." I huff out.

"Semantics." She steps out of our hug and goes to leave my room, leaning against the doorframe as she adds, "Really, thank you, Diego."

"What are brothers for? Now go, before I change my mind." That makes her bolt out.

I'm already in the city a couple times a month with my

current routine. I try to make the trip once every week or so, visiting our customers or helping Mia out if she has a large group. Now that I'll have more time in the city, maybe I could make the most out of it. Maybe even find more restaurants or stores to stock our wine. Something to drive the profits up. Then again, my time might be tied up depending on how involved I need to be with the new marketing firm.

A few days into my new schedule, I'm surprised with how much I'm enjoying the change. Mia wasn't the most organized when it came to delivery orders, but she always got it done, so I didn't need to correct her. Now that I'm doing them, I get to make some changes.

I start by streamlining the process, boxing up all the orders at the start of the week so they are at the shop, ready for their scheduled day of delivery. This past week we've had a decent amount of reservations and walk-ins for the shop, keeping me busy. But all of that is just another drop in the bucket compared to what we need to rescue the business.

One of the bright sides of me being in the city more often is getting more opportunities to eat at my favorite restaurants, including the one I chose for lunch today.

Walking into the tapas bar across the street, I'm greeted by the amazing smell of all the different dishes they offer. I never get tired of their food. The menu isn't huge, but it doesn't need to be, since everything on it is delicious.

Seriously, it's some of the best tapas in Barcelona. Which is probably why Lorenzo was so successful with his expansion. It's normally pretty busy, and with it being close to La Boqueria, a worldwide-famous market and a heavily visited tourist landmark. The bar gets a lot of foot traffic because of it. The same reason we chose this neighborhood for our family's shop.

Lorenzo has put his blood, sweat, and tears into this business and it shows. He said he's even held off on serious relationships because he didn't want anything to distract him from growing. I'm sure that will change at some point; we all get lonely and crave some sort of closeness with another at some point in our lives. Someone to share our wins and our losses with. Someone who can make a house feel like a home when you walk through the front door at the end of the night.

Lorenzo isn't always in when I stop by, but I guess our schedules matched up today.

"Hey, Diego! I'll be right over there!" Lorenzo shouts out.

Luis greets me as I take a seat at the bar. He's been here since Lorenzo opened, in fact, most of the staff has. He takes my order immediately, knowing I already have the menu memorized.

While you can't go wrong with anything on the menu, I always make it a point to order their potatoes. They're done perfectly every single time. Cut into little cubes, then fried, paired with a smoky tomato sauce. You can also order it with a garlic aioli, but I prefer the red sauce. The octopus and clams are also amazing, both melt in your mouth, but today I feel like some chorizo and maybe a couple of meatballs.

"How's it going, Diego?" Lorenzo comes up and pats me on my shoulder before taking the seat next to me at the bar.

"It's going okay." I take a sip of my water. "How's business?"

"Business is good, really good actually." He pours himself a glass of water before continuing. "So, the winery's not doing so well, huh? Have you called that number I gave you for the firm yet?"

I nod. "I left a message yesterday, but haven't heard back yet. I'm taking over for Mia for a bit, so I've been busy getting my new schedule organized. I'm planning on following up with them soon."

"That's too bad about Mia. I'll miss seeing her around." Huh, that's weird. I didn't think Mia came in here. I mean I guess it's not that unusual since she's in the city so often. And the bar is right across the street from the shop and my apartment, which she stays at during her overnights in the city.

Luis arrives with my food as Lorenzo stands up to leave. "Well, I'll let you eat in peace. Hope to be seeing you here more often now that you're spending more time in the neighborhood. And let me know if the marketing firm works out, okay?" He pats my back as he turns to leave.

"Will do. See you next time!" I say as I stab a stack of potatoes. These hit the spot every time, without fail. I definitely need to take full advantage of being so close while I'm filling in for Mia.

After lunch, I head back to the shop and decide to call the marketing firm again. I need to take some ownership in this and try to get the ball rolling. The goal is to secure the winery's future in as little time as possible, showing up for my family in a way I actually know how to do.

"*Bon dia.*" A welcoming voice answers the phone.

"Hi, yes. I called in yesterday in the hope to get some information on rebranding my family's winery. I was wondering if someone would be able to assist me with that today?"

"Absolutely. Let me direct your call to a colleague in that department. Please hold."

Smooth jazz starts playing while I wait on hold. A recorded voice plays over it, listing off all the offices this company had. Sounds like they are spread out around the globe. Pick a continent, and I bet they have an office there.

I go back to cleaning the wine glasses used earlier in the day while I wait. Thankfully, my new routine has actually been a pleasant change of pace. I don't feel cooped up in the cellar or office all day. I do, however, miss my walks around the vineyard, but I can always take a walk around the neighborhood after I close for the afternoon, at least on days we're not open late, and if I'm not rushing to get back to the winery.

The music cuts off and I hear a man's voice over the line. "Hello! My name's Javier. Cecilia said you are looking for help with rebranding your winery? Please, can you tell me a little about your business."

"Hi! Yes, of course. It's my family's winery, and in full transparency, our business is in some desperate need of saving. We won't be operating next season if we don't find a way to increase our profits in the next couple of months."

"I see. Well, we have someone available later this week that I think will be great for your company. She'll be here on a temporary basis, but if it's the right fit, she'll be solely focusing on the rebranding of your winery. Based on her calendar, she can meet with you either Wednesday or Thursday morning. Do either of those days work for you?"

"Wednesday morning sounds great. Let's say ten?"

"Perfect. Wednesday at ten. I'll pencil you in her calendar now. Do you have any other questions I can help to answer before you meet with her?"

"No, I think that's it for now."

"Great. If you think of any before the meeting, please don't hesitate to call and ask."

"Sounds good. Thanks."

"Thank you. Have a great rest of your day. Goodbye." The line clicks shortly after.

Alright, that's one step in the right direction.

Today was one of those days that kept getting dragged out, so I'm not going to be home for dinner. Hell, I might not even drive back to the winery at all. I might just decide to stay at the apartment. I had a late afternoon reservation at the tasting room. Normally, we're closed between the hours of two and five, but if a group calls a week or so ahead of time, asking for a spot during that window, we try our best to accommodate them. After all, we can't really afford to refuse people right now.

I close the shop shortly after cleaning up, deciding to head over to Lorenzo's for dinner since I'm pretty sure there's not enough food in the apartment for a meal.

Last time I was at my place, I only had dried pasta and a jar of chocolate sauce in my pantry, and I highly doubt Mia did any restocking before she lost her license.

It's only five and it's already a full house at Lorenzo's. I wave to a few staff members as I walk in. Working my way over to the bar, I'm lucky to find a barstool that just opened up between a few groups of people. I order a glass of my family's Syrah and of course some potatoes. I'm feeling seafood tonight, so calamari and shrimp it is. Since I'm not starving, those three dishes should be enough to fill me up. Maybe I'll walk to the market after to grab a few things to stock the kitchen, that way I'm prepared for the next time I'm staying overnight.

It's Lola working the bar tonight. She's always friendly but friendly in the true sense of the word, we've never crossed that line nor have I wanted to. She's pretty and nice enough, I just don't have the time for someone. Plus, up until now, I was never in the city long enough for it to make sense to date someone who lived here. But Mia was right, maybe this change will bring a new opportunity to meet someone.

I enjoy my wine and food at a leisurely pace. The crowds are keeping steady. A constant flow of people in and out of the bar, noise from everyone's conversations filling up the space. Tables don't stay empty for long after getting cleaned before another group comes and sits down.

I'm finishing up my wine when a woman walks in, giving me pause on where my focus should be. The delicious meal in front of me or the goddess waiting at the door. She seems unsure of herself while also exuding confidence. It's confusing, but also captivating to watch.

She looks like she's new here, perhaps even a tourist. Definitely here alone. She's wearing a white wrap shirt that's tied around her waist, crossed a little higher above her chest than where I've seen other women position it. The white fabric falls just above her waistline, a little bit of skin playing peekaboo every time she moves. The jeans she's wearing hug her perfectly round ass then fall straight down her legs. My eyes roam back up to her head as she turns, giving me a glimpse of her rosy pink lips and icy blue eyes. Those will be hard to forget. Her hair looks strawberry blonde in this light as it cascades down her back with soft waves. I get a glance at her stunning smile when she looks at me.

Oh shit. I've been gawking at her for god knows how long, and I definitely don't need her thinking I'm looking at her like she's my next meal. I mean, she could be if she wanted to be. Maybe take her back to my place, lay her out on my . . .

I stop and shake my head. Fuck, I need to get laid.

Mia was right earlier. I haven't been on a date for a while. I've just always been so busy helping out around the winery. Or too tired from having such long days. It's easier to just stay in my own world.

But I won't lie, the sound of having more time to find someone if I wanted a casual hookup sounds appealing. But *is* that what I want? I'm thirty-two and honestly, a little tired of that scene. I played that role when I was younger and when I was in California for a bit. I always felt even lonelier afterwards. Always wanting some sort of connection but never being able to get close to someone. I guess that's something I'll attempt to remedy *after* I help save the family business.

During my zone out, I completely miss the group of clearly drunk guys disturbing the woman I was just ogling and having inconvenient thoughts about. She is obviously uncomfortable and —yup, one of them just touched her. This needs to stop right fucking now.

CHAPTER FOUR

EMMA

After I finish unpacking, I'm surprised I'm not struggling with any jet lag. Deciding to make the most of my afternoon, I do a quick trip to the market. It's just a three minute walk down the street. I grab a few basic necessities—eggs, milk, dinner makings, some fruit, espresso grounds, and a few other snacks. Even though my fridge is stocked, and I should probably prepare myself dinner with the ingredients I just bought, I feel like rewarding myself for the successful travel day.

Making my way downstairs, I find the tapas bar is steady with customers, a few tables opening up here and there. I sit down at a small table near the bar and start browsing the menu.

The options all look delicious and with the smaller portions, I could definitely order a few dishes. I'm half tempted to order one of everything, but I know my stomach better. My eyes are treacherous bitches who are always starved when it comes to food *and* men.

The waiter was quick to get my drink order, the house-made sangria. I peeked the advertisement on the chalk sign right outside. I've had sangria plenty of times before, each time a little different depending on the fruit and wine used. It sounded refreshing and if I hate it, I'll just order a glass of red.

I'm still contemplating what to order when a group of guys come in. Clearly tourists, and it's obvious that they've already started drinking. With it being only six in the evening, and a week-day, I'm definitely betting on them being on vacation.

My waiter returns to take my order. I decide on something that looks like fried potatoes, something with chorizo, some cala-mari, and fried balls of some sort. So basically a ton of fried food. Figure I can't go wrong with any of those choices. I might pay for it later, but everything looks so good, especially those damn potatoes.

The guys behind me get a little louder just as I start to feel a presence behind me. "Hi there, beautiful. This seat taken?" He moves in before I can stop him, or really say any sort of response. "What's your name, gorgeous?"

Normally, I'm okay with a fun meet-cute, but this is far from that. The guy smells like a brewery, not the best first impression.

Giving him the attention I so desperately don't want to give, I look up at him with a polite smile. "Actually, the seat is taken—"

He cuts me off. "Me and my friends were going out to a few clubs tonight. You wanna tag along?" What the actual fuck?

"No." I return to my drink, which is clearly more interesting than this guy in front of me. While I'm a big believer in "no" being a complete sentence, clearly this man isn't. His presence still lingering at my table tells me he's having issues understanding the two-letter word.

"Oh, come on," he whines, leaning over the table. God, I can literally taste the beer from him breathing so close to me. "Don't be such a tease." He reaches over and has the balls to grab my wrist. Oh, hell no! Not feeling this at all.

I yank my arm back. "I said no." I point over to the door, "Now leave."

"Hear this guys," he shouts to the guys behind me. I tune out the rest of whatever he is saying as I stand up to leave, but freeze when I feel a soft hand touch my shoulder.

Looking up, I stare into the most gorgeous set of hazel eyes, framed by beautiful long lashes. I don't remember seeing him walk in with these other guys; in fact, I think he was at the bar when I first walked in.

He's tall. Like *tall* tall. Almost six and a half feet if I was guessing. For sure a full foot taller than me.

He's big too. Like muscle on muscle kind of big. Like someone could tell me he's a distant relative to Dwayne Johnson, and I'd believe them. Hell, I'm intimidated just looking at him.

He looks between me and Chad. Now, I have no idea if the guy sitting in front of me is really named Chad, but he just looks like he'd be one. Someone who uses Daddy's—or Mommy's—money and has no respect for others. Like they expect the whole world to revolve around them.

Getting an idea to hopefully send Chad off running, I do a quick glance of my tall stranger's left hand, no ring. Hopefully, he doesn't have a girlfriend either. I look into his eyes, sending him a gesture that I hope conveys a pleading "just go with it" look. Though by his head tilt, I'm not sure he understands.

Fuck it.

I side hug him and nudge my head towards his ear whispering, "Thanks for your rescue. I'm so sorry about this." I catch the confused look on his face, but before he can act, I grab the back of his head with one of my hands and pull him down to my lips, planting a quick kiss on him.

"Hi, babe!" I say in a loud voice, ensuring Chad not only hears me, but knows this impressive gift to mankind is here for me. "I already ordered some food, but I wasn't sure what you wanted to drink."

He pulls his head back up and looks towards Chad, who is still sitting at my table, now looking more like a dog with its tail tucked between its legs. The redwood tree of a man in front of me turns his attention back to me and smiles, causing me to melt right then and there.

"Sorry, I was running late, honey." Pulling me closer, he kisses me again. But this one lasts a little longer than the first. And is definitely more of a *kiss* kiss rather than the barely-there kiss I gave him before.

He deepens it more and it quickly becomes a *really* good fucking kiss. And my knight in shining armor is really selling it by wrapping his gigantic arms around my waist, causing me to lean in closer, forcing me to bring my hands up to rest against his rock hard chest.

Okay, so maybe I didn't *need* to move them up, but can you blame me? I'm pretty sure with all those muscles, this man has bigger boobs than me.

As I'm losing myself in the kiss, I hear a throat clear along with something that sounds a lot like, "You can have her." That wakes me up.

What an ass. I turn and see Chad and his friends leaving the bar. Thank God.

Relaxing my hold on the mysterious stranger, I look back into his hazel eyes and clear my throat. "Thanks for that."

"No problem. I'm sorry you had to deal with that while trying to enjoy your dinner." The waiter appears like his ears were burning, setting down all of the food I ordered.

As I see the stranger turning to leave, I blurt out before thinking, "Want to join me?" I motion to the table filled with food, clearing my throat before I add, "I mean, I have more than enough to share."

He looks to the table then back to me; he's going to turn me down. Which is totally fine. He's definitely not obligated to stay. He saw a person in need of a little help and stepped in; he was just being a good person. Plus, I basically attacked him with my lips. He probably doesn't want to make this any more awkward than it already is.

You know what, no. Fuck that. We are *not* thinking that way.

I'm a fucking catch. "We already kissed, might as well eat dinner together."

He looks around. Searching for what, I don't know. Maybe he's looking for his girlfriend. Or even his boyfriend.

"Shit, I'm sorry. I shouldn't have assumed. You're probably waiting for someone. You can go, I'll just sit here and eat my dinner alone." Oh my god! Emma . . . shut the fuck up!!!

He chuckles as he runs one hand through his curly, chocolate brown hair, using his other to grab the chair that Chad just vacated, taking his seat at the table. Actually, I'm not even sure if you could call what just came out of his mouth a chuckle, more like a husky puff of air.

I can't help but stare at him across the table. He looks like a giant sitting on the small chair, like the chairs used for little children's tea parties. Now all I'm imagining is one of those delicate pink teacups being held by one of his huge hands. Pinky out obviously.

I wonder what else he can do with those big hands . . .

I shake my head, getting the mental image out, and meet his extended hand, "Diego." My hand feels so small as he shakes it in his.

God, is everything on him supersized? I look from his hand, to his arms, to the Henley pulled tight against shoulders and chest, then down lower to his . . . Before my eyes catch up to where my mind is lending them, I stop myself.

Shit. I'm definitely not thinking about his hands anymore. Well, maybe his hands and another part of his . . . I clear my throat, attempting to get my mind out of the gutter before giving my name.

"Emma." But it comes out hoarse, making me grab my drink to relieve my dry throat.

"Emma." He stretches out my name like he's testing it, almost tasting it. "And, no, I wasn't waiting for someone. I'd love to join you." Though his English is great, Diego definitely has an accent.

One that makes me even more intrigued about the man sitting before me.

"Great. You're welcome to anything I ordered." I grab a bite from the potato dish and oh. My. God.

I'm not sure if it's because I haven't had anything decent from traveling today, but damn. These are the best potatoes I've ever eaten. I wonder if Mom or Tory can make something like this. They seem like a pretty basic dish to make. I'm not sure if it's the seasoning, or the red sauce, or the combination of both, but fuck, it's good.

I'm reaching out to grab another forkful of potatoes, when my fork scratches the bottom of the small plate. I can't help but grimace. I hate that sound.

I look to the dish, then over to Diego, then back down to the dish.

"Did you eat the rest of the potatoes?" Asking, hopeful I didn't just zone out while devouring the plate.

He looks down at the empty plate. "That was definitely all you."

"Well since those are now gone, do you want any of these?" Motioning my fork to the other three dishes. He shakes his head.

"So you're just going to watch me eat?" I eye him suspiciously before adding, "I feel like I should be charging you for that." Popping a calamari ring into my mouth, I stop myself from moaning at the buttery taste.

"Oh," he clears his throat and lowers his smoky voice, "I'd gladly buy tickets to that show."

Well fuck me.

I blink widely at his response. Now this is more like the meet-cute I was hoping for. More like meet-hot.

"Well, if you don't want any of my food . . . " I bite my bottom lip and take in a long, lustful look at him before I continue. "Can I get you something else? Maybe you want to order a drink or something else on their menu? My treat, for saving me of course."

He looks over to the bar then back to me, waiting patiently with a soft smile. "I'll order a drink, but a lady never pays." His eyes drift over my shoulder, and I can see him nod to the pretty bartender. She's got great hair.

Within another minute, the waiter appears with a glass of wine, asking Diego if he wants to order any food. He declines but thanks him by name. Interesting. He either comes here often or he's really good at names.

"So . . . we did things kind of backwards." I grab the lemon. "I have your name now, Diego," I say as I squeeze the slice over only half of the calamari, still hoping Diego will share it with me. "But are you single? Do you live in Barcelona? What do you do for work?" I ask all the basic questions, so he can talk while I enjoy this amazing food. Seriously, I'll be needing to make this a regular spot for dinner. Maybe even lunch for those days when I'm working from home.

He takes a sip of his wine then wipes his thumb over the corner of his mouth before the liquid gets a chance to run down his trimmed beard. "I live right outside of the city and work at my family's vineyard."

Inching my head closer, I'm not so patiently waiting for him to answer the most important question. But when he pauses, I can't help but repeat, "And are you currently unattached?" I eye him up and down while popping more calamari in my mouth. It's so flakey and the squeeze of lemon is the perfect compliment to the squid.

"Currently . . . " Now it's his turn to look me up and down. "Yes, unattached." Thank god. That means no woman will come popping out, yelling at me for kissing their man.

While brainstorming my next question, I reach over to fork some more calamari. Dammit. I did it again.

"Seems like you're out of calamari." Diego notes with a smug grin.

"Looks like it. At least I still have the sausage and balls to enjoy." I shrug like I have no idea what I just said. He chokes a little, trying to conceal the noise as he grabs his wine glass.

"I'll let you finish in peace then." I look up, shocked by his quick wit and see him smirking at me.

"Oh, don't you know, it's no fun to finish alone."

"Who said anything about being alone?" Where did this man come from? I've never met a man who is not only a gentleman, but can serve such sexy and witty banter as well.

Fuck, am I already thinking about sleeping with this guy? Not even twenty-four hours in a new country, and I'm thinking about dick. Well you know what they say, work hard, play hard. And I'm willing to bet, Diego plays *hard*.

Oh, good god, Emma. Now that was a bad joke.

Or was it a *bad* joke?

No! No dick for you. Just eat the sausage and balls, like a normal person.

I go to do just that, but as my fork scrapes against the porcelain of the plate, I get the wakeup call I need. Apparently I'm out of chorizo. Goddamnit.

CHAPTER FIVE

DIEGO

She's cute. Like *really* cute. But also, sexy. A combo I don't come across very often. Or really at all, since I'm always locked away in my cave, as Mia would say.

"Well, thanks again for the kiss. I really appreciate you pulling a white knight earlier." After wiping her mouth, she rests her napkin on her empty plate. "Did you want any dessert?"

"Not from here." I look her up and down from where I'm sitting. She's busy doing the same, swiping her tongue along her plump bottom lip. "I've got some chocolate sauce over in my apartment across the street if you're interested."

Maybe that was a tad forward, but what did that one hockey player say? *"You miss one hundred percent of the shots you don't take."* Or was that Michael Scott? And maybe I don't always have to be the grouchy dragon my family paints me out to be.

"Oh yeah?" Emma smiles wide as she reaches into her bag. "Well let me just pay and then—"

"Oh, don't worry about it." I interrupt, freezing her in place. "I come here often, the owner's a friend. I'll square up with him tomorrow, just let me tell Luis we're leaving."

"Oh no. I can't let you do that. You didn't even eat."

"Don't worry." I stand up, holding my hand out for her. "I'm about to."

Emma's eyes go wide as her beguiling mouth drops open. I can't help but bite my bottom lip, attempting to hide my smirk.

"Um yea—yes. Yes, that sounds—" A hint of an accent sneaking out with her stutter.

"Delicious? I thought the same thing." I motion to Luis, informing him we're leaving. "Now let's get out of here."

I lead her out and across the street to my apartment. "I'm on the third floor." She nods as I guide her up the interior stairs, making our way up the two flights upstairs to my door. I unlock and open the door but hold off on taking us through the threshold. "Now, if you want to stop at any point—" She stops me by reaching on her toes with a quick kiss.

Pulling away she adds, "I appreciate that, but I'm a big girl, Diego. I'm not afraid of saying no. Now open up this door, and let's get you some dessert."

Fuuuuuuck.

I quickly usher her inside, not wanting to waste another minute. "My bedroom is to the left, but the dining table is straight ahead." I lick my lips as I stare pointedly at said table. She doesn't even hesitate. After taking off her shoes, she struts straight to it, and I can't help but admire her ass as she walks away from me.

When she reaches the table, she spins back around, facing me with what I can only describe as siren eyes, luring me in.

"Am I putting on a show, or would you like to unwrap me like the gift I am?" She teases with a smartass grin.

Good god, this woman is going to ruin me before I even have a taste.

I march over to her before she can get any further with unbuckling her jeans. Pushing her up against the edge of the table with my hips, I palm her ass in one hand and the back of her head in the other. She's a handful, figuratively and literally.

Sliding my hand down her chest, I pull on the fabric, exposing more of her to me, feeling the soft skin between her breasts.

Fuck. When she said unwrap, she really meant *unwrap*. Her white shirt has a fucking bow in the front, taunting me. With strips of fabric tied around the smallest part of her waist, I literally have to unwrap her. After untying the bow on the side, it falls completely open, exposing the lace bra she was hiding underneath.

It's soft and delicate, leaving me wondering if the woman wearing it is the same. I swipe my thumb over the lace, feeling her peaked nipples through the thin fabric as a gasp slips through her lips.

I kiss along her collar as her hand makes its way into my curls, my other hand moving down to the waistline of her jeans. She's already unbuckled them; I just need to pull them down her rounded hips.

I work the denim lower as I continue to kiss her, lifting her up onto the table when the jeans make it past her knees. They fall off immediately when her ass slaps down on the wood table. Keeping my hands on her hips, I fit myself in the space between her legs, needing to be closer to her.

I move my mouth up to give a sweet kiss on her lips, only to slowly work my way back down, sprinkling her neck and chest in kisses while her hands dig dipper into my scalp.

Giving time to each breast, I suck and nip both nipples, one after the other.

I look up at her before continuing my worship, only to see her head tilted back, eyes closed, and mouth slightly open, whispering small praises and pleas for me to continue.

Switching my position, I kneel between her legs, wrap my arms under her thighs, and tug her closer to the edge of the table, making sure she is right where I need her to be.

My new position doesn't go unnoticed. Emma sits up a little more, peering down at me like the queen she is. "I could get used to seeing you on your knees."

"And I could get used to being between yours." Emma licks her lips as I swipe my thumb up over the small fabric covering her pussy. She's already wet, evidence showing through the little red triangle covering right where I want to be. I kiss the inside of each thigh before hooking my finger under the fabric, bringing it to the side and exposing her fully to me.

Her lips are already pink and puffy, shining with the proof of her arousal. "Is this all for me, Sweetheart?" I tease her with another swipe, but this time, there's no barrier.

"Yessss," her answer more like a hiss.

"Want me to keep going?" My thumb makes another swipe.

"Fuck yes, Diego." I reward her with a single lick.

"I'm going to need to hear you say that again, Sweetheart." Switching back to my thumb, I swipe her again, only slower with a bit of pressure, spending more time on her clit.

"Then make me."

What a little brat, but I do love a challenge. That's the only push I need to start eating her out like the delicacy she is.

I listen to Emma's cues, making sure she's taking as much enjoyment as I am, hopefully more. Emma's good at encouraging me with a "god, yes" or "fuck", even saying my name a time or two. But she hasn't said that special phrase again. Apparently I need to do better.

I lick two fingers of mine while licking the thumb on the other hand. My thumb goes up to tease her hard nipple, rubbing it in slow, sensual circles.

While my fingers play with her opening a bit, my mouth stays busy, switching between sucking and licking a figure eight around her clit. "Fuck, Diego!"

Ah. We're getting closer to the special phrase I want to hear, but we're still not there yet. Maybe she needs a little *encouragement*. I'm not normally a talker, but like me, she might enjoy a little praise herself.

I work my two fingers inside and god, is she tight. "Look at you, taking my fingers like a good girl." I'm so tempted to undo my pants and . . .

No. No, my rule has always been, and *will* always be, to make the woman come first before I'm allowed inside. Hopefully, allowing her the chance to come again when I'm inside of her.

I motion a "come here" while my fingers are inside of her, reaching her g-spot. She screams out, "Fuck yes, Diego!" Proof I hit my intended spot.

Licking her clit once more, I let my thumb take over as I raise, making sure her clit stays stimulated while my fingers are moving inside.

"That's right, Sweetheart. Ride my fingers and take what's yours."

With one hand, I grab hold of the back of her head, licking and sucking on her neck while working my two fingers inside her, making sure to keep a constant rhythm while the sensation builds inside of her. "Don't stop! Don't stop!" I lower my mouth to play with her nipple and after a few sucks, I feel her clench around my fingers. "Yes! God, yes!"

"While I may not be god, I'm definitely having a religious experience right now." I ease her down off her high, not taking my fingers out until she's relaxed, kissing her soft and slow. I stroke my fingers through her hair, taking a moment to stare into her glacier blue eyes. Her wavy hair sticking to her flushed face, cheeks red from her release, but she's eyeing me up and down, almost conspiratorially.

"So . . ." she starts. She's working her hand down my chest as she continues, "How strong's your table?"

Rubbing my nose up her neck, I whisper against the shell of her ear, "Why? Are you feeling up for a ride?"

"Hell yes. And with what I'm feeling pressed up against me," her hands explore lower, playing with the waistband of my jeans, "feels like you're ready to go." She pulls her hand out and taps the space beside her. "So take a seat and let me give you the best ride of your life."

CHAPTER SIX

DIEGO

*Y*eah, we definitely won't be doing any sleeping tonight.

Excusing myself to grab a condom from my nightstand, I come back and find she's moved off the table, now sitting on my couch. "As much as I'd love to take you on the table, I'm pretty sure my knees would be more grateful if we moved to the couch."

"Wherever you want me, I'm yours."

Pulling off my belt, I stalk over to her and stand between her legs. She reaches out her arms, running her hands up my stomach, lifting my shirt as she goes. Because of the mix of our height, she barely reaches my chest, so I take over pulling the fabric off, while her fingers roam my waist.

I unbutton my pants and start pulling them, along with my boxers, down as she greedily admires my exposed body. "God, the amount of muscle you have, it should be studied." I chuckle as I step out of the fabric pooled around my ankles. "Oh fuck me! Now that's," she points unabashedly at my dick, "not even fair."

"Too much for you, Sweetheart?" I taunt as I stroke myself

from base to tip. She just stares at me while biting her bottom lip and shaking her head. "Good."

I grip her under her thighs and pick her up, wrapping her legs around my waist. Spinning us around, I sit my ass down on the couch, positioning her perfectly on my lap with my dick pushed against her wet pussy.

As Emma starts to grind against it, she coats me in her arousal while I grip her plump ass. Fuck, she looks gorgeous, sitting naked, tits bouncing while she grinds against me. I'm not even inside her yet and she's wrecking me for any future with anyone else

"Okay, enough with the teasing." She demands. "Where's that condom?" She is my kind of woman.

I reach over to the edge of the couch, but she eyes my movement and snatches the little foil wrapper before I can. "Thank you!" She quips while plucking the square away from my reach. "I need you in me *now!*" She orders as she shimmies herself away just enough to expose my dick between us, rolling the condom over my hard length.

With protection in place, she straightens herself back up. "Now, where were we?" She lifts herself up on her knees, positioning her opening right over my dick and sits herself down without any warning. I can't help but let out a groan; she hasn't taken me fully, but we'll get her there.

As she takes a minute to get adjusted, I kiss up and down her neck, ensuring she knows there's no rush. When I feel her start to move around, I whisper against her ear, "You're gonna be a good girl and take all of it. Aren't you, Sweetheart?"

She gasps as she takes the final two inches. I sit still, giving her time to recover from my length. I work my thumbs over her tight pink nipples, causing her back to arch towards me. "Fuck, you are a sight I'm blessed to see, Emma."

She crashes her lips to mine and starts grinding her hips while I move my hand south. She's still a little rigid, but relaxes immediately when my thumb circles her clit.

"Fuck. Me. *Diego*." When I hear her moan out my name, that's all the encouragement I need to switch positions.

Pivoting us while keeping myself locked inside of her, I lay her down on the couch. I kneel between her legs, positioning them so they're wrapped around my waist. Once we're settled in this new position, I set a constant pace with my thrusts while continuing to work my thumb, making her even more of a mess around my cock. "You like that, Sweetheart?"

"Fuck yes." She exhales while she reaches up to her chest, playing with her nipples.

"I'm sorry. Have I been neglecting these perfect breasts of yours?" Running my hand up over the skin of her stomach, I reach her right breast, massaging it while I continue my thrusting. She arches into my touch, bringing her hips even closer to mine.

I bend down and give each breast a teasing kiss, nipping the last one a little.

"Are you just going to tease me all night?" She's a little brat, and I kind of love it.

I let out a deep chuckle before bringing her knee over my shoulder, lowering myself closer to her. Thrusting even deeper but at a faster pace, ensuring I'm hitting that perfect spot inside of her.

She moans as I thrust deeply. "Oh my god . . . oh my god . . ." She pants, making me sneak my hand back in between us to play with its new favorite spot. "Fuck, I'm close." She curses, encouraging me on.

"I want to feel you come on my cock, Sweetheart." I whisper in her ear, then give a teasing nibble on her ear lobe. Her moan of pleasure lets me know that tipped her over the edge. I slow my finger tips over her clit, easing her down from her release, but continue to thrust into her a few more times while I reach mine, finding myself almost nuzzling her cheek as we both come back down.

No. No, strings, Diego. Just sex. Just really, *really* good sex.

I steal a quick kiss on her lips, but before I can pull away, she playfully nips at my bottom lip.

"Oh, I'm definitely not done with you." I taunt before kissing both breasts while giving her ass a little squeeze. Pulling myself up on my feet, I look down at her lying naked on my couch. Fuck, she's perfect. I guess the night doesn't have to end just yet. "Want to continue this in my shower?"

The next few hours are a mix of position changes, curses, moans, and orgasms, with a few catnaps thrown in here and there. It's practically a sex marathon for ten hours. We had the table. Then the couch. We rinsed off in the shower, which naturally led to sex on the bench while the water rained down on us.

Opting to go to bed naked was a horrible idea, because as I soon as I laid down, all I could think about was Emma naked, in *my* bed. I *had* to fuck her again.

We both passed out for a couple of hours afterwards, only for Emma to wake me up with her mouth wrapped around my hard cock. Fuck, she even gives great head, maybe the best I've ever had. She did this thing with her hand before sucking me to finish. Swallowed every bit and licked me clean afterwards.

I woke up around half past six, finding Emma passed out in my bed, sheets tangled around her naked body. Draped around in a way to provide just enough coverage while still showing enough to make me want to wake her up for another round.

But we're both exhausted, so choosing the more responsible path, I turn and make my way to the kitchen to make some espresso. It's a crazy thought, but with how well last night went, I can't help feeling we might be able to turn this one-night stand into something more.

I'm standing at the stove brainstorming ways to ask when I feel two arms wrap around my waist. "So last night . . ."

"And this morning." I turn my head to reply but feel her press her forehead to my back. She's so small and pocket sized, especially compared to me. Hell, her hands don't even come close to touching each other right now as they fully extend around me.

I reach up to grab some sugar in the cabinet and see a jar that jogs my memory.

"Oh dammit, we forgot the chocolate sauce." I turn around, hand slipping down to squeeze her ass. "You up for round . . . what number are we on now?"

"I don't know, but at this point, I feel like we'd have a good shot at Trojan sponsoring us after the night we just had." I chuckle as I take the moka off the burner. "What's that? It looks like a cute little teapot."

"It's for espresso. I made enough for both of us, if you want some." I reach over and grab two cups.

"Oh, yes please." She moves to take a seat at the island.

"Need any sugar? Unfortunately, I don't have any cream at the moment." I take mine with a sprinkle of sugar. I find it helps balance the bitterness and highlights the flavor notes of the beans.

Her face puckers a bit before she replies, "God, do *not* say cream after we've had so much sex. It's one of those words for me. But sugar would be great, thank you."

After mixing in the sugar, I bring the tiny cups over to the bar. "One of *those* words? Please explain."

"You know, like moist or panties. While those don't bother me, that *other* word does." A phone goes off but it doesn't sound like one of my alarms. "Shit!" She startles off the barstool. "That must be my alarm. What time is it?"

"Almost seven."

"Shit!" She sprints to my bedroom, where I'm assuming she gets her phone because the alarm finally stops ringing. "I start a new job today and I really need to get home and get ready for my day," Emma hollers from my room.

When she appears again, she's fully dressed and hurries to the bar where she does a quick blow on the tiny cup left out for her. She throws the scalding liquid back and coughs a little.

"Fuuuck, that was hot." She takes a deep breath, forcefully blowing out her exhale. "But so good. Thank you for all of this. Really." And she sprints off without a hug or a kiss. Or even a number exchange.

Fuck! I don't have her number!

I run out into the hall in nothing but my sweat bottoms. "Emma, wait!" I don't hear a reply as I make my way down the stairs. When I step outside, she's nowhere to be found.

Dammit. How did she get away so quickly? Maybe there was a cab sitting right outside? She literally sprinted to get out of here.

Shit, I really fumbled that one. Emma checked off all my boxes, even the ones I didn't even know I wanted.

Good going, Diego. Your first date in over five years and everything was perfect. *She* was perfect. But you were too busy thinking with your dick that you couldn't even get her number.

CHAPTER SEVEN

EMMA

$\mathcal{O}$h my god! I cannot believe I almost ruined my first day all because I got distracted with some hookup. What the hell was I thinking?

I mean Diego was a fine example of what a man could and should be but *fuck*.

I have my own life that I've worked hard for. I don't need a man screwing this up for me. I'm only here for six weeks and after that, the sky's the limit. If he wants me, he can call me, no matter how magnetic our connection was.

Shit. No, he can't. He has no way to get a hold of me. I left before giving my number.

Hell, he doesn't even know I live right across the damn street. I mean, of course he doesn't. He's still a stranger and I'm not about to give all my personal information to him.

Yeah Emma, because after a night spent in his bed, *that's* the part that would be crossing the line.

But all stranger danger aside, he did seem like he's a relatively normal guy. Not someone who would become my stalker while I'm here in Barcelona.

Though I could easily see the roles reversing, I now know where he lives, and something tells me I wouldn't need alcohol to become his stalker. His place is right across the street for goodness sakes. I might even be able to see his . . . yup.

I've definitely crossed over to the line of stalking because I just realized I have the most perfect view of his apartment out my bedroom window. The bedroom window that I specifically picked for its view of the street, even before I had my meet-cute. And depending on where he is in the apartment, I bet I could even see him from this very spot.

In less than sixty seconds, I prove myself right. Looking one floor down, I see the very hot, very sexy, perfect example of the male figure, Diego himself. He's pacing in front of his window in his sweatpants, his *grey* sweatpants. May there be a special place in the afterlife for the person who decided grey was a good color choice for men's sweatpants.

I watch him walk from one side to the other and I can't help but wonder, did I do that? Cause the amazing Hulk to sulk?

Fuck.

No, you know what, it's fine. If things between us are meant to be, he'll figure out a way to find me.

Shaking my head, I tear myself from the distraction before me. I have to be out the door in less than an hour.

Scrambling to the bathroom, I crank the shower on hot. I took two showers at Diego's, one productive and a bit more recreational, but I still feel like I reek of sex. I don't need to get my hair wet, just scrub any evidence off my body before getting ready for my first day. Though even after my shower, I can still pick up on a faint scent, smoky oak and something sweet, almost like berries. Probably just from the wine we had at dinner last night.

My office is less than eight minutes away if I walk. After doing some mental math, I figure that leaves me forty minutes to shower, get dressed, put on makeup, and eat something before heading out the door. I'm normally able to chalk up a one-nightstand to just that, one night, and then move on. But I can't get this man out of my head. Maybe this time could be different, maybe it could be more . . .

I can already hear my sisters in my head responding. "But how can it?" or "You didn't even get his number." or "You don't even know his last name."

All three of my sisters tease me that I'm always walking through life with rose-tinted glasses on, in all aspects of my life. I'm constantly being teased with some variation of "There's Emma with her glasses on again." Whether it's because I ignore all the red flags and only see the good in the men I'm interested in, or because I try not to let a situation determine my happiness, I always try to find some positive spin to it, but not so much that I ooze with toxic positivity. I can be the first person to admit when a situation is shit; I just don't choose to stand in said shit. I stomp my boots clean and keep going with the day.

So maybe he'll find some way to reach out, or maybe I'll see him at the bar again. But if not, he'll forever be known as Diego, The Rock, because of his resemblance to the man *and* how he rocked my world last night. Or even because of his rock hard—

Nope. Definitely a distraction I *don't* need while I'm currently in the shower, attempting to not be late to my first day.

My first day ends up being great. I'm given a tour of the office by someone named Stacia; she's also a transplant from the States, only her contract is twice as long as mine. She introduced me to almost everybody, all seemed nice and welcoming.

"Just about everyone here comes from somewhere other than Barcelona." Stacia adds as we make our way to my new cubicle for the next six weeks. As she gets more comfortable with me, I notice she starts to drop her R's, making me think she's from Boston or somewhere nearby.

"Really?"

"Oh yeah." She nods while giving me a big smile. "So many have fallen in love with the city that by the end of their position, they chose to stay." Doesn't seem hard to do with what I've seen of Barcelona so far. "Well, at least the ones lucky enough to get offered a position here at the end of their contract." Good to know.

She finishes the tour by showing me my desk. It's nothing fancy, just a six by six space, but I don't need much.

My position doesn't require me to work in the office, but it's nice to have the option. There might be days where I won't even go into the office.

The main reason I'm here is to be an account manager and focus solely on the business chosen for me during these few weeks. This will give me the ability to prove my skill to the branch's manager, as well as to the firm in hopes of potential offers from other firm locations.

"Well, that's the tour. I know Javier said he'll be here soon to talk to you. It was great meeting you, and if you need anything, I'm just on the other side of the wall." She taps our shared wall for emphasis.

"Great meeting you, too, Stacia. Thanks for the tour." She smiles then disappears to her side.

"Emma?" I hear a man ask from around the corner.

"Hi, yes. Javier?" I ask with uncertainty. We've only corresponded through email, so I don't know his voice. I also have zero clue on what he looks like since I didn't think to cyberstalk my new manager.

"Yes. Hi!" He greets, hand out for me to shake. "It's great to finally meet you. I'd love for you to shadow me for your first day if that's alright with you."

"Of course. Lead the way." He walks us over to where I remember Stacia telling me his office is located.

"So, Emma, a family business called earlier and said they need help rebranding. I think this would be a perfect project for you. Assuming the client and you mesh well of course."

"Yes, that sounds great." I nod and smile as he motions for me to take a seat in his office. "And when are they hoping to start?"

"I told him you could see him tomorrow morning. Ten to be exact. You'll be working with the son of the family business, and if the meeting goes well, that will be your sole project for your duration here."

"Sounds great. I can't wait to start."

"Perfect!" Javier claps. "I love your enthusiasm."

I'm excited at the prospect of getting assigned a business so quickly. I love hitting the ground running, and there's not too many things I can do around the office in the meantime.

Javier seems like he'll be a pretty relaxed manager. Carefree, but responsible when he needs to be. Throughout my time with him today, I watch and listen while he goes about his daily tasks.

It's great practice for my Spanish as well as my Catalan listening to him talk with everyone in the office as well as on all the phone calls he takes throughout the day. He transitions between all three languages, English, Spanish, and Catalan, effortlessly. A skill I'm hoping to gain by the end of this journey.

"Well, what are your thoughts about your first day?" he asks as we make our way out of the office.

"Other than realizing I need to work on my Catalan," he lets out a chuckle before I continue, "I'm really excited about the opportunity presented here. I truly appreciate you showing me the ropes today, Javier."

"Absolutely. And about the Catalan," He holds his door open, ushering me outside the building, "I'm sure you'll be fluent before you know it! See you tomorrow, Emma."

"Thanks! See you then!" We wave and go about walking our separate ways.

As much as I'd like to go back to the bar, maybe getting the chance to run into Diego again, I have a fridge full of food that I should probably make use of.

Walking home, I take my time. Trying to familiarize myself with the neighborhood around me. When I went to the market yesterday, I just shopped and went straight home, but during my walk home this afternoon, I spot a cute little wine tasting room.

Deciding that would make the perfect thank-you gift for my doorman, I decide to go inside. When I try to open the door though, it's locked and I see all the lights are off.

Shoot. They must be closed for the night. Oh well, I'll just figure something else out.

Manuel is on the phone when I walk in, making it easy to do a quick wave and head up for the night.

I text my sisters while I gather the ingredients for dinner. With the time change, it's roughly lunch time for them.

EMMA:

What's up bitches?

TORY:

Hey there, world traveler! How's Spain?

TAYLOR:

How was your first day at work?

EMMA:

It was good. My new manager said I'll meet with a potential client tomorrow. I'm hopeful it'll be a good fit.

LINDSAY:

Wow. That's great Emma. How was sleeping in your new place?

Shit. I wasn't planning on telling them but since she asked . . .

EMMA:

Yeah, about that.

I actually haven't slept at the apartment yet.

TAYLOR:

Some clarification please.

TORY:

EMMA!

Please don't tell me you already hooked up
with someone in less than twenty-four hours
of being there?

EMMA:

Okay, I guess I won't tell you.

I put my phone on silent before any of their replies came though. As I finish cooking my dinner, I open a bottle of wine to enjoy along with it. As I take a sip of the red, I realize I could've given Manuel this bottle as a gift. Oh well.

I didn't do anything fancy tonight, just some pasta noodles with sauce and a grilled chicken thigh on the side. I opt to eat my dinner out on my balcony, enjoying the sound of the busy city beneath.

There's a slight breeze and with the sun setting, it's a little chilly. Sipping the wine, I savor the pairing with the red sauce. I'm never too good at which wines go best with what foods. If I like it, I just drink it, regardless of what I'm eating.

I finish up my dinner and pour myself another glass, corking the rest of the wine for another day. After cleaning up dinner, I light a candle on the coffee table and settle into a cozy position on the couch.

I packed a few of my books for my time over here, and when I say mine, I mean my sister's. Lindsay's too busy right now to read them anyway. Plus, it's not fair to the books to be put on a bookshelf, only to be ignored for years. They need some attention. Really, it's for the books and not me. Lindsay should actually be thanking me for my services.

Most of the books Lindsay and I read are contemporary romances. Some dark, and some warm and fuzzy. I'm pretty sure Lindsay just buys the cozy ones for me, but I've never told her I'm on to her little sneaky way of building my library. The one I picked out tonight is a fun hockey romance.

Half a bottle and a couple hundred pages later, I find myself second guessing whether or not it's a good idea to go over and knock on Diego's apartment door.

I'm stuck between asking if it's stalker-ish or just me being an adult? He's literally across the street so it would be silly to waste the opportunity to ask for his number, especially when I know where he lives. But then again, I can't quite tell if this is my actual brain speaking or the half a bottle of red. I'm sober enough to realize I'm not sober enough for this decision, so I decide on returning to my text thread with my sisters, filling them in on last night's activities.

Well maybe not *all* of the activities.

EMMA:

Hope you appreciated that cliffhanger.

LINDSAY:

We didn't.

TAYLOR:

Spill it.

EMMA:

I may have met a guy . . .

TORY:

That much we guessed. What we want to know is why you didn't sleep in your apartment.

TAYLOR:

Oh I think we know why.

EMMA:

It all happened so fast and I kinda got lost in the moment.

LINDSAY:

And you slept over?

The night before you started your new job?

TORY:

THAT'S what your concern is?

How about the fact that she went to a
stranger's house and spent the night???

IN A FOREIGN COUNTRY!!!!!

TAYLOR:

Oh please, she's texting us so clearly she's
still alive.

EMMA:

YES! Thank you!

Yes, still very much alive. Maybe even more so
after last night. 😌

And I'll have you know Lindsay, I made it to
the office without being late.

TAYLOR:

Good for you, sis!

TORY:

I'm glad you're alive, but you're sleeping in
your apartment tonight right?

I roll my eyes as I read Tory's message.

EMMA:

Yes, mother.

LINDSAY:

We just want to make sure you're staying safe.

EMMA:

Thanks, I am. Now if y'all excuse me, it's past
my bed time.

TAYLOR:

Night!

TORY:

We love you! Good night!

LINDSAY:

Talk to you soon.

CHAPTER EIGHT

DIEGO

started the closing process early today. Normally, I'd wait until after two but it was the slowest possible day, the shop was basically like a ghost town all day. And it didn't help that I was distracted the whole fucking time with thoughts of Emma. All the things we did. The way her body felt under mine. Hers on top of mine. Her breathy moans. The way she could keep up with me, not just with her body but with her wit. Thoughts of filling that bratty mouth of hers. She left me wanting . . . no, needing more. *Craving* more.

My phone rings, bringing my mind back to the task at hand.

"*Bon dia*, the—"

"Diego, are you coming home tonight or did you decide to make your apartment your new dragon lair?" Always the dramatics with her.

"Hello to you too, Mia. I'll be over soon." I set the phone down, switching it to speaker, while I prepare the shop for closing. Wiping the tables and sweeping the floors are the last things on my closing list. "It's been slow today, so I started cleaning a little early. I'll be locking up soon."

"Sounds good. Mom's on my ass to get you home, which led

her to ask why you're there and not me. And you know what a shit liar I am."

"That you are." I chuckle. "So what'd you tell her?"

"I said I needed a break in my routine, and I missed being home." She answers with a smug tone.

"And she actually bought it?" I ask, doubt clear in my tone.

"Well I wouldn't go *that* far . . . " Mia scoffs. "Look, would you please just head home now, so she doesn't start asking any more questions?"

"Fine, fine." I close the curtains and grab my bag, switching my phone off of speaker. "I'm setting the alarm right now."

"Amazing! See you in an hour or so."

"Bye, Mia." I toss my phone in my bag and lockup.

By the time I arrive back home, dinner is already laid out on the table. I take my seat and plate myself some of the rice and shrimp in front of me.

Dad's at one end of the table, while Grandpa's at the other, leaving Mia to sit by me and our mother across from us.

"How was your day, Diego?" Dad asks after we all dish up.

"It was fine. Slow, but hopefully that will change soon." I take a bite out of the shrimp Mom cooked for dinner. The garlic from the shrimp would pair well with the Sauvignon Blanc of the table, but I don't think wine is best with my current mental state. I'm having a hard enough time keeping Emma out of my head without the help of alcohol.

"Oh yeah?" Mom asks. "Why's that?"

"I have a meeting with the marketing firm tomorrow morning. So if everything works out, we could be implementing some changes as early as next week." I see a glimmer of hope in Mom's eyes but I can't quite read Dad's expression.

Mia elbows me from her seat besides mine. "Wow, bro. Look at you getting the job done."

"Yeah, it's exciting. So with that being said, I thought it'd be better for me to take over Mia's job at the shop for the time being.

Especially since I'll need to be doing a few meetings in the city in these upcoming weeks."

I spare a glance at Mia and she mouths a quick "thank you."

"Well that's certainly understandable." Mom gives Mia and me a knowing look. I've given a legitimate excuse for her to drop the Mia issue for now, but that doesn't mean she isn't still suspicious. "Mia, are you okay with this change?"

"Oh, sure! It works out for everyone." Mia smiles at Mom but it's far from believable.

Shit, she couldn't have sold this a *little* better? I served up a perfect excuse on a silver platter and everything. All she had to do was smile . . . well smile better than that.

"That's great news, son. Let's talk more about it tomorrow night, after the meeting."

"Will do." I agree as we finish our dinner, talking about more mundane things, barely approaching anything else business related.

I follow Mia into the kitchen with the excuse to help her clean up the dishes from dinner, but really I want to call her out for weird behaviour. "Hey, so what exactly is going on with you and Mom?" I make sure my voice is hidden under the sound of the running water from the kitchen sink.

"Ugh, we just aren't seeing eye to eye right now." She pulls a dish out of the soapy water and scrubs a little too aggressively at it.

"So, it's more than your license, I take it?"

Mia puts her soapy hand over my mouth before whisper-shouting, "Shhhhh!!!! Are you crazy!?!" She looks around the kitchen, making sure it's clear before she drops her hand. "Mom has no idea about the license-thing and I would very much like it to stay that way."

I use the back of my arm to wipe the suds off my mouth and beard. "Okay . . . but why? Why aren't you and Mom getting along?"

"It's just . . . " She exhales and turns the water off. "She's been wanting to set me up with some of her friends' sons."

"I'm not seeing how one is related to the other—"

"I told Mom that on the nights I stayed in the city, it was because I was going on dates."

"Okay . . ." I'm really confused now.

"Oh my god, Diego. Think!" She scoffs as she taps her finger to her forehead. "If I'm not going into the city, I'm not going on dates. And if I'm not busy with dates in the city then . . . " Oh. *Oh.*

"That sucks." She curls her lips and gives a look that conveys her annoyance at the situation. "Okay, so you go on a couple of dates? What's the big deal?"

"The big deal? The big deal is I don't want to be auctioned off like a prize to be won." When she puts it that way, I get it.

Mom used to pressure me about settling down in my early twenties, right after I moved back home, but after years of being the recluse that I am, she finally gave up on me continuing the family line. I thought she just lost interest, but apparently she just moved down the line to Mia.

"Maybe I can bring you to the city a night or two during the week, to keep up the charade and all? I'm sure we can figure something out."

"Diego? Mia? Are you still busy with the dishes in there?" Mom shouts from the other room.

"We're just finishing now, Mom. We're off to bed. Goodnight!" Mia rushes out as we finish putting the last dish away. "We'll talk more later. Thanks again, Diego."

I ruffle the top of her head, messing up her hair. "Good night, lil' sis."

Traffic was fairly light this morning, allowing me to arrive a little early to my appointment. I'm greeted by the friendly receptionist, but I don't catch her name as she directs me to take a seat, telling me she'll notify the account manager that I've arrived.

Checking the shop's emails on my phone, I look up when I hear heels clicking toward me.

I stand up, a smirk already painted on my face from the sight before me. "Funny seeing you here, Sweetheart."

She takes me in with a slow, full body look. I don't blame her. I'm halfway thinking I'm stuck in a dream too; one I don't want to wake up from any time soon.

"Diego? What are you doing here?" She takes me in one more time before a look of understanding comes over her. "It's *your* family business?"

"Oh good! You've already met." I was so caught up in the sight of Emma before me, I didn't even realize the man who was trailing behind her. "But just in case introductions haven't been made, Emma, this is Diego Sánchez. Diego, this is Emma Hartman, your new account manager for the next six weeks, as long as everything goes smoothly today. But given Emma's background, I'm sure it will. She's always willing to do anything to satisfy the client. Oh, and I'm Javier." He sticks out his hand for me to shake. "We spoke on the phone earlier this week."

"Sounds great." I drop his hand and immediately turn back to Emma. "Emma, you're hired." Then I turn back to Javier. "So when do we start?" I rush out, still attempting some fraction of professionalism, especially after that comment about satisfying the client.

As much as I need to focus on using this opportunity to grow our family's business, I would be lying if I didn't admit to being a little excited about working with Emma for the next month and a half. Six whole weeks of her attention solely on me.

Well, on the winery. I really should attempt to keep the time she spends on the business separate from the time she spends with me. My family needs this to succeed, so that means I need to keep this as business-like as possible. That might even mean not dating her while she's helping us. But with the way she so obviously checked me out when she saw me, there's definitely going to be dating at some point.

"Oh, hold on there, Diego." Javier chuckles, reminding me it's not just Emma and me. "Let me walk you to the conference room, and you and Emma can talk about the needs of your family's winery and the goals you'd like to accomplish in these six weeks. And then, if it's something Emma believes she can achieve in a timely manner, we'll go forward."

I follow Emma and Javier to the glass room, mentally noting there is absolutely zero privacy in this room. "I'll leave you two to it. Pleasure to finally meet you, Diego, and I wish you and your family the best of luck with your business. Please let me know if there is anything else we can do to be of assistance."

He reaches his hand out for mine and I meet it with a firm grip. "Thank you." I glance over to Emma and smile wide with a knowing grin. "I'm sure Emma will be the perfect fit." Javier smiles as he closes the door behind him, leaving just Emma and me alone in what feels like a giant fishbowl.

CHAPTER NINE

EMMA

J'm a mix of emotions sitting across from Diego. I went into today excited and hopeful that my meeting would result in a partnership with a company I could really see myself helping grow.

Javier told me very little in preparation for this meeting, essentially explaining that it was a family winery, one that was struggling financially and most likely in need of a serious rebrand.

Rebranding is my strong suit. Being able to completely start from scratch, in terms of their image, and working on a new way to market the brand is always an exciting challenge for me.

Finding out Diego is my sole focus for the whole time I'm in Spain shouldn't be distracting, but it is.

Somehow, I'll need to find a way to keep this professional and *only* professional. I don't think I'm even allowed to date a client. I guess I've never been attracted to co-workers or clients in the past, so I've never paid attention to if there was a "no-fraternization" rule. Surely, if we repeated any of the acts we did a couple nights ago, it would be grounds for termination. Maybe I should ask Stacia?

No, I shouldn't even be contemplating it. Strictly client-manager business relationship from now on. Even if *that* client did give *this* manager the best night of her life.

And it wasn't just the sex, even though that was phenomenal. Diego and I just . . . clicked.

It was the instant connection I had with him, with clothes on *and* off. It was all just so easy. So effortless. I don't think I've felt that way in . . . well, ever.

But no, I can't. Six weeks. His family deserves my full attention and hell, I deserve to not throw away a position I worked my ass off for over a man. But I'm not completely naïve to the fact that it's not going to be easy, especially with lines like "I'm sure Emma will be the perfect fit." I need to end that immediately.

"I'm only here for six weeks, so if this is going to work, you can't do . . . whatever the hell *that* was." Getting right to the point, aware I can't get too heated since literally anyone could look in on our conversation. Who the hell makes a conference room made entirely of glass anyways?

"What *what* was?" He takes a step towards me.

"*I'm sure Emma will be the perfect fit.*" I mock, attempting to lower my voice and add an accent so I sound more like Diego. Did pretty damn well, if I do say so myself, but Diego looks less than impressed.

"First off, I don't sound like that." I scoff, because yes he fucking does. "And secondly . . . " He walks over to me and lowers his head so he's speaking directly into my ear. To anyone passing by or snooping on our conversation, it would look innocent enough, but my body is practically buzzing with anticipation of what he'll do next. "You *are* a perfect fit. I thought we proved that the other night."

I feel his warm breath on my neck, making me want to beg for his touch. But when I reach up, he's already pulling out a chair for him. Correction, for me. He's waiting with his hand on the chair. Waiting for *me*. "So, what questions do you have for me? You know, to ensure you're a *good fit*."

"Thank you." I take the seat he offers and adjust myself in the chair as he walks around the table, taking the chair immediately across the table from me. "I have some questions about your social media presences. I'll need a current list of products you offer, along with their prices. And I will basically need complete access to the business, and all that entails. Obviously, not your bank and tax information, but we can start with your daily sales, the amount you need to be bringing in monthly to keep your doors open, and we'll go from there."

"My sister posts on some of those sites every so often but not regularly. I'll ask her to send the login information when she can. We have the vineyard, the cellar, stockroom, and office all on one property about an hour away, while a shop, that includes a small cellar beneath, is in the city." I jot down notes in my phone as he continues. "And I can text you a link to our product list once I get back to the shop. I just need your number." That gets my attention.

I mean, we can't work with each other without exchanging our numbers, so it's harmless. I'm doing this for work purposes only.

"Here." I pass my business card over to him. "It still has the North Carolina address on it, but my cell number is the same. That way you have my number and can send the link when you have time."

He grabs the small card then lifts himself off the chair ever so slightly, putting it in his back pocket. "Great. Thanks."

"Sure thing. I was thinking, if the shop is nearby, I'd love a tour later today. If that's alright with you, and of course, if your schedule permits it."

"Actually, I have a reservation right after lunch, but I could take you there now, if that works?"

"Great. How far is it? The office has a car service we can use—"

"Oh, no." He waves me off as he stands. "I drove here and need to park my car closer to the shop anyway. You can just ride with me."

"Oh no, no. I'm okay. How far away is it? Maybe I can just walk." I'm not about to explain my fear of being in cars to someone I had a one-night stand with.

It's already hard enough for me to use the car service. My justification is that they are trained professionals, who literally drive all day. They have to be safe drivers, right? And that removes half of the risk right there. At least that's what I tell myself whenever I have to ride in one. I know I can never control the other drivers on the road, but thinking about that . . . it will only make me never want to get inside a vehicle ever again.

"Come on, it's less than five minutes to drive there. Why walk when you can drive with me?" He props the conference room door open for me, leaning down when I pass by to whisper, "Plus, I'm sure this won't be the last time you'll need a ride from me." I roll my eyes as I walk past him before he adds, "Since we'll be working together and all that." His voice is a little louder now as we walk across the office together.

I chew my bottom lip, looking for a way out of this. One that doesn't feel like trauma dumping or makes me look crazy for being afraid of cars. I'm sure he thinks the gesture looks more like I'm trying to maintain a professional boundary more than having a panic attack.

"I'm the safest driver, I swear. Never had a single ticket or wreck in my life."

I'm still not comfortable getting in the car with Diego. But this is only the first of what I assume will be several situations where I'll need to share a car with him, especially since I have no vehicle of my own.

My choices are either call the company's car service and wait for their arrival or ride with Diego right now.

I need to get used to it at some point, plus he did say the drive is super short. So I'll be easing myself into this. Dipping my toes in the water before agreeing to a longer drive. I'll just try to focus on something else for those five minutes.

"Fine. Let's go."

We walk out of the building and hop into his car. It's a small SUV, which makes me feel a little more comfortable, since larger and heavier cars statically provide better protection in a crash. "It's just up around the block. Actually, it's just a few buildings down from the bar." He clicks his belt as I do the same before he pulls out into traffic.

"Does it have a black door with a glass surround?" I bet it's the one I tried getting wine from yesterday.

"You know it?" He tilts his head towards me but doesn't stray his eyes away from the road ahead of us, something I appreciate.

"I tried picking up a bottle or two there yesterday afternoon, but you must've closed early." Conversation, this is good. Just keep talking and I'll be fine. Everything is fine. We are safe. Diego said he's a great driver. Everything is—

"Yeah, most of the week we close around two. Unless we have a special reservation." His answer interrupts my inner spiral.

"When do you get most of your traffic?"

"Probably Thursdays through Saturdays. We're open later those days. We close around two then open back again around five for another two hours."

That leaves three hours unaccounted for? I thought the siesta that Javier told me about was optional, but I'm quickly finding out it's more of a lifestyle over here. "Those are the nights that Mia or I stay in the city."

Mia? I thought he said he was unattached? Maybe it's just a coworker?

"Who's Mia?" I blurt out, quickly telling myself it's just for business purposes. I need to be aware of all those working at the winery. I'm definitely not being jealous. Just doing research is all.

Diego chuckles. "She's my younger sister. She was taking care of the shop up until . . . Well, let's just say, we had to switch around a few things, but now I'm taking care of the shop until further notice." There's a story in there somewhere, but it doesn't seem like I need to dig into it any further right now. "And we're here."

See. That wasn't so bad. No close calls. He kept his hands at the proper nine and three position, and used his turn signals even when no other car was around. He seems like a decent enough driver.

After Diego unlocks the door, he turns off the building's alarm and ushers me inside. It's everything I pictured when I heard about the small shop in the city.

The walls are made with a beige-colored rock and clay mixture with oak hardwood floors running the length of the space.

There's a mixture of tables in the main room, most bar height, but there are a few larger six-top standard-height tables. I'm assuming when they have larger parties, they push the shorter tables together to accommodate them.

Peeking to a spot near the desk, there's a good amount of bottles on display, enticing those who enter to buy a bottle while they visit.

"Did you say you had a small cellar here too?" I ask after reaching what I thought was the end of the shop, but Diego surprises me with a hidden door. "Oh, that's fun." He leads me down the steps and flips the light on.

Now this is interesting. The underground cellar is made up of old bricks, which also form the low but vaulted ceiling. Wine bottle storage surrounds the four walls, along with a couple of barrels here and there.

I walk around the space and look back to Diego, who's standing near the wooden steps. "It's like a naughty hole but with wine."

He crosses his arms with a bemused smile across his face. "A *what* hole?"

"A naughty hole." From the look of confusion, I explain. "You know, a place where you're sent for being naughty or bad? Like for a time-out?"

"I have a very different definition for that phrase." Well, when he puts it like that, I guess there could be an innuendo in there somewhere.

"Well . . . moving right along." I walk past a smirking Diego as I head back upstairs. "Do you have any current partnerships with other businesses or tour guide companies?"

"Oh, nothing like that." I hear the click of the door as he closes it behind us. "I've actually never even thought about reaching out to any tour companies, but it sounds like it could be lucrative. Please." He waves to one of the chairs.

He pulls out my chair, pushing me in after I take a seat then walks off to grab some glasses and what looks to be a bottle of water.

"Where do you get your food for the tasting? Who provides the food for your parties here or at your winery?"

He hands me a glass of water as he answers. "Most of the food supplies come from vendors we've known awhile, ones who have a longstanding spot at the market down the street." I take a sip of bubbly water as he continues. "And we don't do any events at the winery. Hell, we hardly do parties here, unless you count a bachelorette party now and then."

Oh man, there is room for so much growth here. Where do I even begin?

"There's a huge untapped market for your family then. Weddings and celebrations would be a massive opportunity to grow your brand, plus increase profits. You could try partnering with a travel group, or even a cruise line, for private tastings. Really, the possibilities are endless."

CHAPTER TEN

DIEGO

It never even occurred to me to partner with a tour guide company, or even a cruise line for that matter. This woman is dreaming big!

Obviously, it makes perfect sense when she says it. It would bring a constant stream of visitors to the shop, and renting out the winery would be a perfect opportunity to use what we already have. We could easily hold two hundred or so outside in the grass field, over by the main building and office.

As Emma continues to talk about ideas for growth and rebranding, I can't help but be consumed with her clear talent and skill for this.

She seems so at ease talking about this kind of thing, and she's filled with creative solutions. With how confident she sounds already, I'm hopeful that she'll provide the solution we need to save the winery.

By the time we finish, it's close to the time of my next reservation.

"So I'll put some things together and get back to you in a couple of days?"

"Sounds great, Sweetheart." She purses her lips at me for the nickname, but her mask slips as a smile threatens to break free.

"Goodbye, Diego." She puts extra emphasis in my name as she waves her goodbye from the threshold, long hair blowing wild as she steps outside. At least I know I'll see her again this time when she says goodbye.

The afternoon passes by quickly, a few reservations and even a few walk-ins. With the day I had, I'd normally opt to stay overnight in Barcelona, but I promised Mia I'd bring her with me tomorrow morning. When the last guest leaves, I set the alarm, lockup, and make my way back to the winery.

"How's city life been treating you? I know before we did this little switch, on the days you drove into the city, you only did deliveries, and maybe lunch with Lorenzo, before heading back to your cave." Mia starts up after we get on the main road.

She loves to jab me with my reclusiveness but really, I see no issue with that. I'm just fine with her being the social butterfly of the family.

"Yeah, it's an adjustment for sure but it'll be fine for the time being."

"Plus, it's more opportunity to have a fling. Maybe if you do, Mom will get off my back a little." She laughs like it's funny to even think of me meeting someone.

"Actually," I start, my voice confident, "I *did* meet someone the other day. Interesting story . . . " I can't help but chuckle because the whole situation is kind of comical when you think about it. I finally meet someone, only for them to be off-limits. "Had a fun night with an amazing woman, thinking I'd never see her again, only to find out yesterday that she's our point-person at the marketing firm."

"What?!" Mia shouts and without turning my focus away

from the road, I can see she's staring me down. "I must've misheard you. Can you repeat that?"

"She's going to be the one rebranding—"

"No," She interrupts. "I'm still at the part where you said you met someone."

"Ha. Ha. Very funny."

"So, she's amazing, huh?"

"Mia, I don't think I've ever met a person like her. But it doesn't matter." I attempt to shrug it off like it indeed doesn't matter, when really, all I've thought about for the last day is that fact that she works right around the corner from the shop. How I'll be seeing a lot of her for the foreseeable future, but I can't do anything about it. "Can't go any further now that she's working for us."

"That's complete bullshit. Who's going to know?"

Turning over to her at a red light, I tilt my head. "Know what?"

"If you're in a relationship with her?" She throws her hands up before elaborating. "It's probably not even a rule. Just something they advise against, so things don't get weird with clients. Could you imagine how awkward it would be to work with the person you broke-up with? That'd be a headache to deal with and a quick way to lose clients."

I nod. She does bring up a good point. "I guess you're right."

"Alright!" She grabs my arm and shakes it. "Who are you? And what have you done with Diego? There's no way my brother would not only be caught up on a woman, but then admit I, his sister, am right? Blink once if you're in trouble."

"Hey, even a broken clock is right twice a day."

"I hate it when you do that." Mia crosses her arms and turns to stare out the window. "You using those phrases only reminds me that you had a chance to leave the country for a bit while I can't even manage to make it out of a two-hour radius."

"I thought you said you were over this? That was over a

decade ago, and it was just for school, Mia. Plus, it didn't even last that long."

"You still got the chance to go. You got to go explore the world, even just for a little." I hear her sigh as she settles deeper in her seat. "The closest I get to doing that is running the shop in the city. And even then," she chuckles, "I was stupid enough to get that opportunity taken away from me."

I reach over the middle console and shake her shoulder a bit. "Hey, it was a mistake. One you're trying to fix." She thumbs under her eye, gathering the tears that fell. "For now, I promise to take you into the city, whenever you want."

"Whenever I—" Her voice turns excited, but I'm quick to rain on her parade before she takes full advantage of my offering.

"Within reason that is." I toss a stern look her way before adding sincerely, "But Mia, I promise, after we get the winery all straightened out, I'll work on getting you out. Maybe book you a trip and let you spread those wild wings of yours."

"If. *If* we can get the winery straightened out." I let the silence sit between us for a minute; not really knowing how to respond.

In one respect, I want to be realistic, because I know that there's just as much of a chance of the winery shutting down as there is saving it. While on the other, I want to put on those rose-tinted glasses and trust Emma to help save our family's business.

"I'll be making deliveries this morning, so you'll be at the shop alone for the majority of it." Mia and I decided to leave for our commute a little earlier this morning.

I have a sneaking suspicion she was ready to go so early because she wanted to avoid Mom.

"Yeah, yeah. I used to do this everyday, Diego. Do we have anything on the books for today?" Mia sasses while adjusting my radio, putting something a little too poppy for my taste, and resting her feet on my dash after she's satisfied with her selection.

I'm more of a fan of instrumental music; I let the beat and rhythm tell the story without the words taking center stage.

"In the afternoon, there are five reservations, all ranging in size, but it's Thursday, so I'm sure there will be some walk-ins tonight, too. You planning on staying at the apartment tonight?"

"Where else? It's not like I can drive home." She huffs out and I'm willing to bet, if my eyes weren't so glued to the road, I'd see her famous eye-roll she loves to dish out. "God, it's only been a week and I hate this."

"Well, *maybe* you should treat driving more like the privilege it is and respect the rules of the road." She knocks her fist into my shoulder. "It'll make the world a safer place." I chuckle.

"Okay, that's enough from the peanut gallery. Plus, I never got in a single car accident."

"Yet." I tack on quickly.

"But seriously, I'll just crash in one of the spare bedrooms. By the way, you really need to get some new mattresses in there. Yours is much more comfortable."

"Wait, how do you know what my mattress feels like?" She's quiet for too long. "Mia, have you been sleeping in my bedroom when I'm not there?" I ask as I pull up to the shop, turning and glaring at her after I've shifted into park.

She shrugs. "What? Your room has the better of the bathrooms. And your bed is so comfortable and surprisingly fluffy. The other bedrooms are stuffy, too."

"Then open the window, Mia! Or buy new sheets for all I care! Don't sleep in my bed." I get out of the car and make my way over to unlock the door. "Please don't say you've had . . . *guests* over and in my room." Even just the thought of that makes me want to burn my bed.

"Ew! God, no! I'm not *that* perverted. Why would I want to have sex in my brother's bed?" She bends over and pretends to dry heave.

"Alright, alright." I open the door and turn off the alarm. "Send me some links and I'll make sure one of the guest beds is up to your . . . What was it? Fluffy?" She nods. "Yes, I'll make sure one of the spares is up to your *fluffy* and non-stuffy standards."

Mia giggles as she starts to open the shop up. "Oh, please do use the word fluffy more in your vocabulary. It helps break down your fire-breathing exterior."

"And with that, I'm out of here. I'll be back around noon."

CHAPTER ELEVEN

EMMA

I'm in the office only a couple of hours on Thursday morning before I decide to leave. It's hard for me to be creative when I'm stuck in a dull space, hearing the conversations of my fellow coworkers.

"Leaving so soon?" I hear as I pack up my things. I turn and see Stacia peeking over the wall. Just the woman I've been meaning to talk to.

"Yeah, I'm just in a creative slump and need a change of scenery." Grabbing my purse, I do another glance around the office to see if anyone is nearby, not wanting anyone to hear my question for Stacia.

"I totally understand. There's this tapas place not too far—"

"Yes! Lorenzo's!" My face lights up, recalling, and maybe even drooling, over those potatoes. Definitely not about how it's the place I first met Diego. And my mind *certainly* doesn't wander off about the events that happened that night after Lorenzo's. That wouldn't be professional at all.

Speaking of professionalism, "Hey, I've been meaning to ask you a question about office relationships."

"*Oh* . . . already have your eye on someone?" She leans in conspiratorially.

"No, not like that. Just curious, if I did, are there any rules against it?"

"No rules, per se, but it is frowned upon. I know a couple of months ago, two staff members were dating and then when they broke up, Sarah ended up leaving that same week." Well that sucks for whoever this Sarah is but doesn't really answer my question. "But then again Sarah might have just switched to another branch. There are so many to choose from; I heard someone say they just opened a branch in Poland!"

"What about relationships with clients?" I ask, trying to steer us back to the question I'm desperate for the answer to.

"Oh!" Her eyes go big as she explains. "Those are *strongly* advised against for obvious reasons, of course." Right, *obvious* reasons.

Only right now, I'm having a hard time naming just one of those obvious reasons. Especially when Diego's face keeps popping into my head. That chiseled jaw line hidden by his trimmed beard. It's not the only landscaping he takes—

"But don't let me keep you from Lorenzo's." Stacia's voice punches right through my imaginary Diego. "It's the best; I'm obsessed. The food there is great at getting you out of any kind of slump."

"I completely agree." I nod, thinking about how out of all the tapas bars I could've walked into that first night, it was fate that I walked into Lorenzo's.

"Well, enjoy! And hopefully you find that creative inspiration soon."

"Thanks, Stacia. See you later!"

The nice thing about my job is that I don't have to feel confined to a desk. Realistically, I can ultimately get my job done anywhere I choose to go.

Even back in North Carolina, I would often walk below to the coffee shop under the office. Or some days I wouldn't even show up to the office, just work from home. There's also this beautiful library that isn't too far of a walk from my apartment in Raleigh. That's where some of my best ideas were created.

The library has this amazing wall of windows with a bunch of seating, making it the perfect place for quiet brainstorming. It really was the perfect place to focus, whether it be for college or work.

I leave the office a little before eleven, and decide to swing by Diego's shop to get a few answers to the questions Javier brought to my attention. Plus, I can finally grab a bottle of wine for Manuel to thank him for helping me the other day.

The shop's lights are on as I approach the door, so I walk straight in. Only the person to greet me isn't my big burly Diego.

She's cute and curvy. Beautiful curly, chestnut hair with a great smile. A smile that gives her away immediately. This must be Diego's sister. Mia, if I remember correctly?

"*Bon dia!*" she greets with a wave.

"*Hola.* Is Diego here?" I look around, trying to spot him. There aren't too many places for a man his size to hide, so unless he's downstairs, I'm betting he's not here.

"He'll be back in an hour or so. But I can try and help you out. I'm the better of the two of us." She winks. I like her already. "What do you need?"

"I'm actually working with him—"

"Oh! You're from the marketing firm. Emma, right?" I nod as she takes a good hard look up and down my body. "Now I get it." She adds with a knowing smile.

"Get what?" I look down at myself and then back to her.

"You're cute. Like *really* cute. Like steal-Diego's-focus cute. But I guess you already did, didn't you." She smiles like the cat who caught the canary.

"From the sound of it, you already heard how we met, but I assure you, I'm doing my best to keep things professional between us. If I had known he would be my client, I wouldn't have . . . " I pause and scoff at myself. "That's a lie. I don't regret anything that happened with your brother that night—" The corner of my mouth starts creeping up in a smile.

Mia holds up her hand to stop me. "Ew, say less. I beg of you."

I laugh. "What I meant was, going forward, I'm keeping this a strictly business relationship."

"Uh huh. If you say so." Giving me a quick eye-roll, she walks up to me and extends her hand. "I'm Mia by the way." I grab it and we shake. "What is it you needed from him?"

"I just had a few questions for some of my proposals, but they can wait until later. What you *could* help me with is picking out a few bottles of wine. They're for me and as a thank-you gift to someone in my building."

"Given you just moved here, I'd say you probably don't know what kind of wine the person prefers. Am I right?" I nod. "So I'd go with our Grenache, that's what we're known for." She grabs a bottle and places it on the counter between us. "But you can't go wrong with our GSMs either." She points to a display filled with, I'm assuming, GSMs. "We have a few, but this one's my favorite." She pulls out another bottle from under the counter. "It's still Grenache-dominant, so it still has all the fruitiness, but it also has the spice from the Syrah and structure from the Mourvèdre."

"Perfect! I'll take two of the Grenaches and two of those GMSs?"

"GSM." She corrects with a smile. "It's short for Grenache, Syrah, and Mourvèdre. GSM is a mix of all three types of grapes." Ah! That makes much more sense now.

She reaches down and grabs two more bottles, placing them on the counter before me. Taking a better look at the label design, and although it does the job just fine, it could definitely use a face lift.

"Which one's the gift?" Mia grabs a wooden box as I point to the Grenache. "Great choice. Is it okay if I put the rest in a wine bag?"

"Yeah, that's fine." I scan my card while she boxes the gift and bags the rest. "Do you know when your brother will be back?"

Mia hands me the wine while looking at the clock on the wall. "I'm not sure, but I do know he'll be the one closing up tonight. Our last reservation should end right before seven. You should come by then."

"Sounds good. Thanks for your help, Mia. I'm sure I'll be seeing you around." I smile and head to the exit.

"Oh, I'm sure you will, too. Bye for now, Emma!" I hear her shout as I walk out the door.

I decide against returning to the office, opting not to walk back to the sad little cubicle because my apartment is just across the street, taunting me to enjoy the view while I work outside on my private balcony.

It took little time to make that vision a reality, setting my laptop and phone on the balcony's table, only going back inside to get a cup of tea and a few snacks.

Taking my seat outside, I jump straight into creating proposals for Diego. I lay out my top favorite proposals and choose to focus on the tour guide option first.

Before digging too deep, I send an email to Javier. He knows the area so well, so I figure he's the best brain to pick for reaching out to any local tour guide businesses. I also make sure to ask if he has any cruise line contacts as well. Can't hurt to dream big, right?

Moving on to the two ideas I'm favoring, I list out the potential costs and profits based on the area. I also create a schedule for the changes, a guide of when and how to implement the improvements.

The plan proposes slowly increasing the costs as we go. Instead of jumping in and spending money the winery doesn't have, the winery can hopefully reap the benefits while making more subtle changes, using the profit from the prior changes to help pay for even more improvements.

After feeling like my thoughts are a little more organized, I call my older sister, Lindsay, for help with the event rental proposal. She gives me some helpful advice on what

Diego and his family should look out for when hosting events.

She's been an event coordinator for almost a decade, and she's a damn good one, even if her social life has paid the cost.

"Honestly, it sounds like they have almost everything they need. Just double check those permits and their insurance. I have no idea about the laws in Spain about event hosting."

"Perfect. Thanks, sis. And you'll send me those brochures so I can use those as examples when making theirs?"

"Emailing them over as we speak."

"You are a rockstar!" My email dings in the background letting me know her email just came through. "I owe you one."

"No, you don't." I hear Lindsay sigh over the line before commenting, "It's been a few days now . . ."

"Uh huh, and your point?"

"My point is, are you staying . . . safe?"

"If by 'safe' you mean not doing any more sleepovers? Then yes." I laugh before adding, "And get this, my sleep-over buddy ended up being the client I got assigned."

"Wait, it's *his* winery?"

"Well, it's his family's but yeah, small world right?"

"Be careful with that, sis." Oh here we go again. "Last thing you want is to get involved with a client. Especially if it goes against your firm's rules." I make a mental note to get clarification from Stacia about that next time I see her.

"I *am* being careful, Linds. We already discussed boundaries and I don't see there being any problems keeping things strictly professional."

"Uh huh . . ." Her voice oozes with doubt.

"Alright . . . well . . . fun talk!" Even a person with noise cancelling headphones could hear the sarcasm in my voice. "Thanks for the help with the proposal. I'll talk to you later."

"Ugh, Emma. I'm sorry—"

"No, it's fine, Linds. I know you're just looking out. But really, I'm fine. I love you very much."

"Love you too, Emma. Good luck with your proposals."

"Thanks! Bye." After hanging up, I open her email and read the short body of text.

Her quick message points out that prices will vary depending on locations and how I should research other wineries in the area to see what the average price is, giving me a great starting point for my cost research.

Thankfully, the winery has most of the facilities in place to host an event that large, and anything they don't have, they can build into the cost for the client. Additionally, I think an exclusive partnership with vendors would be a great route to go, whether it be for chair and table rentals, linens, or even the food.

Liability wise, like she said, we would need to check their insurance as well as double check for any necessary permits for events that large.

One of my other proposals is for a more literal approach to rebranding. Changing all of their labels, any marketing pamphlets, and of course their internet presence. It may seem like a simple cosmetic change, but you sell a lot with looks and having a label that really grabs the eye can make a difference in making someone pick up a bottle or not.

Even though the saying says not to judge a book by its cover, I'm still guilty of doing just that when I look for a new book to read, or a bottle of wine for that matter.

Checking the time on my laptop, I bring everything back inside before returning to Diego's shop, hopefully catching him before he leaves for the night.

CHAPTER TWELVE

DIEGO

"One more reservation, right? You want to take them, and I'll start cleaning up everything else?" Mia's a much better people-person than I am, and honestly, by the end of the day, my social battery is drained, especially on these longer days. I forgot how much energy it takes working at the shop. I'm fine with all of the work that goes into running the shop, I just need to get adjusted to being back around . . . well, people.

"Oh, I was actually going to ask if you could cover me since I'm meeting some friends around seven." Mia is conveniently dodging my stare, doing everything in her power to keep her back to me.

"Yeah, I guess. Go enjoy."

She rushes over to me, squeezing me before grabbing her bag and running out the door. But before she leaves, she tosses over her shoulder with a mysterious smile, "I have a feeling the night will pick up for you too, brother." Whatever the hell that means.

I can't force her to stay nor can I blame her for having a social life when I have zero. Well, that's not entirely true. I have Lorenzo and his employees.

Really Diego? I'm so low on friends that I'm counting Luis

and Lola? The people who *work* at the bar? I never see them outside of the bar. Hell, I don't even have their numbers. I feel like a good requirement for a friend is if you have their phone number, or at least some way to contact them.

Technically, I have the *bar's* number. Does that count?

I continue my pathetic wallowing about my lack of friends while I clean before the last group comes in. I guess I have Emma now too. She could be a friend.

A naked friend.

No, *just* a friend. A business friendship. I even have her number, so she definitely qualifies as a friend now. Come to think of it, why haven't I used her number yet?

But what would I even text her? "Hey, this is Diego. Here's my number" or "Hi, it's me. Diego."

I contemplate a bunch of first text ideas while the next group comes in and gets served. The group's a lively bunch, so I just serve and explain, while they continue to talk and laugh with each other. Seeing groups like this makes me wish I hadn't been so reclusive over the last few years.

They all seem to be having fun. All relaxed, and laughing while sharing stories with each other. Someday I'd like that.

After they leave, I start cleaning up when I hear the door open again. I turn around to greet the newcomer and freeze a little when I see it's Emma.

"Hi!" she greets with a sweet smile and cute little wave. "Want some help cleaning up?"

"Emma, what a pleasant surprise." I can feel the corners of my mouth raising. "I'm almost done here, but feel free to take a seat and keep me company while I close up." That comment makes her smile glow even more as she pulls out the nearest chair.

She's wearing these high-waisted trousers that are fitted tight, sitting right at her waist, with a white button-down blouse, half tucked into her waistband. It looks like she may have attempted to pull it out while walking over here. Her strawberry blonde hair has a touch more copper in it today and flows a little wild down her back.

"I take it your sister didn't tell you I was stopping by?"

So, that was what Mia's mysterious goodbye was all about. I'll have to circle back around with Mia afterwards. "No, she didn't. But I'm happy you're here now."

"I would've texted but I still don't have your number since you never texted me those files." Oh the files! That would've been a perfect first text. "Do you mind if I snag it now?" She pulls out her phone.

"Sure," I rattle off my number and a minute later, I feel my phone buzz in my pocket. "Was that you?"

"Yup! I just texted you." I pull out my phone and I see a text from an international number.

UNKNOWN NUMBER:

Emma - work

Short and simple. Very professional.
I send off my own version.

DIEGO:

Diego - night of amazing marathon sex

Her phone dings, and I watch as the blush floods her face and she bites her bottom lip.

"Now that isn't very professional." She scolds lifting her eyebrow, but she's not able to keep her smile away for long.

"And here I thought that was my identifier?" I walk over to her, taking the seat across from her.

"Pfft." She rolls her eyes.

"Or maybe this is a better one." I'm quick to send off a text from my side of the table.

DIEGO:

Diego - the best sex I've ever had

She checks her phone as it buzzes and slams it down immediately after. "Or maybe I should just input your name as 'Diego - the biggest dick'!" She shoots me a tightlipped smile, but it quickly fades as her eyes widen and her mouth drops as she realizes what she just confessed.

"Far be it for me to correct you." I smirk as I get up to finish closing down the shop. "I wouldn't mind that identifier one bit."

"I'm sure you wouldn't." She mutters before taking a loud exhale. "Switching gears—" Her tone becomes more upbeat. "I came over originally to ask you some business questions, since we're, you know, keeping this a *professional* relationship."

"Hey, you're the one who brought my dick into this." I raise my hands, feigning innocence. "But go on. Ask your questions while I finish up."

"Okay, so . . . " She pulls up something on her phone. "Who is your largest customer currently, wholesale or retail?"

"I'd say wholesale at the moment." I spray a few tables, wiping them down as I go. "We used to get a lot more foot traffic here, but I'm not sure what changed."

"Was it more recent? The change in foot traffic that is."

"Hmm . . . " Coming behind her, I grab both of her wrists in one hand, raising them above her head.

She takes a sharp breath. "Diego, what are you—"

I spray the cleaner, interrupting her train of thought. As I bend lower and bring a towel to the table, I whisper into her ear, "Just making sure it doesn't get too dirty in here." Her breath stutters for half a minute, telling me I've successfully gotten under her skin.

"To answer your earlier question," I keep hold of her wrists while I wipe the towel in slow circles, making sure every inch of the surface is cleaned, but also providing me an excuse to keep my hands on her. "I'd have to see the financials. My sister has been the one running the show for the last couple of years. I only just started filling in this last week." I place her arms back down and continue my closing routine.

Emma shakes her head and clears her throat as I step away.

"Okay, well I guess it's not all that important right now . . . but I'll let you know if I change my mind . . . on the financials that is."

Oh I definitely riled her up. It's cute seeing her get frazzled like this.

Ten minutes later, the shop is all cleaned. And during that time, I've kept my distance, trying to let Emma continue rattling off her questions in peace, but I've waited long enough.

I grab a few things from the stash of food in the fridge, put a bottle under my arm, and snag two wine glasses.

Pulling out my chair with my foot, she asks, "What is this?" Motioning the spread I just brought over.

I pop the cork out and pour us both a glass. "Think of it as product research. You really should taste the wine you're helping to sell. Plus, this bottle was already opened earlier today. It would be a shame to waste it." I slide the wine glass in front of her and take a sip from mine.

"For your information, I actually bought some wine earlier, when I was talking with your sister. A Grenache and a GSM." She takes a slice of prosciutto, folding it into a little square before popping it in her mouth, sucking the tip of her finger as she slides it in. I'm entranced by her dainty finger swiping across her lip then leading down her chin. I follow it down to her exposed chest, then lower, under her . . . I shoot my eyes up to hers. "Tsk, tsk. I thought I lost you there for a minute Diego. This prosciutto is delicious by the way." Shit, did I just imagine all that?

"I pride myself on having the best meat." She chuckles at my innuendo before taking a sip of wine. "Please continue your questioning. I didn't mean to distract you with wine and prosciutto. I assumed if I was hungry, you were probably as well."

"I actually have no more questions to ask. But I appreciate the wine and food."

She gets up to go. "Just because you finished your questions, doesn't mean you have to leave." I look up and catch her eyes wandering down my chest, snapping back to my eyes once she catches herself. I motion my hand over to her chair. "At least finish the bottle with me."

"Trust me, 'everyday me' would have no issues doing just that, and maybe more." She says the last part under her breath, but I still heard it. And is that yearning I detect? "But 'professional me' says this is a bad idea, one that could lead to dangerous places."

"I promise I'll be a good boy." I smirk, causing her to bite her lips. Those lush, pink lips; ones that *I* want to be biting. "I'll even stay on my side of the table."

Her head tilts side to side like she's contemplating the idea. It's just after seven on a Thursday night, so clearly neither of us have plans or else we wouldn't be here.

"No, I should go." But she stays standing right by her chair. So, I get up from mine. She eyes my every move suspiciously.

"If you insist on leaving, let me walk you to your apartment." I grab my keys and head to the door. I look back and find she's still standing, frozen by her chair. "Change your mind so soon?"

She shakes her head. "No, sorry. I'm just across the street. No need to walk me."

"I know, but I want to all the same." I lock up and we step out onto the sidewalk. "Lead the way, Sweetheart."

"It's just the building above the tapas bar."

"You weren't kidding. Well, isn't that convenient."

"It is, if you love a great meal." She turns my way with a coy smile. "Which I know you do."

Now who's the one not being professional? I'm not one hundred percent sure if she meant the double meaning when she said that, but my dick sure is taking it like she did. Especially since the implication means he could get some attention other than my right hand tonight.

But I promised to be good. Good guys don't have random hard-ons while walking women home. That's just called being a creep.

"This is me." She looks up at the building then back to me. "And look at that! We arrived with no ass-grabs or anything for the two minutes it took to get here, it seems like you really *can* be a good boy."

The praise does something to me coming from her, sarcastic or not. In fact, I might even like it more because of her sarcastic tone. What in the world is happening to me?

"I'll be finishing up these proposals and most likely see you early this next week, if that works." She takes a couple steps up the entry, making it so she's almost even to my height.

"Let me know when you'd like to meet, and I'll be there. On my knees if you wish." As I lean in to give her a goodbye hug, I feel her slightly stiffen before returning the gesture, sneaking her arms under mine and around my waist. I hold her for what will never be enough time, but definitely longer than a professional hug calls for. But before I unwrap my arms, I bend down and kiss the side of her neck.

Not as forward as a kiss on the lips, but something more inti-mate than a kiss on the cheek. Before pulling back, I whisper in her ear, "Hope your bed isn't too cold tonight without me in it, Emma."

Her breath shutters for a minute as she holds me a little closer before finally releasing me and whispering. "Good night, Diego."

She turns and walks away, into her building, leaving me here alone, wishing I was going up with her.

CHAPTER THIRTEEN

EMMA

A fucking *neck* kiss!?! Who in the world gives someone a neck kiss for a goodbye kiss? Good god. Can I really be ruined from all future dates because someone, someone who is *supposed* to be a work colleague may I add, decided to go full throttle and give me the *hottest* non-lip kiss goodbye?

I've never been so thankful for my little purple friend. But even that's not having the same effect since meeting Diego.

My vibrator seems miniature compared to what he brought to the table. I don't think I'll ever be able to feel as full as I did with Diego.

Do they sell vibrators in Spain? I might need to upgrade while I'm here to help satisfy the need, but for now, I'll just have to work with what I've got. It's not like I can text him. We're supposed to have a *working* relationship. One that's strictly business, no funny business whatsoever.

Who am I kidding? The forbidden aspect of this is fucking hot, and I'm not even a week into this. Hell, I'm not even a week into being in Spain and I'm already dickmatized. After one time! Well, not *one* time, more like five or six.

Or was it seven?

Okay, let's just say after one *night*. I can read the room, I know at this point, it's not *if* we'll break the rule of not sleeping together, it's *when*.

I've read way too many romances to be as naïve as some of those characters. There's no way I will have enough willpower to hold off Diego forever.

Fuck, I could text him right now and I'm sure he'd come running. Ready to please me with his hands, mouth, or dick. Or even all of the above.

No!

No. You aren't going to do that Emma. At least give it another week. Get through the proposals. Put a plan into motion before completely distracting yourself. Diego deserves that. His family deserves that.

Oh, that's good. Think more about his family. That's killing my ladyboner. His parents definitely deserve me giving their business my full, undivided attention, even if that means denying their son the pleasure he deserves.

Nope, ladyboner back. Fuck. Why did it have to be a neck kiss?

I spend the rest of my Thursday night with my phone put away, in the highest cabinet I could find, while I use my vibrator. Well *try* to use my vibrator. Is there really anything worse than being all worked up, getting close to climax, only for the damn thing to die?

Buzz. Buzz. Bu . . . I could've just used my fingers to finish; I *was* right there. But I knew no matter how much I worked myself, it wouldn't be the release I was craving.

And even if I did continue, I would've been interrupted anyways because my phone rang a minute later. Who is calling me at this hour? Maybe it's Diego? Maybe he's having the same problem, too! Well, not with a vibrator dying . . . or maybe with a vibrator dying. You never know someone's toy preference.

I practically leapt from bed into the kitchen, hopping on the counter like I'm doing parkour. I'm amazed I didn't break the counter. Or my leg.

Reaching up to grab my phone, I'm surprised just how disappointed I am when I see it's one of my sisters calling, and not Diego.

"Hey, sis," I pant. "What's up?"

"Were you just having sex?" Taylor greets.

"I wish." Not even lying a little bit. "No, I just ran across the apartment to grab my phone. What's going on?" I take a seat on my countertop and attempt to calm my breathing.

"I was just calling to check in on you. And I wanted to say that Lindsay and I are down to visit for a couple of days; we just wanted to get some dates that work best for you."

"Oh yes! I'd love that. I'd probably say in two weeks or so? I need to present my proposals and hopefully by the time y'all visit, I'll be working on implementing one or more of the changes."

"Great! I think we're just going to do a long weekend, but we're both excited. Tory doesn't think she'll be able to come, but I'm happily surprised that Lindsay's even *attempting* to make the trip." Wow. That *is* a surprise. She never, like literally never, takes a sick day, let alone a vacation. "My hopes aren't too high with her *actually* making the flight over, so it might end up just being me, but I guess only time will tell."

"At least the thought is there. That's what counts. For me at least." Lindsay and Taylor are twins, and though they used to be the tightest of all us sisters, a couple years ago, a fight happened at one of the holiday parties that drew them apart.

We all had a little too much to drink and got on the subject of Jess, Taylor's boyfriend at the time, but now fiancé. In fact, Jess and Taylor are scheduled to get married in September.

Anyways, Jess isn't a favorite among the family and Lindsay, not so subtly, let Taylor know she deserved better, and something about him being trash?

I don't remember what exactly was said, and really nobody does because of Mom's special eggnog. I think it was my first year drinking, well legally that is, so I was going hard, as was the rest of the family.

Ever since then, they've been less than friendly with each other. Lindsay is truly a busy woman, so she's not at a lot of family get-togethers, and Taylor loves to remind everyone of Lindsay's absence. I think her snarkiness is just her way of dealing with the hurt of missing her best friend.

I wish they would just work it out. I know, or at least hope, they will someday. Maybe after the wedding it will finally all blow over out since the ring would be on, and that would be the end of that.

"Anyways, is it okay if we both stay with you? I wasn't sure how big your apartment is. But if it's not large enough, one or both of us could get a hotel."

"Of course! There's more than enough—"

Taylor cuts me off with a squeal. "Oh my god! I can't believe I didn't ask sooner. Have you seen the man from your first night again?!"

I chuckle. "Yes, yes I have. Get this, he's my client."

"Emma, no! Are you serious?"

"Yup."

"So what are you going to do?"

"Nothing. Well, nothing right *now*. I'm trying to stay as professional as possible."

"*Trying* being the key word there. Emma, I know you. If he didn't leave a lasting impression, you wouldn't be *trying* anything." She has a point there. "It would be easy for you to keep your distance and turn your resting bitch face on without a second thought."

"Hey! It's not my fault I learned my RBF from the queen herself."

"Bitch." We both laugh. "But you're right. I do have the best RBF." We laugh some more before she adds on, "Look, all I'm saying, is it's rare for you to catch . . . whatever it is you've caught. Get your ducks in a row and figure out what you want."

"Speaking of what you want . . ." I add, trying to switch the conversations into her relationship.

"Everything is fine, Em. Jess is fine. Wedding planning is fine. Life is just fine."

"You deserve more than just *fine*, Taylor."

"I'm comfortable and taken care of. I want for nothing." Liar. I know she might love Jess, but she isn't *in* love with him. It's a marriage of convenience, and *not* of the romance book types.

"If you say so." There's a pause before I add, "I'll send you some dates and hopefully see you and Lindsay soon."

"Sounds perfect, sis. Love you!"

"Love you, too." I hang up and decide to take a rinse off before heading to bed.

CHAPTER FOURTEEN

DIEGO

A few days go by without much talk from Emma. We've exchanged some texts, all starting off with questions about the business before moving closer into the grey area of our relationship.

Nothing incriminating though, just in case someone from her office sees. Just a little light flirting before she sends a "goodbye for now" text, ending the conversations every time just before things got too heated.

It took all my willpower the other night not to reach over the table and kiss her. And saying goodbye . . .

Well, let's just say the neck kiss was just as much of a tease for me as it was for her. I went home and couldn't get her off my mind all weekend. I found my gaze constantly drifting over to her building when I was at the shop. Wondering if she was inside, thinking of me as much as I'm thinking of her.

Emma reached out late Monday, asking for a meeting on Tuesday. Obviously I agreed, but only under the condition I take her to the winery so she knows what we are working for. With a little extra push, she agreed for me to pick her up early in the morning, allowing us to spend the majority of the day together.

I spent the night in town, since there was no sense in driving home tonight, only to get up early to drive an hour to pick her up for the winery, then to return to the city a couple hours after that.

Since the shop didn't have any reservations for the day, I took the liberty of closing it with a sign apologizing and stating business hours will resume tomorrow. Tuesdays are normally slow anyway.

Hell, almost every day is slow; that's why we hired Emma.

As I open the door to her building, I'm greeted by a young man, hair slicked back with a faint mustache. Looks to be about Emma's age. He seems decent looking enough; not sure how much I like that.

"*Bon dia.*" He smiles and waves.

I politely wave back, but my attention is stolen as soon as Emma walks down the stairs. The first thing I see are her over-the-knee brown leather boots, ones that lead my eyes up her legs.

She's wearing some type of tights, giving coverage to keep it professional. A brown skirt sits at her waist, the kind with little pleats folded on the sides. She paired it with a white button down blouse, a little beige sweater vest pulled over.

Her hair is mostly tied back away from her face but not fully up. A few wavy strands frame her face while the rest cascade down her back. She's holding a jacket in her arms along with her purse, smiling when she sees me standing here.

"Good morning, Emma." Her eyes light up with surprise from hearing her name on my lips instead of the nickname I've come to enjoy using. *See,* I can be professional I want to say but refrain.

"Hi there."

I grab her coat from her arms, linking her arm with mine, and lead her out to my car, making sure to wave again to the man behind the desk. I'm sure it won't be the last time I see him and I don't want to give him any reason to deny me entry in the future.

"I'm glad you brought your jacket. Sometimes it can be a bit cold up there." I open the car door for her, closing it when she's sitting comfortably inside.

After taking my seat, I notice she's quiet this morning. Not sure if it's this meeting that's making her nervous. Maybe it's meeting my parents? But she's a professional. I'm sure she's used to meeting all sorts of people.

Emma's smart and creative. She seems to care a lot about what she does. Plus, she has multiple plans to help bring in more money in order to save the winery, so my parents are going to love her on that alone.

Before pulling out, I tune my music to one of the newer albums Mia introduced me to. It's still instrumental, but it's a nice change from my normal rotation. The car fills with the soft sound of an acoustic guitar and I'm ready to go. "All good?" I ask. When Emma nods, I pull out into the street.

I'm used to a quiet drive to and from the city, so it takes me a few minutes to realize that maybe I need to start the conversation this morning. "How was your weekend? Did you do anything fun?"

"Um, actually I did. I walked to the *Sagrada Família*. I think I'm saying that right." I nod, she did just fine. "Had an early lunch right outside, then took some time walking around the museum below. Ending my time walking inside the church itself."

Sagrada Família is the largest unfinished Catholic church in the world, and if memory serves me right, it's the tallest one as well.

"What did you think? I haven't been inside for a few years."

"It was beautiful. I haven't seen anything like it," she comments, awe and wonder clear in her voice. "All the colors inside were spectacular. I felt like I got there at the perfect time, too. Since it was midafternoon, the sun was shining bright, illuminating all the beautiful colors of the stained glass windows around the church, especially the yellows, oranges, and reds. It created this amazing glowing effect inside."

It's easy to imagine myself back inside the church. I remember it just as she's describing it.

"In some areas, it felt like I was getting wrapped in a rainbow, and that's just inside! I could spend all day looking at the design on the outside of the church. All that detail . . ."

"It really is something. It's been under construction all my life, so whenever I'm over there, there's always something new to see."

We talk about a few of my other favorite spots in the city. Antoni Gaudí is naturally one of my favorite architects, so Park Güell is another treasured spot of mine. I tell Emma about all the spots in the city where people can see his work, which leads me to Saint George's Day.

"*Casa Batlló* was actually inspired by Saint George's story. The building is covered in roses in celebration on Saint George's Day. So next week, if you're in the area, you can see it in all of its glory." It's a beautiful site to see. Really the whole city is.

"Saint George's Day, what's that?"

"It's your classic 'knight in shining armor saving a beloved princess from a dragon' story. You've never heard of it?"

"No, I'd love to hear the story, if you don't mind sharing it?"

"Well, I'm not the best story teller, but I'll give it a go. A long time ago, there was a town that had a menacing dragon wreaking havoc on the people living there. He demanded daily sacrifices from the town to appease his hunger. The people would draw names to decide the grim fate of those selected.

"One day, the princess was called to be the sacrifice for the day. But before she could get eaten by the dragon, *Sant Jordi*, also known as Saint George, a literal knight in shining armor, appeared, He slayed the dragon, thus rescuing the princess from her horrible fate, as well as saving all the people in the town from a future fate.

"A rose bush sprouted from the dragon's blood that was spilled that day. Saint George picked the most beautiful rose and gave it as a gift to the princess.

"Today, Saint George's Day is celebrated on April twenty-third with roses and books. Around a hundred years ago, the day was combined with World Book Day which honors writers Miguel de Cervantes and William Shakespeare, who both died on April twenty-third as well.

"It used to be that men gave those they loved a book and a single red rose, but now, anyone can give and receive the gifts."

"That sounds like such a special day."

"It really is. The city is a mess if you are trying to drive anywhere, but also filled with so much exciting activity. Most busy streets have vendors selling roses or books. Some of the squares are even closed, providing markets around the city for those celebrating the special day."

"I'll have to mark it on my calendar."

"The shop is closed for the holiday, so I could take you out that day." I say hopefully. "Be your unofficial tour guide for the city's festivities."

"Diego." She turns her head towards me. From the corner of my eye, I catch the side of her mouth creeping up. "I thought we agreed we'd see each other only in a professional setting. That sounds an awful lot like a date."

"Oh no. Far from it actually." I shake my head with a mock frown.

"Oh, please *do* elaborate." Waving her arm in front of her, she motions for me to explain, seeming a little more relaxed than she was earlier.

"Think of it as . . . " Tilting my head, I ponder the best wording. "*Market research.*"

"Market research?" she repeats, incredulously.

"Yes! Market research. We could spend the day together, obtaining which selling techniques work best in this region of the world." A completely valid reason. "After all, there are so many businesses offering specials that day. We can see which ones work best based on the size of the crowds they are gathering. Or even which ones catch our eyes. Saving the ideas so we can integrate them into our marketing strategy for the winery."

"Wow. I'm impressed. That was a very creative and thorough answer to how this *wouldn't* be a date." She chuckles.

"You should know I love being creative." I turn and give her a saucy wink. "And are you in need of a reminder on how *thorough* I can be?"

I hear her mumble something like "Longest car ride ever" before turning onto the road right before my family's driveway.

CHAPTER FIFTEEN

EMMA

J've never had so many conflicting feelings being inside a car before. By the end of it, I couldn't tell if I wanted out because of my fear of cars or if I wanted to stay in the metal deathtrap just for the chance to see how Diego would remind me of his *thoroughness*.

But in the end, Diego chose for me, exiting the car soon after parking it.

When I first got in the car, I was anxious for all my regular reasons, especially once we got out of the city and onto more rural roads. Thankfully, there wasn't much silence on the ride, which helped to distract me. I know Diego said he wasn't a storyteller, but I was captivated by the story of Saint George. And date or not, exploring Barcelona during the celebration sounds like a wonderful opportunity. I would be a fool not to take the opportunity of being guided around the city by a local, right?

And that's all it is, a tour by my client. One might say, it's not much different than what's happening today.

What was it Diego called it? Market research? Yeah, sure. We'll go with that.

I feel like we are always flirting with the line between professional and not. Okay, maybe flirting is putting it lightly. It's like I'm saying no with one hand while pulling him closer with the other. I can't help it; the attraction with Diego is magnetic. Sometimes I don't even realize we're flirting until we're already on wafer-thin ice, skating a fine line between professional and not. Both of us waiting to see which one will fall into the ice first.

We haven't kissed or touched, at least not inappropriately, since we established the ground rules.

But wait, what exactly would you call that neck kiss?

Ughhhh. That fucking neck kiss.

Now *that* was a good kiss without it being a "real" kiss.

"Emma?" Shit, was Diego calling me this whole time.

"Hi, sorry. What's up?" Diego chuckles while holding open my door. My door . . .

"Oh shit, sorry." I step out of the car and take in the view in front of me, and what a view it is. Rolling hills, vineyards sweeping over most of the land, with a castle-like structure sitting in the middle of all of it. It's simply incredible.

"This is . . . wow. Yeah, people would definitely get married here. Hell, *I* would get married here."

"Good thing you're about to meet my parents." Did I really just say I would get married here?

Diego answers my internal question with a chuckle. "You did." Shit, I must've said that part out loud.

"Sorry, it's just . . . it's better than I imagined it would be. The photos online are great, but don't even scratch the surface of the beauty before me right now." I do a three-sixty, attempting to take everything in. "Yeah, we definitely need to get some new photos in order to do this place justice."

"Why don't we stop by and meet my family first, then I'll give you a tour. Sound good?"

"Sounds great." We walk up the driveway to what looks to be the bigger of the two buildings. Both are made of these large stones, giving an old world, castle feel. These buildings must have been built centuries ago, and yet here they stand, still as beautiful as ever.

You don't see architecture like this back in the States. I'm not sure how large their estate is, but I don't see any other structures or neighbors, just green surrounding us. I sneak a peek of the vineyard hiding behind the building, but from what I can tell, there's a green belt surrounding the structure. A perfect spot for events.

Diego opens an oversized wooden door for us to walk in, and I can immediately tell this is where the bulk of their process is done.

There are barrels standing up everywhere with a corner filled with larger equipment, I'm guessing that's where they prep the grapes before putting them in these barrels.

The room has a subtle smell of alcohol lingering, but there's more to it. Like a mixture of all the wines I've ever tasted before. There's oak, red berries, smokiness, a little bit of pepper, and something else. Yeast maybe?

Pausing our walk, I say, "This may sound silly, I know most of these barrels are aging the wine, but what does the equipment over there do?" I point to the corner. "I actually don't know much about the process of making grapes into wine."

"Over there," he points to the corner where all the unfamiliar equipment is as he explains, "is where we destem and crush the grapes, then ferment, press, and macerate the grapes. Each wine variety requires a little different process." He continues to explain as we start walking again. "Afterwards, we barrel the wine for aging, though most of these barrels are empty, cleaned and sanitized, ready to be used in a couple of weeks. We store the ones aging underneath the building, in the cellars."

We walk closer to a door at the end of the room. "And how long do those barrels sit there for?"

Diego opens the door for me, and his hand glides against the small of my back as he ushers me in, giving me instant chills. He continues walking like the action didn't just shake me to my core.

"It depends on the wine. Some of them only sit for six months while others can stay in for three years, but we only have a few of those. For our family, most stay in the barrel for eight to ten months." We take a flight of stairs up, Diego's hand finding that spot on my lower back again. I bite my lip to give my mind something else to focus on instead of his touch.

Upstairs looks to be an office, and turning the corner, his hand drops from my back as we run into a woman who has the same smile as Mia and Diego.

"Emma, this is my mother, Elena Sánchez. Mom, this is Emma. She's from the marketing firm. I was going to introduce you and Dad to her before giving her a tour."

"Ah!!! Emma!" She greets me with an embrace and kiss on each cheek. "Yes, it's so good to have you here. Thank you so much for your help. Diego has told me you are anxious to start implementing some changes."

"Yes, I am. You have an amazing estate here, Mrs. Sánchez—"

She waves me off with a playful scoff. "Oh, none of that. Elena, I insist."

My smile turns more genuine with the friendly correction. "Elena, then. Pleasure meeting you. I look forward to helping grow your family business." My smile grows a little when I add, "And of course, seeing you more as well."

Elena wiggles a finger in my direction. "Oh, you're a keeper!" She returns my smile with a warm one of her own. "Diego, your father's in a meeting, so go ahead and give her the tour now. He should be done when you get back. Are you staying all day?"

I exchange a questioning look with Diego. Keeping eye contact with me, he shrugs when he answers his mom, "We'll have to see how the day unfolds itself. I don't want to hold Emma here captive." The corner of his mouth creeps up, a mischievous glint in his eyes.

"Please, that's exactly what a dragon like you would do." I hear another voice join in before I see her face. Mia walks out with a teasing smile. "Good to see you again, Emma."

"Dragon?" I question out loud. Must be an inside joke.

Diego leans closer to me but doesn't whisper, letting the current company hear. "Mia always thinks it's hilarious to compare me to a dragon."

"Because he's broody, likes to keep to himself, and . . . " Mia starts listing the reasons off on her fingers.

"*And* guards the things he loves so fiercely," their mom interrupts. She tosses Diego a look I can't quite decipher. "And he's always been very passionate about people he cares for."

"And on that note," Diego says a little louder, "we're out of here. See you all around lunch." He grabs my hand before I can register that we're leaving.

I toss out a quick, "See you ladies later," before being whisked away by Diego.

"Don't forget to grab a radio, Diego!" Elena shouts as we exit.

Diego leads us to a spot where a couple of side-by-sides are parked. "Hop in."

"Don't I need a helmet or something?" I doubt I need one, since it looks like a heavy duty golf cart, but you can never be too safe. Especially when you're off-roading.

"No, I won't be going fast today. Just buckle-up, stay seated, and you'll be fine." Fine. I'll be *fine*. "Ready? Let's g—"

He stops himself and unbuckles his restraints, hopping out the vehicle to retrieve something. He holds a radio up before tossing it in the back then rebuckling himself. "Forgot the radio. Let's go!"

CHAPTER SIXTEEN

DIEGO

Driving up to my favorite spot on the property, it's a little too loud to carry-on a conversation, with the cart being exposed to the elements and there being a mild breeze. I turn to see Emma taking in the vast landscape surrounding us.

We have acres of vineyards, all a sight to see. But my favorite view is on the top of our highest peak, where you get the best sight of the whole estate. You can see everything from up there, rolling hills covered in green vines and trees, with the main building and our family home at the base of it all.

The best time to visit is right at sunrise, the sun shines beautifully on the hills surrounding the property. If it's cold enough, you may get lucky to see a small layer of fog blanketing the area, giving the vineyard an ethereal glow, filled with oranges and yellows from the rising sun.

Currently, all the vines are just starting to bloom. Most have bright green leaves sprouting, as well as a few blooms hidden under the foliage.

These grapes won't be ready until the fall, but it's always something special to see these plants come back year after year. Some of these vines are even older than me.

Our family has been fortunate with the production on a lot of these vines; we haven't needed to replant as often as other vineyards have. Grandpa insists it's the soil, and while I agree that is definitely part of the reason, I think we give our vineyard a lot of meticulous care and attention. The placement of the vines, as well as the favorable weather, makes for a great environment for the longevity of the plant, too.

About four years ago, I got the opportunity to help plant a new block of vines. It was small, but a project I'm proud to have played a part in. The old ones in that area weren't producing any more, so it was time for new life.

Last year, my vines were mature enough to start producing a decent crop, though Dad and Grandpa strongly believe the grapes aren't label worthy for another few years.

That being said, they weren't interested in the grapes for the business, so I was able to experiment a bit with them. In the end, I was able to create a few barrels from them. They should be ready to taste soon, too.

We reach our destination roughly ten minutes later. I park us close to the vineyard, but without disrupting the vines.

"I can't believe you grew up here."

I peer over the estate. "It's pretty special. Some days, when I need an escape, I just lose myself walking through the rows." Letting out a chuckle, I add, "Mom can always tell I'm 'in a mood' because I *conveniently* forget to bring a radio.

"Even as a young kid, I'd walk all the way up here some days, just to get some alone time. There's something to be said about the outside world not being able to reach you when you're out here. I love it. No noise, just nature."

"I like the sound of that." We stand there for a few minutes, just soaking in the view and the quiet surrounding us. "So, are all the grapes the same variety, and you just change the process for different wines? Or do you have different types of vines?"

"Over there." Positioning myself behind her, I bend down close to her ear, pointing to the east side of the property while placing my other hand on her hip. "That's our Grenache, which makes up the majority of our crop. It's what we use to make our most popular bottles."

I slide my hand up her body, guiding her head in the other direction, letting my hand linger after. "Toward the west, that's our Mataro, or Mourvèdre. It's small, but enough for what we need. Then to the south, near the house"—I slowly move my hand down her arm, raising it with mine as I point in that direction—"is our Shiraz, or Syrah. Those three, are the bulk of our grape varieties. We have a few experimental vines around the property as well." I lower her hand back down where it was at her waist, squeezing it a little before letting go.

Emma clears her throat before turning around to face me. "Well that was . . . " Our hands touch as we reach up to her face, both attempting to tame a wild strand of her hair. "Thorough. That was very thorough."

"That's the second time you've needed reminding of how thorough I can be. Maybe you *do* need another lesson in my"—my eyes lingering on her mouth as I finish my thought—"thoroughness."

"I don't think I've heard that word being said so much in under a span of a minute." She looks off into the distance and she puffs out under her breath. "Nor did I ever think that word could get me so wet."

I chuckle, not knowing if she meant to say that part out loud or not. "Ready to move along? I can show you a few good spots for events?"

"Yeah, that sounds great." I turn, but she stops me in my tracks, grabbing my hand. "Thanks for taking me up here. It's beautiful and a very special place indeed." She gives me a soft smile, and I can't help but return the gesture.

"Of course," I bring my other hand up, entwining my fingers in her hair while my thumb strokes her cheek. I move my head to the other side of her face, whispering softly in her ear. "You're kind of making it difficult for me not to kiss you though." She pinches my waist. "Oh, you don't want to do that, Sweetheart." I pull away just enough to look her in the eyes.

"And why's that?" She tries to say it in her brattiest tone, but the last word comes out breathy.

"Because I like a little pain with my pleasure." I smack her ass and quickly turn, returning to the side-by-side.

"Fuck me." Emma grumbles before joining me. I internally answer *just tell me when*.

She hops in, buckling herself quickly before commenting, "You know, you're making it really hard to keep this business relationship professional."

"And you're making something else really hard, so it looks like we're even." I catch her looking down at the bulge in my jeans, eyes lingering a bit too long for it to be accidental before she snaps her head up in surprise. "Like that look right there . . . you're practically drooling."

"I am *not* drooling." She drags her thumb over the corner of her mouth. The movement should not be as sexy as it is, but here I am, rock hard and ready to jump her whenever she gives me the green light.

"Okay, maybe I am, but that still doesn't change the fact that we can't do this." She waggles her fingers between us. Her eyes return to my crotch before she adds, "God, Diego. It's like a fucking beacon. Now that I know it's there, my eyes can't help but look."

She shakes her head like she's physically trying to get the image out, while I can't help but chuckle at the whole thing. "No, we can't cross that line . . . at least, not until we have some plans for the winery put in place."

"So . . . we're talking about a couple weeks?" I can do that.

"As long as everything goes right, yeah. Two, *maybe* three weeks. Can you handle that?"

"Sweetheart, I already got a taste, and I'm addicted. These next couple of weeks might be torture, but knowing you'll be the reward waiting for me at the end, makes it all worth it." I turn on the cart before adding, "But I'm still taking you out on Saint George's Day."

"Right. Like you said, it's for *market research*." I know she's wearing a cheeky grin without even turning my head.

The tour passes smoothly, walking the different sites for events, giving her a tour of the cellars, all before heading back for a quick lunch with my family.

Our day is filled with flirty banter and subtle touches, all of it walking that thin line we just re-established. Honestly, this pining is making her even more irresistible. Normally, I would question if the attraction is there only because I know she is forbidden, but I don't believe that's it with Emma.

She's so smart and talented with what she does. She's confident and knows how to get the job done, in more ways than one. From what I've seen, she has a very special skill set that makes her perfect for her position.

It was no surprise hearing that a promotion brought her to Spain. She definitely seems like a "work hard, play hard" kind of woman. When she puts her mind to something, I could see her doing everything in her power to make it happen; determined and strong-willed. But she balances it all so well, still making it so she's adored by everyone who meets her, all falling under the spell that Emma's presence puts on them.

Her beauty is unmatched by any other, too. Bewitching me from the very first time I saw her at Lorenzo's. She has a soft and delicate exterior, but I'll never let that fool me again. How can such a ray of sunshine be so bratty at times?

But I love the sweet and sour of Emma. She reminds me of those little sour candies I had when I went to California for college. They had them in all sorts of colors and were dusted in this sour powder, but the gummy was sweet. What were those things called? Sour Farm Babies? Tart Patch Kids? She's my own version of those little candies, but even more addicting.

When we get back to the house, Mom already has lunch waiting for us. We exchange introductions with Dad and Grandpa, before sitting down and eating together.

While eating, Emma walks my family through a few of her proposals, most of it in Spanish. Nothing too formal, just overall ideas and how she expects to put them into motion. Anything she has issues with translating, she leans on me to help with.

"I, for one, am very excited about the potential for an event space," Mom starts, switching to English. "I've always thought the property was gorgeous and I can only imagine the weddings and events that will be held here. Plus, a part of me always loved the idea of party-planning." Mom *has* always loved to throw parties, and I'm sure this would be a great change of pace for her. She's had the same office routines she's had since she married my father.

"Oh Elena, do you know what Pinterest is?" Emma asks, but Mom shakes her head. "Oh, I *have* to set you up with an account on your phone. It's a treasure trove full of all sorts of ideas. It's where I get most of my creative inspiration."

"Sounds fun! I'd love that, Emma."

"Can you tell me more about how the tour guide idea would work?" Dad asks in Spanish.

"Essentially," Emma starts, switching back to Spanish. She's doing a seamless job at switching between the two languages. "We'd partner up with a tour guide company, local or international, and provide ticketed, pre-selected, wine tastings at your Barcelona location." Dad nods and I'm certain that's all the approval we will receive from him.

"Now, the only thing I'm concerned with is the financial burden of printing all new labels for the rebranding." This time, it's me asking the question. I bring this up because the other two options don't seem like they have as much of an upfront cost, unlike this one.

"We could always start small. Maybe start with swapping out

the wine labels that are running low." I nod and Emma continues, "If all goes well, we'll continue with the transition, incorporating the new logo on more labels as well as everything else."

"There's a few of the GSMs that are running low now," Mom adds. "In fact, I was about to place an order so they'd be ready for the next run, but I can hold off if we wanted to try a new design."

"Perfect! I can come up with a few designs, then print some samples to give to Diego by the end of the week. You can all decide over the weekend on which one you'd like to go with, then I'll send them to the printer."

"Sounds great." I agree.

"I could even switch out the logo on the website and social media pages, since those don't cost anything to change." Emma looks around the table before asking, "Did any of you have a design in mind?"

We haven't changed the logo since . . . well definitely longer than I've been alive, maybe even longer than Dad, too. In the end, we decide we don't have too much of a preference, just something simple yet eye catching.

I'm excited for the change that's coming. Of course, I hope it brings in the income needed to save the winery, but it's refreshing to have a new face come in and switch things up.

Emma is so optimistic, and brings a new kind of energy into the winery that I haven't seen in . . . well, ever. We've always done the same thing, day in and day out. The only change being some of the revolving labels, but even that took some arm twisting.

Dad and Grandpa only started experimenting when we had a year that required it. Whether it was because we had a low harvest and had to get creative, or when we had an excess and had the grapes to spare.

A few of those creations made it into the general rotation, but most got shelved for a later date. No matter how small of a batch, every recipe gets written down and saved, just in case.

Every now and then, we'll reach for an experimental label and surprise ourselves with the flavor profile it brings. Five years ago, we all enjoyed a particular blend that Mom had made, and now it's one of our best sellers. It's always a small batch, so it costs almost double our most popular Grenache, but it sells out every year. If only we could have that happen with more of our bottles, maybe then we wouldn't be in this predicament.

"Well, I think that went well." Emma begins, tilting her head with a squint to her eyes while we walk out to the car. "Don't you think?"

"You did great. I can tell my mother loves you already. I think I even saw a smile from my dad, and he's a tough one to impress." The corner of my mouth pulls up as I get a glimpse of her smile.

"And Mia is so much fun."

"She gets it from me." Emma laughs, only it's a little too hard. "What? You think I'm lying? Who do you think taught her how to be so fun?"

Emma tilts her head back and forth a minute before responding, "Given by what occurred at lunch, probably your mom."

"I'm going to ignore the fact that you just made a 'your mom' joke."

She gasps. "I can't believe you even know what a 'your mom' joke is."

"Well, I *did* go to college in California." We both laugh.

"But seriously, Diego," Emma grabs my hand as we approach the car, "thanks for such a special day."

"Any excuse to spend the day with you, Sweetheart." I give her ass a little pat as she gets in the car, only for her to whip her head back in my direction. I raise my hands up. "Must've been that damn wind."

"Sure, sure. I've got my eyes on you." She motions two fingers to her eyes then points them towards me, sporting a menacing look. Or at least, it *would* look menacing if she wasn't fighting so hard to keep her smile from slipping.

"Keep watching, Sweetheart. It only gets better from here."

CHAPTER SEVENTEEN

EMMA

After my day with the Sánchez family, the rest of the week went by in a flash, filled with brainstorming, calls, and so many emails. I'm pretty sure my spacebar is sticking from all the emails and documents I've written.

After picking up the samples from the printshop on my way to the office, I receive a text from Diego, chuckling when I see his name light up my screen.

DIEGO - MARATHON MAN:

Are you free tonight?

I really need to change his name. To anyone else, the name looks innocent enough. Professional even. But whenever I see it flash up across my phone screen, another part of me lights up and wishes it was vibrating. And that's been the common theme of this past week.

He's kept things . . . friendly, and maybe a bit flirty. A lot of innuendos, especially while texting. Nothing that would get me in trouble with work. Just a few quick texts here and there. He blames it on keeping tabs on the progress, but I like to think it's more than that.

EMMA:

I was just going to ask you the same thing. I
have a few things I'd like to show you.

DIEGO:

I like the sound of that.

EMMA:

Samples. I have samples, Diego.

DIEGO:

I like that slightly less than what I was
thinking, but you should come by the shop.

I'm staying in town tonight, so no rush on
time.

EMMA:

Sounds great. I'll wrap a few things up and be
on my way to you.

DIEGO:

And here I thought you were only good at
unwrapping.

Okay, so maybe our texts aren't as inconspicuous as I thought. I let out a laugh under my breath, but startle when I hear a knock on my cubicle.

Javier peaks his head in, "Emma, do you have a minute?"

"Hi, um, sure, yeah."

I can't quite determine his mood based on the look on his face. I'm not aware of any issues . . . shit. Maybe someone *did* see my texts.

No, there's no way. It's not a company phone so they don't have records on my texts. Plus, nobody has been close enough to read my texts. Unless . . .

Oh my god! Did Stacia say something? No, surely not. It's probably nothing.

"Follow me to the conference room?"

"Sure thing." I stand up and follow him to the fishbowl.

When we turn the corner, I see a man already sitting in the conference room. A man I'm sure I've never seen in the office before.

Javier opens the door for me while introducing the stranger. "Emma, this is Roger Jefferson." I grab Roger's outstretched hand. "Roger, this is Emma. She's the one heading the family winery I told you about." A welcoming smile spreads across Rogers's face.

"Oh, perfect! Emma, it's truly a pleasure to meet you." We all stay standing at the end of the room as Roger continues. "Javier let me know you may have a winery willing to partner with a cruise line for wine tasting excursions."

"Oh." I look at Javier who subtly nods to me with a warm smile on his face. "Yes, I do. They already have a shop with room for tastings established; it's over by La Boqueria. I was thinking it would make a great excursion, wine tasting followed by a small shopping trip at the market. Or even just the wine tasting would make for an excellent experience." I cut myself off before I ramble any more. I still have no idea who this man is or why he's here; but clearly it has to do with the winery.

"Yes, I think you're right. We have a few other wineries around the city we partner with, but it's always great to add another. Would you mind if I got your contact information? That way I could have my team tour the shop before going any further?"

I pull out one of my business cards from my wallet. "My cell is the best way to reach me."

"Great, thank you! We just need to make sure the space can hold the number of people we need for the excursions. Oh, and to taste the wine of course," he chuckles.

"Of course. I'm sure Diego would be happy to schedule a tour and trial run for your team. Just give me a call and we can set something up soon."

"Perfect. Well, I have to get to another meeting while I'm in town, but thank you so much for your time, Emma." He shakes my hand once more as he says goodbye.

"Javier." Roger pats his back. "It's great to see you, too. Don't be a stranger!" Then he's gone. That's it. We didn't even sit down; it was so fast.

"So, *who* exactly was that?" I ask once the door is shut, leaving just Javier and me in the room. I'm still uncertain what exactly just happened.

"Roger is an old friend of mine. He travels a lot for work, so it's hard to nail him down. But he was in Barcelona and I thought he'd be a great contact for you." Javier ushers me out of the conference room as he continues. "He's the lead shore excursion coordinator for Royal Cruises." I swear my eyes double in size as soon as he says it.

"Holy sh—crap." I correct myself, remembering I'm still at work. "Holy crap." I second, needing my brain to catch up. "Javier, this is an amazing opportunity. Thank you so much for making something like this happen."

"Like I said, I wasn't sure if our schedules were going to match up, so I didn't want to get your hopes up or promise anything I couldn't follow through on. But I'm glad it was able to happen," he continues to talk as he escorts me back to my desk, "and I hope the trial run goes well for the Sánchez family. This could mean big things for their business. It was a great idea, Emma. You should be proud you thought of it."

"Thank you, Javier. Well, I'm off to see Diego now. I'll be sure to tell him the amazing news."

"Have a great weekend, Emma. Let me know if you need anything else from the team." I go to leave but a thought hits me, causing me to turn back around.

"Actually, I do have a bit of a random question for you, Javier."

"Sure. What's on your mind?"

I look around, making sure no one is in ear shot before I ask, "Is it against the rules to—" Only his cell phone rings, interrupting me before the rest of the question makes it out of my mouth.

Javier turns his phone over. "Oh, shoot, I have to get this. But real quick, what was your question?"

"Is it against the rules to date a client?" I hurry out before I lose the nerve, the words blending together as I ask.

Javier just shakes his head and chuckles. "I knew there was something between you two." He lifts his phone up to his ear before adding, "Just don't make it my problem and I'm good with it."

"Thanks, Javier!" He smiles and waves, mouthing his good-byes before he greets the caller.

Well that answers that, only I'm not exactly sure what to do now that I know Diego's not "off-limits."

On one hand, all I want to do now is jump his bones.

Jump his bones, are people still saying that?

But on the other hand, I still feel a little conflicted about dating a client.

Putting my feelings aside for the answer of that particular question . . . holy shit, that meeting!

I am beyond excited to share all this news with Diego. Not only do I have some kick-ass label designs, but I'm still stunned by that surprise meeting. A freaking cruise line is interested in Diego's shop! After gathering my things, I head out for the day, making my way over to meet Diego. It's a beautiful spring day.

The sun is in full force, but the breeze is keeping the heat away. The energy here in Barcelona is always buzzing, so full of life, but it doesn't feel like everyone is rushing to get to one place after the other, like how it is back home.

Really, the whole lifestyle here in Barcelona seems more my speed. There's more passion in the work that people do, and it shows. From the product quality, to the attitude people have while they work. A lot of having to do with the overall outlook on society's view on work, making sure it's not the center of your life.

Most people I have encountered during my short stay, actually enjoy the work they do while also setting a healthy boundary with work. The overall work environment here is centered more around a "work to live" mentality rather than the hustle culture over in the States. Something Lindsay, my workaholic sister, might want to look into.

I've said it before, and I'll say it again: my motto is work hard, play hard. Life is too short to save up for forty or so years, only to then enjoy the fruits of my labor after I retire, *if* I'm able to retire.

And, honestly, I've always hated the idea of a nine-to-five job. I chose a profession and company that allows me to be on the move if I needed or wanted to. It helps keep the creative juices flowing, as well as help protect me from burnout.

Now that I'm thinking about it, this has been the only project where I've been actively thinking of the client at almost all hours of the day. Thoughts filled with ways I can satisfy Diego.

I take a deep breath and a mental image of me doing just that appears, causing me to almost walk into a planter box.

So, maybe not *always* work related, but I really do take his satisfaction seriously in terms of rebranding his family business. I know there's not much time for me to help flip their financial situation around, but I have a great feeling about all of these changes I'm proposing. I guess only time will tell.

CHAPTER EIGHTEEN

DIEGO

I'm setting up for a reservation when the door opens and a strawberry blonde beauty walks in, making my night better by just walking through the door. She has a faint blush to her cheeks from her walk over. "Hi there, Sweetheart."

"Hi. I've got some fun news for you." She struts closer to me in a flowy olive dress, a cheeky smile painted on her face. The dress leans a bit on the modest side, with its high neckline and flared skirt. From what I can see, I think she's hiding those thigh-high boots from the other day under her dress. I'd like nothing better than to sit her down on one of these tables to find out if I'm right, checking to see what else she's hiding underneath.

"Is it something I get to," I give her an exaggerated slow once over, imagining what's beneath the green fabric, "unwrap?" My eyebrows dance with the insinuation.

"Only if you ask nicely." She flutters her lashes as she stands before me.

Rubbing my hand down her arm, I'm *trying* really hard to keep this as professional as possible, but failing miserably. "You already know how much I like to get on my knees for you."

She runs her tongue over her bottom lip while staring me

straight in the eye. "Prove it." So she wants to play sexy chicken? Oh, it's on.

I'm about to do just that when the door opens again. Shit. It must be the party coming in a little early. Emma gives me a minute of coverage, allowing me time to adjust my pants, before she moves over to the checkout counter.

"Hold that thought." I whisper under my breath before greeting the group. "*Bona tarda.*"

"*Hola!* I know we're early, but we figured we were in the area already." A woman says, leading the group of ladies to the table I had just finished setting up. I knew ahead of time that this group would be on the larger side. When one of the women called, she said it was for a mini-bachelorette party, but the size is anything but mini.

"It's no problem. We're happy you're here and congratulations to the bride." I wave at the table in front of me. "If you're ready to start, please take your seats and we can begin the tasting."

The next hour passes without much fanfare. Emma helps me without a second thought, pouring wine and refilling waters when necessary. We're in such close proximity, it's easy to sneak my hands on her. A palm on her lower back. My fingers grazing hers in passing. Whispering softly in her ear what I need her help with next, all while I hold her near me. Swift but intimate all the same.

As Emma helps me finish the tasting, we have a couple of shoppers come in, making me need to sneak off in between pouring wines to help them check out. It's nothing unusual, since the shop is normally run by one person. Though, it would be helpful to have two people in the shop on days we know we'll be busy with reservations, allowing one person to focus on the group and the other on the customers shopping.

I'd love to hire someone, but we don't have the funds. I really should thank Mia for all the work she does over here, since she's been doing the bulk of it for the last couple of years.

All of my teasing interactions left me buzzing with a need for more. One look at her after the group leaves, and I can see she feels the same.

Before letting myself get too distracted with Emma, I start cleaning up the shop. Technically, we have another thirty minutes or so before the shop closes, but I think I'll call it an early night. "Thank you for this evening. It was nice of you to stick around and help. "

She helps gather the wineglasses, walking them to the back to be washed. "Of course. I was already here. Plus, I still have to tell you the good news."

"Please do." I encourage as I collect dirty plates off the tables.

"A large cruise line is interested in partnering with your tasting room! They want to do a trial run tasting. You know, to check out the space and the wines. I'm not sure on the time yet, but probably in the next week or two." She rushes to get the words out, voice climbing higher and higher with each new sentence. She is practically jumping up and down with giddiness.

"That's great news!" Setting down the plates I was carrying, I rush over to her, lifting her in my arms and squeezing, kissing her on her cheek as I do. "When did this happen?"

Emma's stunning eyes stare back at me then trail down to my lips as she bites hers, feet still dangling from me holding her up. She doesn't respond to my question, focused on something else entirely.

"Emma . . . " I kiss her again, a little lower on her chin as I set her feet back down on the floor. Peppering kisses down her neck, she melts into my embrace, arms roaming my waist. With my head bent down, lingering in the space between her neck and shoulder, I whisper, "Do I need to repeat my question, Sweetheart?"

Emma pinches my side and I let out a chuckle. "You tease." She's so playful today, probably because of the good news.

Running her hands up and down my chest, "I had an impromptu meeting with my manager and his good friend. The friend turned out to be the lead shore excursion coordinator for a major cruise line. How amazing is that?!" Her smile is back in full force, crinkles forming around her eyes from the joy on her face.

"That's incredible, Emma!"

My arms are still wrapped around her as we get lost in each other's eyes. Neither one of us wanting to move away from each other. Both needing to stay here, in this moment. But as luck would have it, someone chooses to ruin it for us, interrupting us with the sound of the damn door opening. Never thought I'd see the day where I was getting cockblocked by a customer. Should've locked up before we started to clean.

I give her hip a little squeeze before dropping my arms and turning to greet the intruder. Thankfully, they just need a few bottles of wine.

After purchasing their bottles, I walk them out the door, making sure to lock it behind them. But the moment is gone, I can see it in Emma's face when I return. Clearing her throat, she's back in "Work Emma" mode.

"So I left the samples on the counter for you to take home to your family. Talk it over and let me know by Monday morning which one you decide." She tucks a piece of hair behind her ear before continuing, only for it to fall immediately back in her face. "If for some reason you don't like any of them, just let me know and we can go back to the drawing board. It'll just take a few more days for the redesign."

I'm slow to approach her, not wanting to spook her, but I don't want her to leave. I grab her petite hands in mine, taking any chance to touch her. "Thank you. I'm sure one of these will be perfect."

I'm running through excuses in my mind for her to stay, when she interrupts my thoughts. "I should probably go before we do something we promised we wouldn't. I crossed the line before. We were playing with fire."

"Sweetheart, when it comes to you"—I grab her head in one hand, bringing my mouth down, stopping a hair's breadth before touching her lips—"I'm not afraid to get burned." And I kiss her.

I kiss her without any restraint. I kiss her with all the want I've been trying to stifle down these past weeks.

I'm done with the waiting. I'm done with the tormenting. I've had nothing but her on my mind since she walked into my life. I meant what I said, I'll dive straight into the flames for the chance to be with her. You hear about those people who fall fast and hard, never thinking it could be you. But here I am, happily taking the plunge.

Moving my other hand from hers to her waist, we fall into a familiar rhythm. Her hands roaming my back as we continue our kissing. I sling an arm under her ass, picking her up and carrying her over to the counter.

Easing her on the edge, I push my body between her legs, making her straddle my hips. The countertop is a little taller than the tables, but she's still a significant amount shorter than me even with the added height, causing me to have to bend down to give her the care and attention she deserves.

I work my hands up the skirt of her dress as she opens her mouth to let my tongue in. Tracing the leather seam of her boots, following it up until I feel her exposed thigh. The shop fills with the sounds of our panting and moaning. My fingers explore higher and higher up the length of her thighs, pulling the fabric of her dress up as I go, continuing to kiss her deeply. I show her how much I've missed us these past two weeks.

"Wait, wait," she pants as she pulls away. "You locked the shop's door, right?"

Smiling, I nod and move my fingers up to graze the wet spot on her underwear. I groan as I run my hands back and forth along the damp fabric. "You sure know how to compliment a guy."

"Who said that was from you?" I punish her with a nip on her bottom lip.

"Brat." Hooking my fingers under the lace between her legs, I tease her wet opening, softly stroking my fingers in taunting, feather-light touches.

"Please . . . " she breathes out. Leaning her head back, she allows me access to the expanse of her neck, my dick getting harder from her plea. "I know my 'brat' only gets you harder."

I can hear the teasing tone in her voice, tempting me to bite down on the pulse point on her neck. Nothing hard. Just enough to punish her a little.

But she's right. I do love her bratty side. Especially when it means I get to have her like this.

The shop's phone rings, but I'm determined to let it fade into the background and go to voicemail as I work two fingers inside of her. Her gasp is loud enough to block out the rings, bringing my focus back to her.

Even with the thick material of her dress, I can see her nipples are hard, teasing me through the dark green material. The only way to reach the little peaks is by taking her whole dress off, and I'm not about to stop what I'm doing. At least, not this time around.

Lowering my mouth, I suck at her breast, soaking the fabric with my mouth before moving to the other one. My head is low enough now that she works her fingers in my curly hair, holding on tight for what she knows I'm about to do.

I pull the skirt up and around her waist with one hand, while continuing to thrust my fingers in and out of her with the other.

"Is this," she pants while I continue thrusting my fingers, "your way," *thrust*, "of thanking me," *thrust*, "for a job," *thrust*, "well done?" *thrust*.

I give a slow and thorough lick up her slit. "If you keep talking, I'll give it something else to do with that smart mouth of yours."

CHAPTER NINETEEN

EMMA

Jesus fucking Christ. The mouth on this man. Literally *and* figuratively.

I am not shy in the bedroom. Matter of fact, some men have told me I'm *too* bossy, some even going as far to say bitchy, in the bedroom.

Hey, it's not my fault they can't find my clit. Most times, I'm even sporting a buzzcut down south and they still can't find it. Hell, with some of the male population, a woman could have a tattoo pointing to it saying "press here for a good time," and some would *still* never find it.

But those guys aren't Diego. He *knows* what he's doing. And he can play both dom and sub, which is a pleasant surprise.

He takes well to my brattiness and has some of his own. I like the little bite he gives back to my bark. I need someone to keep up with me, and Diego does that and more. Him teasing to shut me up by shoving his dick in my mouth might come across as degrading in some social circles, but somehow it ignites the fire within me even more.

While I'm tempted to say some smartass remark just to see if he'll make good on his word, I can't.

His mouth feels so fucking good, and I selfishly want to see how far his devotion will go.

And after getting the green-light about this relationship from Javier, only to be tormented with all of Diego's lingering touches earlier, I can't wait any longer.

I spread my legs a little farther, letting his tongue reach even deeper, places no other man has explored with their mouth.

You read about people getting devoured, but experiencing it with Diego is more than I could have ever imagined. Our first time together on his table was phenomenal, but somehow this is even better now than that first night. He's eating me out like he's been starved, given his first meal in weeks, making sure to lick the plate clean, not wasting a thing.

The hairs from his mustache and beard, mixed with the light rubbing from his thumb on my clit, send me flying off the cliff in no time. My grip in his hair tightens while my pleasure crescendos. His tongue working me through my orgasm, slowing its pace until my senses return, then comes to an end.

He kisses the inside of one thigh, then the other. Swiping two fingers along my slit, he gathers the wetness collecting there before fixing my soaked panties to their previous position.

Adjusting himself so I'm face to face with him, and in the most seductive way humanly possible, Diego brings the same two fingers up to his mouth and sucks slowly so as to not waste anything, keeping eye contact with me the whole time.

This puts a whole new meaning to "tasting room." Though I'd call it more than a tasting with how *thorough* of a job he just did.

God, I'm never going to be able to use, or hear, that word without blushing now.

I clear my throat and pull my skirt back over my legs, before the images I'm conjuring in my mind become a reality. "Clearly our professionalism has been thrown out the window." I chuckle as I fix his tousled hair.

"And hopefully it never returns." He smirks before kissing me on the lips, slightly pulling away afterwards. "If that's alright with you, Sweetheart. I'm all for it, but if you need to slow down, or take the weekend, I understand."

"It's not that . . . " I swing my leg over and hop off the counter. Really, I'm not sure why I'm pushing back on this. "It's not *technically* against any rules. Actually, I just asked my manager for clarification on that before I came here." I sit back down in the nearest chair and sigh.

God, does it really matter? I mean I just let my *client* eat me out while inside the shop I'm supposed to be focused on rebranding.

"It just goes against what I believe the definition of a professional relationship should be." I say defeated as I grab my stuff. "I've never dated a client or coworker before." I admit.

"And yes, I know this is different since *technically* we had a relationship before I even knew you were my client, but . . . "

Psh, *relationship*. More like twelve hours of mind-blowing sex. A night that almost could've resulted in the worst UTI of my life had I not been staying hydrated and peeing after almost every time we had sex.

I've always sort of rushed the *after* part of sex in the past, and what better way to get out of a guy's bed than by saying you need to use the bathroom.

In fact, Diego's the first guy I've voluntarily snuggled with after having sex. Not sure if I want to analyze *that* right now.

"*But* . . . " he starts, "it sounds like you have a few things you want to sort through," I look up and see his soft, hazel eyes, a little bit of gold rimming the edges, "and I get that."

"You're right." I exhale. "I'll take the weekend to figure out what I'm okay with and then I'll let you know." Diego bites his lip and reluctantly nods.

"You're still okay with me taking you out on Tuesday, right?" He runs his fingers through my hair, lingering there while he waits for my answer. But I can't for the life of me think of what's happening on Tuesday.

"Tuesday?" I ask with my eyes closed as he works his fingers deeper into my scalp. God, his hands feel *incredible*.

"Yes, Tuesday. Saint George's Day? You said you'd help me with some market research . . ."

Right, right. Now I remember.

"Yes. Of course. How could I forget the very important *market research* we need to conduct?" I mock, but still don't open my eyes under his damn hypnotic touch.

Seriously, his hands are god-blessed. No matter where they touch, I'm putty beneath them. He could be rubbing my wrist and I bet he would still get me hot all over.

"I'll be there. But for now," I pull my head up and away from his magic hands, "it's probably time for me to go. Please, do look at those labels and let me know. I appreciate any feedback."

"I'm sure they're perfect." He softly grips my chin, swiping his thumb casually across my cheek. "Thank you for everything today and I'll text you with our choice."

"Sounds like a plan." I look down his chest, and then even lower, noticing the very impressive bulge in his trousers. "Looks like you may need some assistance with that." I add, looking pointedly at his dick.

"As much as I love the thought of you providing me some *assistance*, I think we both know, if you don't leave now," he sighs as he brushes a strand of hair out of my face, "I'll be bringing you back home with me. And though we might make it to the bed, we'll be doing everything but sleeping in it." When he puts it like that . . . "And you just said you needed me to give you the weekend to *think*."

Right. Think. I did say that.

His smirk alone is dangerous, and so goddamn tempting. But he's right. It'd be marathon sex, round two. Before I say just that, my phone dings, pulling me back down to reality.

I look down and see it's my sister. It's been a few days since I've talked to them.

"I'll see you Tuesday?" I ask over my shoulder as I gather my bag and jacket.

He nods. "Tuesday, but I'll lock up and walk you to your apartment, Sweetheart." I smile and we leave the shop together.

As I make my way to the steps, he swoops his arm around me and steals one last kiss. This isn't some goodbye peck, it's a melt-me-into-a-puddle kiss. A remind-me-again-why-I'm-leaving kiss. An I-don't-want-this-moment-to-end kiss.

My phone rings again, and like a gentleman, Diego pulls away a little and stares pointedly at my purse. "Someone's trying awfully hard to get ahold of you." He kisses the back of my hand before lowering it, allowing him to back away completely. "I'll talk to you soon."

"Goodnight, Diego." He casually waves his hand goodbye as I slip inside the door.

I quickly walk across the entry, not stopping until after I've climbed the four flights of stairs, locking my door as soon as I make it inside my apartment.

Leaning up against the door, I melt onto the hardwood. Now that Diego's beautiful face isn't here, and his magic hands aren't on me, I can think a little more clearly.

Obviously, it's not the brightest idea to be in a relationship, even if it's just sex, with a client. And can a relationship ever be *just sex*?

Even if it could, I have enough self awareness to know that we are far past the point of no-feelings sex. There are certainly feelings for me, and I'm willing to bet there are for Diego as well.

And really, we started this *before* we knew we'd be working together. That's got to count for something right? Plus, I'm only here for another few weeks. Why not enjoy the time I have left with him?

The sex is mind-blowing, like out-of-this-world good. And the man himself is unlike any other I've met. Broody yet sweet. Almost like he came from one of the books I read.

What are they called? Burnt cinnamon rolls? Crunchy on the outside but sweet and gooey in the middle.

My phone chimes again and I finally pull it out, seeing that the Girls' chat has a few new messages, but Taylor has called a couple times as well.

Before responding to the text thread, I call Taylor. She picks up on the first ring.

She rattles off questions left and right before I even say hello. "There you are! Where have you been? Isn't it close to eight over there? I thought you'd be done with work by now?"

"Hello to you, too, Taylor." I chuckle as I get myself off the hardwood floor. "And to answer your questions, I was with a client."

"The client you're trying *not* to sleep with? How's that going by the way?"

"Not good." I bit my lip while the image of him between my legs pops up in my head. "Well, he's fantastic, but it's clearly a losing battle. I can't stay away from him, Taylor."

She "hmms" before asking, "That good, huh?"

"Beyond good, Taylor. The things he can do . . . "

"Alright, alright. That's enough. I get it. He's great in bed."

"And on the table. And in the shower . . . "

"Enough, Emma!" She laughs. "I get it. He's a real winner in the sex department. So, you're going for it then?"

"I think I am." I guess it's just that easy. "I don't want to live a life full of what-ifs."

"I know what you mean." She adds quietly, and I can't help but think she's thinking of her own situation.

"Plus life always has a funny way of working out, you know?" I add. "So why not dive in?"

"God, how are you always so positive and optimistic, Emma?"

"Put me in a car and I'll prove you wrong." I try to chuckle, but it sounds forced. Visions of that day briefly flash in my mind.

"Still struggling with that, huh?" Her tone is sincere. We all have our own quirks from that day. Most of us have done therapy at one point or another in our lives because of the crash and the effects that happened to our family afterwards.

"Yup." Popping the P. "But how are things with you? Excited to spend a few days over here?"

"I am." I can hear her taking a deep breath. "Happy to escape a little and visit you. It looks like Tory won't be able to come after all."

There was a brief window where Tory thought she could snag a couple of last vacation days for a visit. Lindsay was even going to cover Tory's airfare, since she's been trying to save up for her trip this fall with her daughter, Haylee, but another nurse quit a couple days ago, so she felt like she needed to stay behind.

"Yeah, she messaged me. But I got a text from Lindsay saying she bought her ticket, so that's a good sign."

"We'll see if she actually gets on the plane though." Taylor huffs.

"When are y'all going to move on? You used to be so close and I hate seeing how distant you've become."

"Honestly," she sighs, "it's gone on for so long now, I'm not sure where to even begin, even if I *did* want to fix it."

"Well, you have to start somewhere, Tay. Anything is better than this. I love you both too much *not* to intervene in some capacity."

"I love you too, no matter how meddling you can be. I'll let you get back to your night. Talk to you soon, sis."

"Can't wait to see you. Bye!"

CHAPTER TWENTY

DIEGO

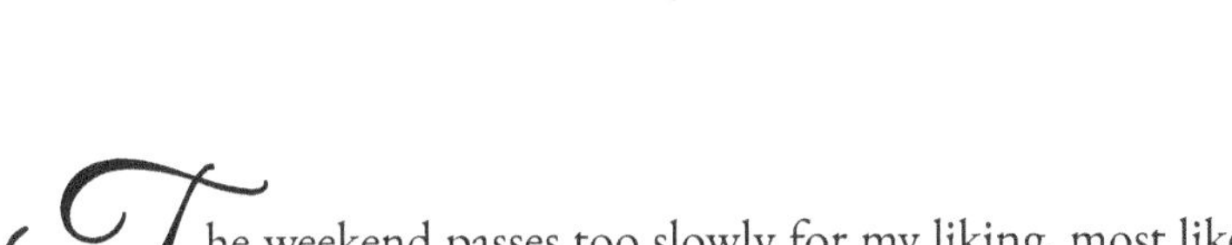

The weekend passes too slowly for my liking, most likely due to Emma's absence.

My family loved all three of the designs Emma printed, but ultimately one design won over the others. While the other two designs were professional and accomplished what they needed to do, the third design incorporated our family's coat of arms, taking a more modern approach to the eagle and crown symbol. Ultimately, it was an easy decision.

In the past, the winery used a variation of the mark throughout the business, in fact, you can still find it hiding in different parts of the property.

I texted Emma our selection on Saturday night, after I got back to the winery, which led to a late-night text session. Nothing too vulgar, just some friendly flirting. As much as I wanted to turn the conversation into sexting, I promised to give her space, so there I was, trying my damndest not to ask what she was wearing.

Thoughts of her naked, writhing beneath me, stayed with me long after our goodnight text. Keeping me up in more ways than one throughout the night. I don't remember a time I was constantly this turned on, finding release in my fist, only to wake up a few hours later and repeat the same process.

In fact, my appetite for sex has been nonexistent for the last few years, but with Emma, I'm ravenous. I've been around other beautiful women in my life, and have had no problem keeping my hands to myself. In fact, in the past, I was known for moving *too* slow or even being too quiet. I'm not one to rock the boat or make the first move.

And the more I think about it, Emma and I started out of convenience, for her protection. I didn't walk over to her in the hope of asking for her number. Not even a thought of bringing her home. No, I saw a person in need of help.

Really, Emma was the one to make the first move. The first several moves actually. She's the one who kissed me first. She's the one who invited me to sit and have dinner with her. She's the one who asked if I was unattached.

Emma's the one who brought me out of my cave and into the light. And god, is it bright and beautiful under the light she shines.

When I'm not thinking of her body, I'm consumed with how creative and intelligent she is. Always confident and optimistic about what the future will bring. I'm already pulled into her orbit, and I don't see myself being able to leave.

I'm pulling out of our main driveway on Monday morning when my phone goes off. My car screen lights up with Emma's name, strange. Normally, she'd text me. I press the accept button on my steering wheel after a couple rings.

"*Bon dia,* Sweetheart."

"*Bon dia,* Diego. Sorry to call so early. I just got off the phone with the printer and they said they could deliver the new labels on Thursday. Does that work for you or do I need to rush the order? I wasn't sure if the winery was completely out of labels yet."

"Thursday is just fine. We won't be needing the labels until next week anyway. We have a few to last us through the week if we need them, but most of our production won't start until the end of the month."

"Perfect timing then. Okay, and next up—" A motorcycle comes racing down the other side of the road, loud enough I miss what Emma says.

"I'm sorry, Emma. I missed that last part."

"Are you driving right now?"

"Yeah, you grabbed me on my way into the city."

"Oh, I'm sorry. I didn't mean to distract you."

"You're not dis—"

"Just call me when you get to the shop if you can. Thanks, Diego!" The phone clicks letting me know she hung up.

What was that? She knows it could be an hour before I reach the city, so whatever she has to say must not be *that* important.

I try not to think about it for too much longer, instead I play the latest album that's been stuck in my head ever since Mia suggested it. Every once in a while, she sends me a link to an album with me in mind. They're always instrumental, and some just work their way in my head, leaving me no choice but to listen to them on repeat until I tire of them.

This one is no different. By the time I pull up to the shop, the album is one song shy of finishing. And because this album is my current obsession, I know exactly what song is left in the lineup, so it plays in my head as I unlock the door and disable the alarm.

I get everything situated before opening the shop and then call Emma back.

"Are you finished driving?" she says in lieu of greeting.

"Yes, I'm in the shop now. What was it you had to tell me?" I take a seat behind the counter and start up the computer while I wait for her response.

"You remember Roger, the cruise line guy?"

I nod, but vocalize my response when I remember she can't see me. "Yes, I remember."

"His team emailed me this morning saying they could have a couple of people from the company come by on Thursday or Friday, whichever day works best for you."

"My schedule is pretty open here at the shop. What about yours?"

"Mine?" The word is voiced in confusion.

"Yes, your schedule. I'm assuming you'll be here with me. Am I not right in that assumption?"

"I guess that does make sense. It's just that my sisters are supposed to be arriving on Thursday for an extended weekend with me. But I'm sure they'd be fine exploring the city or hanging around my place while I'm helping you. It is my job after all."

"Why don't you bring them by? We could do the trial run together while your sisters enjoy their own tasting at another table. It's not like the cruise line reps are going to rent out the whole shop for this. I still have to be available for other customers if they walk in."

"That's a fair point." There's a pause on the phone, making me feel good to be the one who found the creative solution this time around. "Friday it is then. How does noon sound?"

"Great. I'll block off a portion of time so no other reservations will interrupt us; we'll just work with the walk-ins if and when they come in. I'll be sure to mark a table for your sisters as well." She's only briefly mentioned her sisters before. Hell, I don't even know how many she has. "How many seats should I reserve for everyone? Your sisters included."

"Hmm. I'd say four. Two at one table for the cruise reps and two at another. I'm guessing I won't be needing one since I'll be your assistant for the hour."

Assistant . . . an image of her bent over a desk, skirt pulled up with her ass out, immediately comes to mind. I'll have to keep that thought for later.

"And just so you know," she adds, "one of my sisters is a total wine snob. So feel free to tune her out. At least, that's what I do whenever she's on her high horse. I still love her though, even when she has her nose so far up her wineglass she can't see in front of her." She giggles and I join in with my own chuckle.

"Sounds like a plan. I'm spending the night at the apartment, hoping to start the morning off early with you." I clear my throat before continuing, "If that's okay with you, that is. I have a spot with a view in mind for breakfast"

"That sounds great. What time would you like me ready? I can even meet you at the shop, if that's easier."

"No, I'll pick you up at your apartment. I won't be opening the shop anyways because of the holiday." And like hell is she "meeting me" anywhere. I may not be a gentleman, but I sure as shit won't be accepting anything other than me picking her up. "How does nine sound?"

"Nine's perfect. I'll wait for you downstairs."

"Can't wait! Be sure to wear some comfortable shoes, there'll be a lot of walking. Bye, Sweetheart."

"Bye, Diego."

I hang up and take a deep breath, readying myself to start the day. And no sooner do I release that breath does the door open, bringing in the day's first customer.

CHAPTER TWENTY-ONE

EMMA

"I'm sorry, Emma. I really wanted to go, but it's just not in the cards for me right now."

I started my day off great. Amazing news from the printer and cruise line reps, then a great call with Diego, only for the good news to stop there.

My phone buzzed with a text from Lindsay, asking me to call her when I had a moment. I knew as soon as I read the text that she was going to cancel on me.

Something came up and she had to cancel, so now it's just Taylor coming.

Tory, I understand. She's a single mom with a daughter still in high school, and she works her ass off nursing. So when her co-worker quit, she understandably picked up more shifts to cover the absence. The hospital is hoping to have someone hired soon, just not soon enough for Tory to still make the trip.

Really, the sisters who are in most need of a vacation are the ones not going. Don't get me wrong, I'm sure Taylor has her own stress in life right now too, but she doesn't have a job or career. And her only responsibilities currently are keeping her and her fiancé's apartment presentable and being arm candy for him during the *many* business dinners and events they go to. Seriously, Jess and Taylor's calendar is filled almost every single night with dinners or functions.

Even me, being the people-person I am, hate the idea of never having time to myself.

But since Taylor is the only one with the semi-flexible calendar, she'll be flying alone to visit. But knowing her, she probably sprang for first class seats, so I don't feel too bad for her traveling alone.

"I know you are. And I promise I'm not trying to give you a guilt trip for not coming. I just miss you and was looking forward to spending some quality time with you. But I get it. Work comes first." Lindsay has always put work first with literally everything in her life since graduating college. She's worked hard to get where she is in her career, I just wish she'd live a little, you know?

"I promise I'll be at the next sisters' brunch when you come back into town."

"Are you, Taylor, and Tory not doing them while I'm gone?" Lindsay has been flaking out more recently on the monthly brunches us sisters do. But it's strange for Tory and Taylor to cancel them altogether.

"Oh I'm sure Taylor and Tory are, but you know my schedule. It can be so unpredictable." Or she just has a knack for keeping busy with work during all hours of the week.

"Whatever you say, Linds."

"Hey, I'm sorry to do this but my other line is ringing."

"Sure. I guess I'll just see you when I get back. Text you soon. Love you!"

"Love you, Em!" The line clicks as we end the call.

I'm not surprised at her canceling. I *am* surprised at the authenticity of her apology though. It really did seem like she wanted to come. And who could blame her? Barcelona is one of the most beautiful cities in the world. Full of culture, art, and scrumptious food *and* men apparently.

Maybe that's what Lindsay needs. A European vacation of her

own, to find some balance, and maybe even her own adventure with a special someone.

Nothing long term, just a quick vacation romance. I'm not sure she's even gone on a date since starting the job she's at now, and that's been . . . god, almost ten years. I'd be pretty uptight too if I hadn't had dick in a decade.

Now that's not fair. Just because she hasn't told us about a guy, doesn't mean she hasn't dated or had her fair share of one-night stands.

She could totally be keeping her sex life under wraps. Though I'm not sure why, since the rest of us girls talk about it so openly with each other. Then again, Tory hasn't had sex since conceiving Haylee, and Taylor has had a monogamous relationship with Jess for the last five or so years. So I guess that means I'm the only one really talking about sex.

Oh well, it's sex. Nothing to be ashamed of. A woman's got to have her orgasms, whether by a man or by her own hand. And frankly, sometimes all us women want is a great *O*, and not the baggage a man can bring to the table.

Though Diego doesn't seem like a man with baggage. Or maybe his baggage is hiding under all those muscles and I'm just blissfully unaware of it, floating down the river of denial with a wineglass in my hand.

I'm at the office until two, then go home to put together some renderings of what the winery could look like when rented out for events. I'm hoping to do a test run next week. It'll give me a chance to show the Sánchez family how perfect the property would be for dinners or weddings, though I'm pretty confident I've already sold them on the idea. I also hope to grab some photos and post them on their website and social media pages, giving potential clients a peek at what their event could look like. It gives the customers something to visualize. As the family rents out the space, they can add more photos from those events and grow the collection even more.

I've already talked to a few vendors about partnerships with the winery, most of them are even willing to let us rent some items for the mock event. The photographer we are using said they may be able to provide an hour of service depending on the day we choose, and if all works out, we'd only have to pay for the images we used, given we recommend them as a photographer to all our potential clients.

The last thing I have to figure out is food. I know Diego already has an established relationship with Lorenzo, and he owns a few tapas restaurants, but when I reached out last week, I didn't get a response. Perhaps if I ask Diego to give him a call, I'll be more likely to get a response. Or maybe Diego and I could stop in to the bar one afternoon, maybe even have a redo of the first night we met.

Obviously, not with the drunken jerks. And perhaps he would actually *eat* the food this time, instead of staring at me while I scarfed it all down.

But it is damn good food, and I know if it was *my* wedding or party, I'd definitely be more than satisfied with Lorenzo's food. I'm sure if I reached out again, and was given the time, I could secure some type of catering deal with Lorenzo.

There's a chime from my laptop, notifying me of an email from Javier reminding the office about the firm's closure for the holiday tomorrow, so I'll be free as a bird to enjoy some "market research" with Diego.

Pretty sure we're past the point of pretending our relationship is only professional. Hell, anytime we're alone, he gets his mouth or hands on me in some way shape or form. And something tells me tomorrow won't be any different.

CHAPTER TWENTY-TWO

DIEGO

The first thing I do on Tuesday morning is purchase a single red rose from the vendor in front of my apartment. I opted for only the rose, instead of the roses with an ear of wheat. Even if the wheat is the more traditional option, I don't want to scare Emma off with the symbol of fertility.

After crossing the street to Emma's building, her doorman greets me with a wave when I walk in the lobby, turning to take a seat on the bench inside, but I stop when I hear footsteps descending the stone stairs. The person turns the corner for the last few steps, and I'm greeted by a beaming Emma. God, she truly is radiant.

It seems she took my advice; she's wearing tennis shoes paired with jeans. Her top is tucked into the denim, I don't know why she's torturing me again with a high-necked shirt. First, that sweater vest, then the high collared dress the other day, and now this. It's practically a turtleneck.

"Hi!" she greets as she kisses both my cheeks, her jacket swung over her arms brushes against me. "Is it breezy outside? I wasn't sure if I needed—" She stops herself when she spots the lone rose

I'm holding. "Is that for me?" Biting her lip, she looks at me while raising one of her eyebrows.

"That it is. It's a tradition for the holiday. And no, it's not too cold. Actually, you could probably leave your jacket here if you wanted to."

"I can store it down here until you get back, Miss Hartman. That way you won't need to run up those steps again."

"Oh, that would be terrific, Manuel. Thank you!" Emma hands off her coat, keeping her rose in one hand and grabbing my hand with her other. "Okay, let's go!"

Our walk should only be about fifteen minutes but ends up taking almost double that length due to Emma's intrigue. Tables and vendors line the sidewalks, slowing our pace dramatically.

Most people are selling books and roses, while others are selling other trinkets and such. We pause briefly at a few book stands, but continue after I promise to stop at as many book stands as she'd like, *after* breakfast.

We reach the restaurant near the crowded plaza a little later than I had hoped, but luckily I know the owner here, too. He and his family go way back with ours. He was kind enough to save Emma and me a table outside, facing the festivities happening out in the plaza.

Tables and people fill the plaza. Honestly, the joy surrounding us is infectious. In my opinion, this holiday is better than Valentine's Day, the most commonly compared holiday to Saint George's Day.

After ordering our breakfast, we fill our time talking about our upbringing. The journey it took to get us to this moment in our lives.

"North Carolina was all I knew and when I got wind of this position, I had to at least apply. The worst they could do was say no, right?"

"Clearly they loved you, because here you are," I add.

"And here I am." She chuckles and god, do I love that sound.

"So, you said you did some schooling in the States. What was it like?" she asks before taking another bite of her egg dish.

"It was a good change of scenery. I enjoyed visiting California and learning some helpful things for the winery. But it was nice to come back home."

"Where in California did you go to school?"

"UC Davis in northern California. They have a few wine programs over there. Surprisingly enough, it was my dad's idea. He thought it'd be lucrative to get a little more education, hoping it could help to grow the family business. Unfortunately, my dad didn't think my sister needed to get the same opportunity. Something I'm hoping I can make up for in the future." Finishing my last bite, I lay my napkin over the cleared plate.

"Look at you, being the thoughtful older brother." Emma has a twinkle in her eyes.

"Just looking out." Our waiter comes over so I can pay the bill. "You ready to continue on?" She nods and after taking one last sip of water, we walk out of the restaurant. "The next stop is just around the corner."

Every year, I'm astounded by the crowd size. And it's not just tourists either; there are so many locals or people, like me, who live just outside of the city, who come in for the day to celebrate.

We walk another few minutes, her hand in mine, feeling like two fish swimming against the current. It's even busier this year compared to years past.

I pull her close to me once the building's in sight and situate us on the opposite side of the street, so we can have the best view.

"This is absolutely stunning," she says with awe, looking at the rose covered building in front of us.

"I present to you, the *Casa Batlló* or *Casa dels ossos*, the House of Bones. Designed by Antoni Gaudí." I stand behind her, wrapping an arm around her waist, while the other hand wraps around hers. I raise them together to help point to various spots of the house while I explain the meaning behind them.

"Remember the story I told you about Saint George?"

She nods and rests her head on my chest as I continue. "The house is said to be a symbol of his battle with the dragon." Bringing our joined hands up, I point to the top of the building. "The roof is modeled after the spine of the dragon. You can see the iridescent scales used as roof tiles covering the top. And over there—" I move our entwined hands to point to what looks like a chimney with a cross. "If you use that creative mind of yours, you can see the lance he used to puncture the dragon's back."

I wrap her even closer in my arms, continuing my description of the work of art in front of us. "You see that window at the top? That's the attic and inside is what's called the 'dragon's ribcage.' You can actually get a peek at the *Sagrada Família* from that window, another work designed by Antoni Gaudí. Then the balcony right below is said to be the princess' balcony."

"Of course, because there wouldn't be a story without the princess."

I nip at her ear and she giggles. "Smartass." Rolling my eyes, even though she can't see them. "They're kind of difficult to see because of all the roses, but underneath all the red petals, you'd find uniquely shaped pillars and balconies. They're said to represent the bones of the dragon's previous victims."

"Now that's just morbid." She's not wrong.

"And finally, if you were to go inside, you'd find the staircase whose rail is made to look like the dragon's tail."

"And is the inside as spectacular as the outside?"

"Absolutely, just not a tour you'd want to do today." I turn her so she's facing me, the crowd continues to grow making me anxious to leave the area. "So, books?"

"Books!" She throws her hands up and cheers. I can't help but laugh, finding her joy contagious.

"Perfect. Stay close and don't let go of my hand. It gets busier throughout the day."

She eyes me suspiciously but holds her grip tight with mine as we continue walking.

CHAPTER TWENTY-THREE

EMMA

Walking back through the plaza, we roam about the various vendors, stopping at the several tables offering books. There are so many.

Old and new. All different genres, too. Some tables are organized while others have piles of books to sort through, it's like your own little treasure hunt with those vendors.

Most of the books are printed in Spanish or even Catalan, but every couple of stalls there are some English ones. My Spanish is pretty good, but not well enough to enjoy a book written in the language.

The weather is perfect for a day spent outside, browsing books and enjoying the energy from the city. Kids are dancing and laughing, some exchanging roses while giggling afterwards with friends.

There's a bunch of noisy chatter filling up the air mixing with the music a nearby band is playing. Smiles are on almost every face you look at. People exchanging hugs and kisses. Some are sweet and simple, while others are filled with a little more passion. Love is given so freely around us. It's refreshing, and such a beautiful sight to see.

I hear Diego's voice before I feel his presence at my back. "Find anything you like?" His breath warm against the shell of my ear.

"No, as beautiful as all these editions are, nothing is really jumping out at me at the moment."

"Well that just won't do. After all, I can't let the day pass without buying you at least one book." He grabs my hand and pulls. "Come. I know a place where we might have better luck."

The music picks up in the square as we pass though. Couples pairing up and starting to sway to the music. I stop to take in the sight, pulling my phone out to capture the image in front of me. Wanting to seize the moment, I call out, "Hey, Diego?"

"Yes?"

I turn my face to look at him, extending my hand out his way. "Want to dance?"

"I could never say no to you, Sweetheart." He takes two steps and wraps me in his arms. I rest my palms on his chest, rose still in one hand, and we rock back and forth enjoying the slow swaying of the slower music.

Our movement quickly changes as the rhythm of the music picks up. I think the song must be a popular one because people of all ages come rushing in and dancing around for the fast paced song.

Diego doesn't miss a beat though, completely surprising me, and starts swinging me around and around, matching our steps to the people around us. I'm quickly overtaken with a fit of laughter. Enjoying the pure jubilation that surrounds us. There's clapping and stomping from both kids and adults alike. All enjoying the music.

The song comes to an end and a slower song starts playing. "One more?" Diego tosses me a roguish grin.

I smile. "Thought you'd never ask." I lay my head to rest on his chest, ear pressed so close, I can hear the beat of his heart. I stay like that for the rest of the song, wrapped in his arms and not wanting to be anywhere else. He kisses the top of my head before resting his cheek on top.

We come to halt, and I pull away slightly to gaze on his face. He returns my stare with one of his own. Eyes pulling me in. Lips begging to be kissed. God, I want to kiss him. And why shouldn't I? We're both—

Diego's lips on mine interrupt my thoughts. I guess he was thinking the same thing.

The world around us melts away. It's just Diego and me. Lips on lips. His hands on my body; mine on his. Neither of us holding back in this magical moment.

We kiss for what feels like hours before separating. "Now let's go get you some books." Diego gives my ass a tight squeeze before finally letting go.

An hour later, I've hit the jackpot. Diego walked me to a secondhand book store, and they had a whole section of books printed in English. And would you believe it, most of them were romance books!

All I can think is I've died and gone to heaven when a kind woman directs us to the stash. After he gets me situated with the pile of romance books, he goes to check out some books of his own.

Diego comes walking back after his own scavenger hunt, putting his few treasures down on the table next to me. "Looks like you've found a few." He motions to the stack of twenty or so books I've accumulated.

"Well I can't get *all* of them. How ever will I get them home?" A look of . . . something flashes before Diego's face, but I'm not sure what it was. Surely not sorrow at me mentioning going back home. "After I finish this pile, I'll sort through the ones I put aside over here." I motion to another nearby stack. "After that, I'll narrow down my choices, one last time before deciding on which ones to buy." He arches his eyebrow at me while picking up a couple of the books on my "maybe" stack.

"Double Teamed? Room for Three?" Well, I guess there's no

reason trying to hide what I read now. "I'm sensing a theme here, Emma."

"If the theme is cozy double penetration, then you'd be right."

Diego curses, shaking his head with a chuckle afterwards. "Well, now we have to wrap it up."

"Oh?" I turn in my chair, making my eyes go all big and doe-like. "And why's that?" With a sneaky suspicion, I look down at his pants and find his dick fighting against the denim. "Did I say something to upset you? Or are you just having a *little* problem over there?"

"Fucking hell, Emma." Diego clears his throat as he not-so subtly adjusts his pants. "You're going to pay for that *little* comment. Come on, let's get your books and head out."

"But I haven't even sorted through them yet." I whine.

"Then I'll get them all. It's a fifteen minute walk back to your apartment, and I'm not going to waste any more time in a place we have to keep our clothes on." He walks around the corner and returns with a mesh basket. "Put whatever books you're interested in inside the basket and let's go."

I don't protest any further because by the look in Diego's eyes, he won't take no for an answer. Plus, all these books are at a relatively good price because they're all secondhand, so really I'm getting these for a steal.

The line for checkout takes about ten minutes, and by some form of magic, the walk back is even faster. Then again, I'm practically being dragged the whole way by the brooding dragon named Diego. Honestly, I am half surprised he doesn't just throw me over his shoulder to carry me the rest of the way home.

Diego opens the door to my building, clearly only one thing on his mind. I greet Manuel and grab my coat I left earlier, while a very impatient Diego waits by the stairs. I hear him mutter something about the "damn broken elevator" before we start our ascent.

Once we're in the cover of the stairwell, Diego can't keep his hands off of me, which is a talent all in itself because the man is carrying bags filled with a considerable amount of books. He's practically a walking romance library.

Our giggles and laughs echo through the stairwell. Luckily most people are out celebrating the holiday, but I know Manuel can definitely hear the commotion from his spot downstairs. I'll have to apologize for that tomorrow.

I hustle up the flights of stairs, eager to see what awaits me once we're behind locked doors. Diego's rubbing my ass and kissing my neck between steps.

Even though I take the lead during the second floor's stairs, he's catching up quickly.

On the landing of the third floor, he surprises me by grabbing my neck and pulling me into a lip-locking kiss. Only to smack my ass a second later, ordering me to keep marching immediately after.

By the fourth floor, he's stopping but only to palm my aching pussy through my jeans before he hurries up the steps, leaving me wanting and honestly, a tad angry because he's in the lead in this little race of ours. Fucking tease.

By the time we make it to my door on the fifth floor, we're both panting and flushed. My underwear is a slippery mess, expecting some attention after all those teasing touches and kisses.

I fumble with my keys, and finally decide to give the door a good shove with my hip, almost eating shit when the door swings wide open.

Diego follows me though the threshold, carrying all the books like the gentleman he is, while his devilish smirk tells a different story.

I take a good hard look at him while I catch my breath, admiring him in his dress shirt, unbuttoned just enough to expose a bit of chest hair, sleeves rolled up to show off his veiny forearms. And his ass, god damn. I've never been an admirer of asses until now. I get a perfect view of it as he turns to put the books down on the kitchen counter; so firm, jeans fitted tightly around his muscular shape.

All I can think is how we are *so* far past a professional relationship at this point.

I lock the door and silence my phone; there's not a way in hell I'll be letting anyone interrupt us. We both kick off our shoes, clearly not planning to go back out any time soon. It's barely after one in the afternoon, but I'm already giddy for bed.

We have a mini stare-down with each other before he marches over to me, picking me up in one fell swoop. I instantly wrap my legs around his waist before he shoves me up against the wood of the door, kissing me with all the fire he's been holding back.

It's hot . . . and wild . . . and god, I just want our clothes off already.

He breaks our kiss and stares at me with a knowing grin.

"Okay, Sweetheart. Now be a good girl, and go get your vibrator."

CHAPTER TWENTY-FOUR

DIEGO

Her shock is obvious. "What?" I ask. "You think I believe a sex-goddess like you doesn't enjoy pleasure by her own hand?" She still has her legs wrapped around me, frozen there in utter disbelief. Whether it's that I called her out for having a vibrator or that I'm open to wanting to use it with her, I'm not sure.

I move my head so I'm nuzzling the side of her face. "Come on, Sweetheart. Bet it's a pretty color, too." I force her ever further into the door, my hips closer, erection pushing into her showing my intent. Her sharp gasp gives her surprise and arousal away. "How about you stop me when I guess the color, hmm?"

I kiss her cheek, light and soft. "Pink?"

She shakes her head.

I kiss the side of her chin. "Yellow?"

She shakes her head again.

"Hmmm . . ." I mutter against her throat. "Purple?"

She nods as I suck on her neck a little.

"Ah, purple." I move a hand down between her legs, lightly rubbing the denim that's pulled tight. "I bet it's all charged up and ready to go. Probably hiding in your nightstand, yeah?"

She nods again, squirming around my hand. I kiss her neck some more while letting her rock on my palm a few times.

"Fine," I breathe out, placing her legs down and stepping out of our bubble. "If you won't get it . . . " I give her a once over, god, does she look desperate for a good fucking. So that's exactly what I aim to give her. "Then I will."

I take off sprinting down her hallway, not exactly sure where I'm going. The first few doors are shut, which leave the two in back.

The first open door leads to a bathroom, not the room I need. Which means the door at the end of the hall is hers.

I hear her rapid steps nearing, so instead of racing into the bedroom, I stop in my tracks. I turn around quickly, and she does exactly what I want and runs right into me, giving me the opportunity to pick her up and throw her over my shoulder.

"Seriously, Diego?!" Her voice is high pitched and breathy. I love it.

I smack her ass and she moans. Fucking *moans*. "I see I'm not the only one who likes a little pain with their pleasure."

"Fuck you, Diego!"

"I hope you will. Over and over today, and all through the night. You might want to draft an email to your boss now, because you won't be going into work tomorrow. Not with all the plans I have in store for you."

"Oh, big talk," she mocks over my shoulder as I march over to her nightstand. I smack her ass again. Naturally, she has two nightstands, so I pick the side with the most clutter.

I open up the top draw and *bingo*. A bright purple vibrator sits pretty right inside. "It looks as if we've caught ourselves a rabbit."

I throw Emma onto the bed, legs hanging off the edge. "Unbuckle your jeans, Sweetheart."

This is the most compliant I've seen Emma, because she rips her belt off and unbuckles her jeans in less than twenty seconds, attempting to shimmy out of her denim like her life depends on it.

I won't lie, I'm enjoying the show, but I'm ready for the main event.

"Let me help you with those." After taking my shirt off, I run my hands up her thighs to her black string thong. I wind the string around a finger on both sides, bringing them down with her jeans. Exposing her perfectly swollen pussy, so wet it's glistening.

"Now take off that damn shirt."

She looks down at her shirt and back up to me. "What's wrong with my shirt?"

"You keep wearing these high-necked tops. Leaving me unable to give your breasts the worship they deserve." She laughs, free and wild. "Are you doing it on purpose? Are you finding this amusing to torture me so?"

"No," she laughs out, but catches her breath soon after. "My breast size is the only thing on my body I'm self-conscious about. I find it amusing that you're complaining about not having them on display, when there's nothing *to* display."

"Oh, Sweetheart." I move my hands up under her top, exposing more skin the higher I reach. "I wouldn't change a thing about your body; it's perfect." I bend down and kiss each breast over the fabric of her bra. "I'm enraptured with every part of you."

She helps me take off the rest of her shirt. Arching her back, she allows me to unclasp the hooks from her bra. I slowly pull the straps down her arms but leave the cups in place. Giving her time to adjust and be comfortable without it.

I've already seen all of her on that first night, but this feels different. More intimate. No one is hiding under the guise that this is only for one night like we were when we first met.

Bending my head to her navel, I kiss a path up to the fabric still covering her breasts. Biting it then dragging it off her body, leaving her utterly exposed on her bed.

"I'm going to call time-out for a minute." I reach back over to the nightstand and twirl the purple vibrator around my hand. "As much as I'd like to use this toy on you while you ride me, I want to check your limits. We can still have fun with this, without the double penetration." And if I'm being honest with myself, I'm a little intimidated, too, just thinking about the logistics of it all. Especially because I've never done anything like this before, and I don't want to do anything to hurt her.

"It's something I've never done, but am very interested in." She bites her lip at her confession. "But not today. I just want to enjoy my time with you." I let out the breath that I guess I was holding, and smile down at her. "I don't want to take it off the table though . . . just not today."

"I'll try anything with you. So no DP tonight, but let's see what else this toy can do."

I'm all for a helping hand in the bedroom. I think of toys as teammates, all with the same goal in mind. After all, you can't achieve a grand slam without the bases being loaded.

I raise the purple toy up to Emma's face. "Suck on it." She does as told and I reward her with a few teasing strokes up and down her opening. Teasing her with kisses up her thigh, wrapping around her hip, along her waist, and stopping on her right breast. Her skin is already pebbled, nipples hard and erect.

She's starting to squirm around my hand holding the vibrator between her thighs. "Fuck, you're pussy is so needy." My dick is protesting the fact I still have my jeans on by leaking so much, I'm sure I'll have a spot. Why haven't I taken my pants off again?

"Diego," she pants. "I'm close."

With that encouragement, I ease the vibrator inside of her. Positioning those little silicon ears so they rub up against her swollen clit, while giving her the fullness she's so desperate for with the vibrating wand.

"Ohmygod!!! Ohmygod!!!" Wetness covers the toy and my hand while she comes, thrusting her hips and making the vibrator slide in and out of her.

I lower the speed, but keep the vibrator in the same position, allowing her time to ride the high all the way. God, she is practically glowing from her climax.

"Fuck, Diego. We are, for sure, doing that again later." She brings her body upright so she's eye level with my chest. "But I couldn't help noticing, we haven't improved your . . . " She looks pointedly at my crotch and then meets my stare again. " . . . *little* situation over there."

"You and that word." I step back and undo my belt, looking down at her with mischief in my eyes. "Guess I'll just need to fuck it out of your mouth."

I drop my jeans and boxers, exposing my rock hard dick. She immediately slides off the bed, positioning herself on her knees between mine, then starts sucking.

CHAPTER TWENTY-FIVE

EMMA

EMMA:

How much sex is too much sex?

TORY:

Jesus, Em!

TAYLOR:

You're going to have to stop this sexcapade at
some point, because I'm landing in less than
twenty-four hours.

Winery guy?

EMMA:

Yes, couldn't keep away.

LINDSAY:

As long as you remember it's temporary. Just
don't get attached.

EMMA:

Too late.

The rest of yesterday went a lot like our first night together, only even more sex.

Nothing was rushed. We enjoyed giving each other pleasure, as well as lingering in the after effects.

I woke up in the middle of the night, wrapped up in Diego's strong arms, legs braided together, with nothing but my sheet and each other's naked bodies keeping us warm. And my first thought was, "I could get used to this."

We had sex a few more times throughout the night.

Diego's stamina . . . it's on the level of a Greek god's. And I say that confidently, even knowing I obviously have zero experience fucking a Greek god.

God, I'm not even making sense, that's how good the sex was. He literally fucked me senseless. I guess that will happen after seven orgasms.

That's right *seven*.

Maybe he was right, maybe I would need to miss work on account of being so thoroughly fucked because right now, I'm too tired, and sore, to even *think* about getting out of bed.

I'm going to correct my earlier statement about Diego being a burnt cinnamon roll. This man is a gentleman in the streets, but a damn freak in the sheets. And I can't believe he was willing to make my book dreams come true with his offer of double penetration.

I won't lie, I was a little nervous. Hence, why I turned him down. It's not like I'm vanilla in the bedroom, I've just lacked partners who have been open minded to experimenting with me.

Reading has always been a safe space to fantasize about new positions or activities without feeling the judgement or shame from others.

Diego is actually the first of my partners who looked at one of my books and didn't get weird or judge me about it. And to make things even better, he used that knowledge and applied it to our relationship in the bedroom. What more could a girl ask for?

Diego leaves the apartment a little before nine after a short round of playing in the shower. I don't even know how either of us had the energy for that.

It went from "Hey, let me help you rinse off before I leave" to "Let's have hot and heavy doggy-style shower sex up against the glass," adding another orgasm to my tally.

Diego had to do a few deliveries this morning before opening up the shop, but before he left, he gave me the most tender kiss I've ever received. And if I didn't know before, that kiss solidified me falling head over heels for the man.

Thursday came quickly. Everything with Taylor's flight went perfectly and according to plan. The driver dropped her off around mid afternoon, giving her time to unpack and relax a little before heading down to the tapas bar.

As luck would have it, Lorenzo's here. I excuse myself from Taylor for a brief moment, allowing me the opportunity to talk some business with him.

"That sounds like a great opportunity. I'm actually in the process of opening a new restaurant not too far away from the winery. It'll be a perfect spot for food prep."

"Perfect! I'll call you later with some more details. Thanks so much Lorenzo!" He smiles as I wave my thanks and head back to my table.

"Is that your mystery man?" Taylor nods over to someone when I return to my seat.

"Who?" I look over my shoulder. "Lorenzo?" She nods as she takes a bit of calamari.

"God, no. Though he's nice enough"—I give him a quick once over—"and certainly good looking enough. But no. Diego's finishing up at the shop and will be driving back to his family's winery after closing. You'll meet him tomorrow though."

"Oh? Why's that?"

"Because we, my dear sister, are going to do a little wine tasting." God, this food is somehow even better. I need to make it a point to eat here more.

"Ah, mixing business with pleasure?" Taylor gives me a knowing look as she sips her wine.

"As a matter of fact, I am. A cruise line is interested in partnering up with their tasting room and they needed to make this week work for their schedules." Taylor gives a knowing look before I add, "Diego was nice enough to invite you to do a tasting while we do a trial run with the reps. If you don't have a problem with it, that is."

"As long as it's good quality wine, I won't complain."

"Perfect. We'll probably go out with Diego and maybe his sister for dinner later that night, too, if you're okay with that."

"Yeah, that's fine. I'd like to get to know the man who's been tying my sister up." I give her a smirk. "Oh god, Emma! I'm speaking figuratively." She takes a sip of wine and shrugs before adding, "But good for you."

We finish dinner and walk up the four flights of stairs to the apartment.

"God, I'm exhausted." Taylor announces as soon as we walk through my door. I'm sure the jet lag is getting to her.

"Feel free to go to bed. My brain is still running a hundred miles an hour with the event next week so I'll be up for a while. I still have a few things I need to iron out." I say, leaning against the kitchen counter.

"Need any help with anything?" Taylor offers.

"Thanks, but I'm good. Lindsay actually sent me some elegant but easy outdoor ideas from some snapshots of events she's organized, so I'm going to use those as a starting point."

She nods, "She definitely has experience with events."

"Yeah, I'll probably just scroll through Pinterest most of the night looking for more ideas, see if any inspiration sparks."

Every vendor I reached out to has agreed that next Thursday works the best for their calendars. Since it will be the beginning of

May, the weather should be perfect for our outside gathering. The whole family will be there, as will some close family friends, and each vendor will have a spot at the table, if they choose to join.

The look I'm going for is leaning towards rustic elegance. Lots of natural wood textures, wine bottles as centerpieces, and plenty of soft light, candles and stringed lights.

"Okay. I'll see you in the morning then."

"Sounds good. Sleep well, Taylor."

"You too, sis." She closes her door as I make my way to my bedroom.

After getting myself ready for bed, I nestle into my fluffy comforter, getting situated for a late night of pinning, room lit by the soft glow from the street lights below and my phone.

"Thanks, Diego and Emma. It was a pleasure to meet you both. Everything was phenomenal and I hope we'll see you again sometime soon. Enjoy your weekend." One of the reps, Ashley, says as the two of them get up and leave.

"Thank you! Pleasure meeting both of you ladies," I add as they walk out the door.

"Well, I think that went well," Mia says to us after we come back inside. Everything went as smoothly as it could have gone. Both women seemed interested in the brand and loved all the wines they tried. Deep-rooted wineries with a rich history is what they said they're looking for. Businesses passed down across generations. They especially enjoyed that all the food is also sourced from another long established, local farm.

Diego did amazing, too. He was a little stiff at the beginning with introductions, but once he started talking about the wines and history of the business, he was a natural. So confident and warm. Charming, too. Not the grumpy dragon he's often painted as by his family.

Before we walked them out, they said we'd hear from them by

the end of next week. Apparently, they've been scouting this whole week and are continuing to do so throughout the weekend.

I'm not sure how many other wineries are in the running, but I feel fairly confident in our chances. The Sánchez family has built such a great legacy, and their products resemble that.

Taylor's the biggest wine snob I know, and even she's impressed with the wines she sampled today.

"Do you know if any stores sell these back home?" Taylor pours another glass, this one resembling more of a true pour instead of a tasting. I chuckle as I start cleaning up all the glasses from the reps' tasting.

"They aren't sold in any stores—" Diego starts.

"Yet! Not sold in stores, *yet*." I interrupt, bumping Diego's hip before I clear off another table. "The plan is to get the new labels on, establish the new rebranding while reaching out to the list of international retailers I'm currently compiling." Taylor nods as she sips her wine. "But, you can always buy them online and have them shipped to you. It just might take a little bit to reach you."

"And the overseas shipping is a bitch to pay," Mia adds as Diego walks over and wraps his arms around my chest. My hands are quick to clasp around his forearms, enjoying his nearness.

He gives me a quick kiss on my cheek and whispers in my ear, "You were perfect today. I couldn't have done it without you. Thank you." He gives me a squeeze and another kiss, this one on the top of my head.

"Well aren't you two adorable?" Shit. I forgot she was here. Taylor has never been one for PDA in the time she's been with Jess, but teenage-Taylor was a different story, so I'm sure she's uncomfortable with the display.

"Sorry, Taylor." I drop my hands, but Diego keeps his arms in place.

"You two ladies have any dinner plans? I'd love to take you all out in thanks for today."

"I have something a little later in the night, but I'm free for a bit right after closing." Mia looks to the sisters as she wipes down some tables.

"We don't, but we ate at Lorenzo's last night already."

"Then it's a good thing I know of more than one place to enjoy a delicious meal," he whispers in my ear, giving my ass a teasing squeeze. I think I hear Mia make a barfing sound behind us. Raising his voice so Taylor can hear, he adds, "Why don't you ladies go back home and I'll pick you up after Mia and I close? Say a little after seven? But I'll text if it's going to be later."

Taylor's first to respond. "If your taste in food is as good as your taste in wine, then I'm in." I guess that settles that.

CHAPTER TWENTY-SIX

DIEGO

During our walk to dinner, I learn that Emma actually has three sisters, Taylor, Lindsay, and Tory. Taylor and Lindsay are twins, about five years older than Emma. Then Tory is another five years older, and has an eighteen-year-old daughter, Haylee. They seem to be a pretty close family from what I can gather.

Walking into one of my favorite spots, the restaurant is buzzing with energy. Tables filled with people enjoying dinner. Live music playing in the back. People lined up at the bar, enjoying a lively Friday night.

Thankfully, there isn't an issue getting a table for the four of us and we're quick to be seated.

"This place looks *fun*!" Emma comments as I pull out her chair.

"Because it *is* fun!" Mia cheers.

"It's a vibe for sure." Taylor agrees as she takes her seat.

"Enjoy!" The host adds before leaving.

The ladies all scan the menu before Taylor asks, "So, what's good here?"

"Honestly? Everything," Mia comments and both of the sisters laugh at that.

"I can order my favorites if you like; we can always order more afterwards," I offer, not even picking up the menu since I practically have it memorized from all the years I've been coming here.

Emma looks at Taylor and she nods. "Yeah, that sounds good!"

I order our food and a bottle of wine as soon as our waiter greets us, a bottle that doesn't last long after Taylor decides it's a good idea for us to play "Never Have I Ever."

Taylor claims it's just to break the ice, but I have a sneaking suspicion it's her way to get some information out of me.

We're about four questions in when I pour the remaining wine into Emma's empty glass.

"Your turn, Diego," Taylor cheers before taking a bite of the food that the waiter just dropped off. She mutters "shit" around the mouth full of food. She's definitely feeling the wine now. "This is delicious."

"Diego hasn't steered me wrong with food while I've been here," Emma praises.

"Yeah, for someone who doesn't come into town a lot, he sure knows the best places to eat," Mia says around a mouth full of shrimp.

"Thank you ladies. Now, let's see." I rub my beard as I contemplate my next question. "Never have I ever . . . kissed more than one person within the span of twenty-four hours."

All the ladies take a drink while looking at each other in shock, only to finish their drinks and start laughing hysterically.

I give Emma a look and she shrugs. "What? It was college."

"A game of 'Spin the Bottle' in high school for me." Taylor nods and finishes her glass.

"Just a regular Friday night for me." Mia winks before adding, "Another bottle?"

"Here, here," the sisters cheer with Mia and I can't help but laugh.

"Alright, one more bottle." I order another while Emma starts asking her question.

"Okay, my turn." Emma eyes Taylor with a knowing look. "Never have I ever . . . laughed so hard I peed myself . . . as an adult."

Taylor shakes her head. Then I laugh as she takes a sip of her wine. "You bitch," she mutters under her breath.

"Play nice, ladies," I caution as I take another bite.

Mia smacks my shoulder. "Shhh, I want to see where this goes."

"Oh no, it's on." Taylor blots her face with her napkin before continuing. "Never have I ever set a fire in the kitchen."

"Oh my god! That was one time!" Emma complains. "And it was only in the microwave!"

"Wait, wait, wait. I need more detail on this, Sweetheart."

Emma finishes her glass of wine before explaining. "I was like eight—"

"Try twelve." Taylor adds.

"Fine, twelve," Emma rolls her eyes, "and I was cooking instant mac and cheese and forgot to add water before cooking it—"

"So it caught fire in the microwave!" Taylor interjects, a little louder as the alcohol takes full effect. She points to me with the wine bottle before she refills Emma's glass. "Never have I ever kissed someone when I didn't know their first name."

"Hey," I start, then take a sip. "I thought we were friends." I wonder what else Emma told Taylor about that first night. "Plus, it's not even your turn."

"Yeah, it's Diego's," Emma scolds.

"Fine, fine." Taylor waves her hand to me. "Diego, your turn."

"Alright, never have I ever . . . played on a sport's team."

"Never?" Emma questions, taking another sip from her glass. I think she's working on glass three? Maybe four?

"Yeah, surely you played football or something during

school," Taylor adds after sipping from her glass. "Wait, is it football or soccer here?"

"*Fútbol* is soccer here," Mia comments as she takes a sip of her wine.

"But no. I didn't have time as a kid since I was busy helping out at the winery. But Mia here," I bump her shoulder with mine, "joined a community league a few years ago."

"Oh!!!" Emma and Taylor shout, raising their fists in the air. "Go Mia! Go Mia!"

Mia takes a bow. "Thank you, thank you! Okay, my turn. Never have I ever had to sleep outside in a vineyard."

I take a sip of my wine, eyeing Mia the whole time.

"Why'd you do that?" Taylor laughs out.

I clear my thoughts. "When I was a teen, I went out on one of my walks around the estate to clear my mind—"

"Which he still does to this day," Mia chirps from beside me.

"Yes, well, I took a nasty fall and twisted my ankle pretty bad. I couldn't walk on it so I had to wait until someone found me the next morning. Thankfully it was summer, so the temperature at night wasn't bad at all. It just felt like I was camping under the stars."

"Oh my god, you poor thing!" Emma's face is furrowed as reaches over to rub my arm.

"Our mom bought radios the next day."

"And she's been insistent about us using them ever since." Mia grumbles before she redirects the conversation. "Okay! Emma, your turn!"

"Well speaking of childhood . . . " Emma starts but pauses with a hiccup. "Never have I ever been flunked out of a class."

"Oh yeah?" Taylor tosses the glass back, a little too aggressively, before adding, "Never have I ever been afraid to get in a car. Beat that!" Taylor declares proudly, like she just won the game.

I look at Emma and see her face completely drop. Something's definitely not right. I reach over and touch her thigh. "Emma, are you—"

"Can I offer you some dessert?" The waiter interrupts. "Maybe even some more wine?"

"I think we're good on wine, but . . . " I look at Emma and she has a soft smile on her face as she nods, "yes on dessert."

I order our desserts and the sisters share a look of understanding. I'm not exactly sure what just happened but clearly the promise of a sweet treat is distraction enough.

Both of them sober up a bit as we enjoy our desserts but the table remains quiet. We pay the bill shortly after and all walk out.

"Since I'm in town, I'm meeting up with someone—" Mia turns to go the other way.

"I'm not so sure I feel comfortable with you walking alone after all the wi—"

"I'm fine, Diego, I'll see you back at the apartment later. Stop being so grumpy." Mia waves me off. "Emma, it was great seeing you again! And Taylor, it was fun meeting you!" Mia waves and walks the opposite way down the street.

I make sure to walk Emma and Taylor all the way up to Emma's apartment, ensuring they make it up safely. After giving Emma a kiss that was over far too quickly for my liking, we exchange our goodbyes and I leave her to enjoy the rest of the weekend with her sister.

CHAPTER TWENTY-SEVEN

EMMA

Taylor and I slept in on Saturday, attempting to sleep off the lingering effects of the alcohol from the night prior.

When I finally do get out of bed, I walk over to the room Taylor commandeered and crack open the door, peeking in to ask, "Can I tempt you with a boozy brunch?"

I hear a groan before Taylor answers, "Literally, the only way you are getting me out of bed today." I point a finger gun at her before turning to leave but stop and face her when she says my name. "Emma . . . about last night . . . "

"Don't worry about it, sis." I give her a warm smile. "Now get your ass up and let's go to brunch!"

"Ugh!" she whines as she dramatically covers her face with a pillow. "Why do you have to be so loud?" she grumbles, her voice muffled by the pillow.

We are both slow to move; but eventually, make it out of the apartment.

Walking over to the plaza where Diego and I ate a few days ago, we approach the busy restaurant. I remembered seeing they offered a special weekend breakfast, plus the food was great last time I ate there.

Luckily, we get seated fairly quickly and immediately put in our order of mimosas and pastries. Because what better way to get over our hangovers than by eating carbs and drinking more alcohol?

Our waiter is super speedy with our drinks and returns almost instantly with two glasses.

"So spill," Taylor says as she takes a huge drink of the orange beverage.

"What?"

"Oh, don't *what* me. Tell me about Diego. It seems like you're doing more than just sleeping with him."

Not even going to attempt to beat around the bush about it when it was so obvious yesterday. "God, I don't know, Taylor." I take a sip from my drink before elaborating. "It just feels . . ." I look around trying to come up with the right way of phrasing it. ". . . right, you know? I really don't know how else to describe it. My instincts are telling me that he's good for me. So, I'm enjoying . . . whatever this is, while I can."

"Mhmm." The waiter comes by, dropping off the food and asking Taylor if we want a refill.

Shit. Did we already finish our first round?

"We tried doing the whole 'professional boundaries' thing"—I throw air quotes around the last part as I roll my eyes playfully—"but you saw how that worked out. He can't keep his hands off of me. And Taylor, the things he says . . ."

She holds up her hand for me to stop. "I get it." And then she shrugs. "I mean I guess I don't, but I get the picture you're trying to paint."

"You're telling me you never felt that way with Jess? Even at the beginning?"

She readjusts in her seat then picks up the flakey pastry in front of her. "Nope." She opts for taking a bite instead of continuing.

I have no idea what we ordered. We just asked the waiter to bring over a few of his favorite pastries; after last night, we really just needed something to soak up the remaining alcohol.

"He was sweet and kind at the beginning, and all that. I just never had that . . . 'movie magic' or whatever with him." I guess it's just an air quotes kind of day. "Or really anyone. Jess was the first person to take me seriously, and then it was just . . . I don't know. What's the right word . . . convenient, I guess."

"But you love each other, right? I mean, I'm sure you do, y'all are getting married in a few months . . . right?" Concern is clear in my voice, after all, I'm not hiding it.

It's just us right now, no other people around who Taylor has to continue the charade for. And normally, she doesn't open up about her relationship with Jess, unless she's drunk or *very* overwhelmed, which happens almost never. She's guilty of bottling up her emotions; "storing them away in the attic" Mom always used to say when referring to Taylor. The only problem with that is one of these days, that attic has to be cleaned out, or else it will overflow to the rest of the clean house below.

"Yeah, we've been together for five years now, so marriage is the next natural step. He'll make a great husband." Well, that didn't answer my question at all.

"Okay . . . " I stretch out the word while slowly nodding my head. "That's all fine and dandy, but do you want him to be *your* husband?" I'm attempting to be delicate with this topic, but feel like I'm failing miserably.

"Sure. I'm one lucky girl." She's wearing the fakest smile I've ever seen as she takes a sip from her glass, not-so-subtly changing the subject back to me. "So, what are you going to do when you have to move back?"

I exhale, letting out a long breath. "I've thought about it a little, but tried not to dwell on it. We're still new, so why not enjoy our time right now? What was that thing that Mom always used to say?"

"It's warmer in the sunshine ," Taylor starts it, but I join in after a couple words, "than hiding in the shade."

"That's the one." I toss a finger gun her way while I click my tongue.

"Yeah, but you're kind of forgetting a pretty big part. She always ended it with, 'but be careful not to get burned'."

"Eh." I shrug. "I guess I'll just need some sunscreen," I add with a cheeky smile.

"Whatever you say, Em."

Taylor's flight leaves around lunch tomorrow, meaning she won't have much time for anything tomorrow, so we decide to squeeze in a bit of sightseeing today before we head back for the night.

"Have anything in particular you want to see?" I ask as I pay the bill.

"Maybe just some stops on our way back? I'm not sure how much energy I have after last night."

"Fair. Maybe just a few easy sites then. I'm pretty sure the Cathedral of Barcelona is nearby, so we could do that? Then maybe we can hit the Picasso museum afterwards?"

"Oh!" Taylor's eyes sparkle. "Yes, that sounds fabulous."

Since it's so close, the Cathedral of Barcelona is our first stop.

The area is busy with tour groups, so we opt to just walk up the steps, and not actually go inside the cathedral, taking time outside to appreciate the gothic architecture of the building. The stained glass looks beautiful out here, so I can only imagine being inside and viewing it as the sun illuminates it. I sort of wish Diego was here with us. He did such a great job explaining *Casa Batlló*, and something tells me he would know a thing or two about one of Barcelona's more popular cathedrals.

After taking a few photos, I pull up the map of the surrounding area on my phone.

"So according to this, the museum is only about five minutes," I look up and double check the signs, "that way." I point in the direction the map shows.

"Why don't I check online to see if I can buy the tickets before we get there?" Taylor offers.

"Oh, smart!"

Taylor successfully purchases two tickets before we walk up to the museum. And it was smart thinking on Taylor's part because there's a decent line as we approach the doors.

Once inside, we take our time going through the buildings and seeing all the pieces out on display. While there are a few other artists on display, the vast majority of pieces are from Picasso himself. Sketches and drawings, as well as paintings, line the walls of the buildings.

"He really did have such a range. Some of the landscapes here are absolutely breathtaking." I say in awe as we look through the pieces on display.

With the little knowledge I have with art, I'm used to seeing most of his artwork have a lot of colors. Most of the pieces I remember have dramatic lines, making his art more memorable because of his geometric approach to his artwork. I would have never guessed that some of these pieces were done by him.

"He's one of my favorites." Taylor grabs my hand and turns to face me. "Thanks for taking me here today."

I squeeze her hand. "You're welcome, sis."

As we finish browsing the last gallery, I get a hankering for . . . well, I don't really know what, but I'm definitely hungry.

"One more stop?" I ask with a pleading look.

"I don't know, Emma." She sighs.

"Pleaseee," I beg. "I'll make it worth your while." She tilts her head from side to side. "Come on . . . I promise it'll be our last stop for the rest of the day."

"Fine, fine. Where are we off to now?"

After a quick ten minute walk in the direction of the apartment, we make a quick detour at *La Boqueria*.

The market is crazy busy, and of course it is because it's a Saturday afternoon, in May.

The aisles are stuffed full of people, both sightseeing and

shopping. Diego once told me that there are a few other markets that he favors, but this is the most well-known spot. Taking Taylor's hand, we dive into the crowd and explore.

The aromas are all over the place given the mixtures of offerings provided inside. A plethora of spices ignite my senses one second, only for florals to take over in the next. I could easily see someone going into sensory overload with all the smells, colors, and sounds all stuffed into one space.

A fruit stand on one of the corners steals Taylor's and my attention. Bags of produce hang above us while we wander the space, checking out the fruits and vegetables on display.

Some are easily identifiable as ones we've seen before, while others aren't as recognizable. There are a few that look unfamiliar to me, even with the shopping I've done in town these past few weeks. I snap a few photos of the more exotic looking produce, and with the promise to come back another day, we start veering to the nearby display of cured meats and cheese.

After waiting for our turn, I ask the man at the counter for a sample of his favorite meat, and he hands us both our own pieces of the mystery meat. Its smoky flavor would make a great compliment to one of Diego's wines.

As we finish eating, the man offers a cheese for us to try as well. It's creamy and pairs perfectly with the meat we just tasted. With a nod from Taylor, I order a small amount of each for us to take back to the apartment before we continue our exploring.

We walk a few more aisles, craving something sweet after the saltiness from the cured meat sample, and as we turn the corner, we stumble upon a couple sweet treat stands.

One is lined with colorful candy-filled baskets while the other has clear bins neatly displayed, all full with a wide selection of chocolates, truffles, bars, and bark, just to name a few.

I turn and look at Taylor. "Which one looks better?" By the twinkle in her eyes from the stand she's looking at, I already know.

"Chocolate," we say in unison.

We each pick out a few pieces for ourselves, and then a few more adventurous choices to try together. We have the woman helping us throw in anything we missed that she enjoys, before paying, then doing one more loop around the perimeter before heading out.

Walking to the edge of the market, the scent is one you can expect when we hit the seafood area, and although the smell may not be the best, the fish selection looks incredible. Whole fish, filets, and many options for shellfish. I really need to make it a point to come here more for my grocery shopping.

One of the last stands we visit is bursting with beautiful flowers of all types and colors. "These would make beautiful centerpieces for that dinner you're planning." Taylor points to a bucket of stunning white roses.

"I agree." I walk over to admire their beauty. "If they have some on Wednesday, I may have to get those in addition to the greenery and baby's breath I was planning on buying."

Taylor takes one more look at the flowers then turns to me. "Ready to head back?"

"Yup. I'm not particularly hungry, so I'd say we have all we need in these bags for tonight's dinner." I tap the paper bags filled with our edible treasures.

"Add in some wine, and I'm fine enjoying a little *girl dinner* tonight."

"Sounds perfect to me." I reach into the bag with all of the chocolates, grabbing two of the truffles inside. I hand one to Taylor and pop the other in my mouth. As soon as the chocolate treat hits my tongue, it completely melts in my mouth. "Holy shit, this is *good*." Rubbing my fingers together, I brush the excess cocoa powder off my fingers.

Taylor inspects hers before taking a small bite. "Damn, that *is* good." She pops the remaining chocolate ball into her mouth, then copies my motion by rubbing her fingers together, removing all evidence of the dark treat from her hands.

She turns to me and laughs, and that's when I see it, it's like a scene out of Bridesmaids. She has chocolate smudged on one tooth. I can't help but break out in laughter. "You have . . . " I start, but my laugh makes it hard to get another word out.

"Emma, that sugar went right through you." Taylor laughs even harder, looking at me and shaking her head. But her talking only shows off her chocolate covered tooth even more.

"Chocolate," I finally blurt out. "You have chocolate," I try to settle my laughter but can't, "smeared across," I laugh again, "one of your teeth," I finally get out.

Her face instantly drops. "Oh my god! I do?" She starts frantically scrubbing one side of her teeth.

But I can't help my laughter that continues, I'm practically wheezing at this point. "Other side!"

She switches sides and cleans it off within a matter of seconds. "Is it gone?" She smiles widely, showing nothing but her perfectly clean, perfectly straight teeth.

"Yes, no more chocolate making you look like you were in a bad bar fight." I try to say stoically, but start laughing again almost immediately after.

Taylor joins in the laughter before asking, "Was it really that bad?"

"Personally, I think you made missing a tooth look good." That earns a playful shove as we walk up the steps to my building, and I open the door before continuing. "I'm serious, you could rock a missing tooth, Taylor."

Our laughter echoes off the walls, filling the stairwell. "You know, as tempting as that sounds. I'm not so sure I could. But thanks for the encouragement."

I walk to the kitchen as soon as we're inside the apartment. Grabbing a bottle of wine in one hand and our chocolates in the other, I raise both in the air in offering. "Chocolate wasted or *wasted* wasted?"

"Since the car service for my flight is picking me up at eight tomorrow, I'd say chocolate wasted." I nod my head, setting the bottle on the counter. "But one glass wouldn't hurt."

"There's the wine-loving sister I know and love." I go back and grab the bottle, glasses, and opener, then head to the couch.

Grabbing the remote and one of my books on the table, I ask, "Now, books or tv?"

"Any of those romances sports related?"

I gasp. "Oh my god!!!"

"What?" She shrugs like what she said isn't a big deal.

"Lindsay said she tried to get you to read romance for *years*, and that you never showed any interest in them."

"That's because I didn't have much of a need for them back then. Now . . . " She looks down to her lap, fiddling with her fingers. "Well, let's just say I have a lot more time these days. Reading has helped make my days a little more . . . interesting," she takes a deep breath before adding on, "and a little less lonely, if I'm being honest."

"Oh, Taylor." I wrap my arm around her, squeezing her close to me. "I get that." I hold for a minute longer, squeezing her one more time before letting go, then open the bottle in front of us. "Lucky for you, sports romance is one of my favorite subgenres." After passing off her glass, I reach over and grab the book I just finished. "This one's about two rival rugby players who both fall in love with the same reporter."

"Oh, I do love a love-triangle."

"I hope you love DP, too." I let out a nervous laugh.

I mean I've never talked about my reading preferences with Taylor. Tory, sure. Lindsay, absolutely. But Taylor? She's always been off limits with that topic, so I don't want to scare her off.

"That's actually a favorite micro-trope of mine," she adds nonchalantly, and I almost spit out the wine I just sipped. "What?" Taylor shrugs. Who is this woman sitting next to me?

"I just never thought I'd hear the day, honestly." I hand her the book and grab one for myself. "I hope you enjoy it as much as I did."

We both start reading, being careful to avoid smearing chocolate when we need to turn the pages.

"Hey, um . . . " Taylor starts up, flipping the book over her knee, "Don't tell Lindsay about this, okay?"

"Yeah, sure. It'll just be between us," I promise before adding, "But when you're ready, I'm sure she'd love to hear about the books you read."

"I'm sure she would. Thanks, Em." I send a sincere smile her way, and then we both continue reading and snacking for the rest of the night.

CHAPTER TWENTY-EIGHT

DIEGO

These past few days have been crazy.

During the weekend, we had a steady flow of people on Saturday, so by the time closing time came, I was ready to head out.

Since Emma was spending some bonding time with Taylor, I went home for the remainder of the weekend, enjoying the quiet back at the winery. But it wasn't as refreshing as I had hoped.

I think with Emma in my life, I may actually prefer living in the city.

Monday morning comes and I start my early morning routine of getting the orders all situated before heading into the city. Grabbing my phone to double check the order printout is accurate, I see I missed a call from Emma, probably while I was packing up the car.

We might not have seen each other this weekend, but we definitely stayed in contact. A couple calls. Some work related and others not. It's no surprise which ones I enjoyed the most.

Later in the day, I get an email from Emma saying we have an issue with the printing company. Something about an ink issue and the colors weren't printing correctly. She assured me they are working on it, and the labels should be ready to use by next week, which will be tight, but as long as that's the last delay, it should work out just fine.

We're busy filling some of the wine bottles this week, but we can hold off on labeling since it's all the same vintage. We have a few leftover labels from the old design, but not enough for all of the bottles being filled.

Since there's so much going on at the winery this week, I'm not able to see Emma until the mock dinner event on Thursday evening. It's something that is supposed to showcase the potential of our winery for future weddings and other events.

In typical Emma fashion, she conjured up a way to get almost everything donated for the night. Enticing the vendors with exclusivity contracts for future events. The only things my family is having to pay for are the flowers and food.

The flowers will be picked up by Emma the day before and arranged during setup. And Lorenzo, being who he is, gave all the food to us at cost. He's bringing the food and then staying to enjoy the dinner afterwards.

I'm not one for parties or fancy dinners, but I find myself excited to see what Emma has planned. She's already told me that she plans to be cooped up in her own cave the majority of this week. Finalizing everything and working on a few other projects for the winery.

It really does seem like it's possible to save the business after all. When I first heard the plans from Emma, it all sounded great but I had my doubts on if it would actually make a difference. She's put in the work and done a damn fine job at securing our family's future.

With all the time alone these past few days, I've been finding myself thinking about what will happen when she leaves. We haven't talked about the future at all, but I find myself wanting a future with her. If there's a way to get her to stay, I want to do it. Hell, if there's a chance I could move *with* her, I'd do that too.

"So, I was thinking . . . " Mia says. She begged to tag along last night since we're not opening the shop tomorrow allowing us more time to set up for the dinner party.

"Yes?" I draw out as I unbox a few bottles.

"Maybe I could move into the apartment for a bit." I stop in my tracks. "Like I can live here while I wait to retake my driver's test. And you can go back home. You know, return to your cave and all."

Well that's not happening. I'm not sure when it happened, but the thought of going back to my old routine doesn't sound appealing in the least.

Don't freak out. Knowing Mia, there's probably more to the story.

And then it dawns on me. "Did Mom try to set you up again?"

She covers her face with her palms and throws herself in the nearest chair. "Was it that obvious?"

I chuckle as I put a plate of food in front of her before returning back to the shelves. Normally, I go to the apartment or hang out with Emma during siesta, but today, after I dropped off some lunch at Emma's door, I'm doing a quick inventory of bottles before the new stock comes in, hopefully sometime next week after those new labels.

"I have to get out of there, Diego! She's driving me crazy! Please switch back with me?" I turn to face her, finding her pouting out her bottom lip and gripping her hands together, attempting to plead with me.

"Mia, that's the exact face you used to ask me to switch in the first place." What number was I on? One hundred sixty-eight? Or was it seventy-eight? Shit. Now I have to recount.

"I know, I know. It's just—" She gets up and starts walking towards me. Fuck. I lost count again. I might as well stop counting until she's done talking at this point. "Oh my god! You *like* her. Don't you?"

"Who?"

"*Who*? Who, the man asks. The man who historically uses every excuse he can find to stay locked up, hidden away in his lair. Away from all of society." She brings her hands up in a swooping motion, almost sloshing the wine out of her glass. Mia really has a thing for the theatrics. "A man who used to spend a Saturday night alone, walking around a vineyard, rather than go on a date." Mia's standing by me now, arms crossed and wine glass dangling in one hand.

"But now . . . now he's fine with socializing. Fine with staying in the city, instead of the comforts of his family home." She's laying it on a little thick now, but she just taps her chin and continues her tangent. "It couldn't have anything to do with the beautiful woman who came wandering into his life, whose goal is to save the family's livelihood, would it?"

"First off, it's fucking weird when you talk about me in third person like that. But secondly, you're completely right." I forget my current task, choosing to join Mia with a little midday glass. "And she only has two weeks left here." I take a larger than socially acceptable swig of my wine. "How did this even happen, Mia?" Looking over to my sister, I find her smiling from ear to ear. "And what part of what I just said is making you look like . . . well, how you look right now?"

"I'm just so happy for you, brother. You deserve to find some-one." She walks back to the chair she was at, settling back into her seat again. "Well that, and because once I tell Mom, she'll finally get off my back." We both start laughing. "But seriously, why hold back? This could be something amazing, Diego. You chase her until the very end." I think I'll do just that.

"Thanks, sis." I salute my glass her way, before finishing it off. "Now get over here, and help me count these bottles."

CHAPTER TWENTY-NINE

EMMA

*T*he day couldn't go any better. I started the morning with a call from the printer, letting me know the problem with the ink was solved faster than expected. They gave me the option to have the labels delivered on Monday, or I could pick them up today. I chose the latter, that way we could have the labels on a few bottles at the party tonight.

After trying to focus my mind on the goal for the day, I reluctantly get into the vehicle sent from the firm's car service. The driver greets me and I realize it's the same one who picked me up from the airport a month ago. Wow, has it already been that long?

Thankfully the drive is smooth and nothing of note. The skies are clear today, not a cloud in sight. Perfect for an outdoor dinner party. Today's going to be a good day.

A few hours after being at the winery, setup is complete. It went relatively quickly since all the vendors' deliveries arrived on time. It's still light out, so I don't have the full effect with the candles and string lights, but everything looks exactly how I wanted it.

Natural wood tables decorated with linen runners, candles in various sizes, and rose centerpieces are set up in a square design in the green belt near the winery's building. I originally planned on only doing some sort of greenery or just baby's breath, but after seeing those roses the other day with Taylor, I couldn't help but buy a few at the market yesterday. In the end, it added a level of elegance that was missing to the tables.

There's supposed to be around fifty people in attendance, a respectable size for the winery's first event. Food will be served buffet style and bottles of wine will be spread throughout the tables. Since I was able to pick up the labels today, I asked Mr. Sánchez if he could gather a few of the new bottles and label them before dinner, that way we can put a few of them out on display, showcasing the wines while also announcing the rebranding. He seemed to think it was a great idea and agreed to grab them before dinner. I even got a smile out of him.

Diego wasn't here most of the day because he was assisting with a few deliveries nearby, but I had plenty of help from Mia and her mom.

After changing into my dress for dinner, I walk back out and rearrange a few things before feeling like everything is right where I want it to be.

"Looks good, right?" I look over to Mia.

"I didn't know this place could look this good," a familiar smoky voice calls from behind me. I turn to find Diego walking toward us. "This all looks incredible, Sweetheart. And you look every bit of the goddess you are in that dress." I beam from the praise as he steals a quick kiss. "I need to rinse off and change out of these clothes, but I'll be back in twenty."

"Sounds good. We're basically finished out here anyway." I look around and take in all we accomplished.

"Well, in that case." He loops his arms though mine, bringing me closer to him with his hands on my ass. I swear, he's obsessed with it. "Wanna join me?" He winks as he flashes me a grin.

"Yeah, so I was fine with the kiss," Mia interrupts, "but inviting her to take a shower with you, in the shower I use too, is where I draw the line."

I bury my head into Diego's chest. "Sorry, Mia."

"It's not you who should be apologizing," Mia replies.

Diego chuckles, causing my head to bounce from the movement. "Alright, I'll get out of here." He kisses my head before sliding his arms out. "I'll be back, ladies."

"Bye," Mia and I say in unison.

I walk around the tables, doing my final inspection before people start arriving. "So my brother, yeah?" I look up and find Mia's curious gaze.

"Yeah, he's pretty amazing." No sense in hiding my feelings now.

"Have you told *him* that?" What does that mean? "By the look on your face right now, I'm guessing that's a no."

"I was planning to after tonight was finished."

She walks toward me. "My advice, you tell him sooner rather than later. He's a real catch, Emma. But so are you. I know your time here is running out, and I'd hate to see you both miss out"— she waves her hand back and forth between the house and me —"on whatever this is."

"Thanks for the push, Mia. My sisters would probably do the same thing if the roles were reversed."

"Sounds like you've got some smart sisters." She winks while she lightly elbows me. "Seriously, Emma, I've never seen my brother like this before. You've really brought him out of his shell these last few weeks."

"Like you said, he's a real catch."

Mia gives me a quick hug before saying, "I'm going to change. Do you need anything before I do?"

"Nope. Everything is ready to go. Food should be here any minute, and then it's showtime."

"I never even thought of turning this piece of grass into something like this. You did good, Emma."

I'm proud of myself for the transformation but it's nice to hear the praise.

The dinner is an absolute hit.

Mr. Sánchez announces the new branding once everyone has found their seats, and it's received with hoots and hollers. We cheer with each other for new beginnings and enjoy a fantastic meal afterward. The conversations are flowing easily, complimented with the soft music playing in the background, the music a compilation of songs Diego plays at the shop.

I'm finishing my plate when one song in particular stands out by its familiarity. After focusing on the beat for another few seconds, the song title immediately comes to me.

I lean over to Mia, who's sitting on my left, "Is it just me or does this song sound an awful lot like an instrumental version of Taylor Swift's *The Man*?"

Mia covers her mouth with her hand, almost spitting out her wine. "Because it is." She laughs. When Diego turns to look at us, she leans in close to my ear. "Sometimes I like to fuck with my brother by getting him hooked on instrumental versions of popular pop artists. He claims he 'could never like that music.'" I laugh at her scarily good impression of her brother. "The funny thing is, there's no way he'll ever find out because he's so against listening to songs with vocals." She sits back in her chair, taking another sip of wine. "It's a harmless prank. He used to play it in the office but now that he's working in the city, I can't help laughing knowing he's playing those songs the majority of his time driving me. Or that he's made those songs the main music playing in the background at the shop."

She takes another sip, then grabs my wrist, laughing under her breath. "Last week, when he brought me to the shop, I caught myself singing along with the music. Thankfully, he never caught on."

"Well, your secret's safe with me." I laugh a little more but stop when I feel a hand on my shoulder. I don't have to look across the table to know I'll find Diego's chair empty.

"Keeping secrets already?" I hear him question before feeling him lean in close over my shoulder, lips touching the shell of my ear. "Are you at a spot where I can steal you away for a minute?"

I turn my head over to him and find a soft smile painted on his face. "With you, always." I excuse myself from Mia and follow behind Diego. Once we're a little farther away from the party, he slings his arm around my waist, bringing me close to his side. He places a kiss on the top of my head as we walk side-by-side toward the main building. "What was that for?"

"Thank you. For all of this. It was a great night. And I," he sneaks another kiss, "have just the thing to take it over the top."

I immediately light up. "Oh yeah?" Are we about to fuck while everyone is still out enjoying the party?

"Yeah, Sweetheart." We walk a couple more steps to the doors that lead down to the cellar. Diego walks down to open it up before holding out his hand to help me. I gladly accept his help, using his hand to steady myself while I walk down the weathered stone stairs in heels. Note to self, never wear heels in the grass *nor* when walking over centuries-old stone. You'd think I'd have learned by now, but nope.

Diego's quick to flip the entry light on and the room fills with a warm glow. Nothing too bright, just enough to help us not trip on our own feet. We walk through the lines of bottles and barrels underground. Wood on the barrels stained by wine, red markings around the silicone stoppers. There are stacks and stacks of barrels, all laying on their sides. All tucked in their cradles, waiting to be woken up in a few months, or even years.

There are years, maybe even decades, worth of wine just sitting here. It's evidence of all the blood, sweat, and tears this family has put into this business.

I stop and run my fingers over an engraving on one of the barrels. It's the original logo of the winery, forgotten by most. The one I saw on an old post from their social media talking about the vineyard's history.

It stood out to me when I first saw it. That's where the idea for the new logo came from. I asked the design team to incorporate it into one of the designs, and as fate would have it, it was the family's favorite design.

Diego looks back at me. "Sorry. It's just a little bit farther." I smile and nod, walking through another archway. The new room is a little darker, but I'm still able to see my feet easily. Diego flips on another light and a lantern-light fixture brightens the room.

"Would you like to taste a barrel with me?"

I won't lie, I really thought we were coming down here to have hot cellar sex, even if I'm not entirely sure what that would look like. But this is something else I've never done before, and am eager to try.

"I'd love to."

He pulls a device from a near-by table that almost looks like a turkey baster, only longer and made of glass. He uncaps a circle on the side of the barrel, inserting the baster into the barrel. Deep red liquid fills the tube and he then transfers the liquid into two wine glasses. He puts the baster down, and hands a glass to me while keeping one for himself.

I've learned a thing or two from the last few weeks around Diego, so without missing a beat, I take a big sniff from the wine glass.

"What do you smell?" He's observing me, and I realize I'm the only one of us smelling the wine.

"Um . . . red berries," I take another sniff, "cinnamon maybe?" He nods and raises his glass, toasting before we both take a sip.

He keeps the wine in his mouth for a little bit, nodding his head side to side. I'm not sure if he finds the flavor lacking or is enjoying it. For me, it's pretty damn smooth. He spins the wine around in the glass before bringing the glass to his nose, taking a big inhale before taking another sip.

"Anything special about this barrel?" I ask before taking another sip.

"It's made from vines I planted a few years ago." He seals back up the barrel. "This barrel is mine, from start to finish."

"And what are your thoughts on it?" I move closer to him, wrapping my arms around his neck, glass still in hand.

"Honestly," He takes another sip before setting his glass down on the small table next to us. "I wish I made more." He lets out a soft, smoky chuckle, and I can't help but join in on the laughter alongside him. "It's pretty damn good."

"Yeah, it is! You should be proud of yourself, Diego." Feeling his palm slide down my back, inching closer to my ass. I look down and then back up to his face, the corner of my mouth creeping up. "You feel like celebrating?"

He gives my ass a squeeze and repeats the phrase I said to him earlier. "With you," he bends his head down close to my mouth, "always."

CHAPTER THIRTY

DIEGO

"Ou look utterly delicious tonight, Sweetheart." With the help of her dress' slit, I sneak my hand up her thigh, pulling the silky material up, baring more of her to me.

Slipping my hand farther up to her hip, I find her completely bare. "Fuck, Emma. Were you not wearing underwear this whole time?"

"When I changed, I had a feeling tonight might end in a little . . . you-and-me time. So I gambled." She cups my hard dick in her hands. "Looks like I chose correctly. Time to pay up, Diego." She gives a tug at my waistband. "Take those off. Now."

"As you say." I strip off my pants, enjoying the hungry eyes Emma's giving me. I can see them clear as day, even in this low light. "Now ass up, Sweetheart. I'm about to fuck you over this barrel and really make you mine."

"Fuck, that was hot, Diego." She obeys and drapes herself over the curved wood.

I run one hand down the exposed skin of her back, bringing the other hand up her skirt, relishing the feel of her round ass in the palm of my hand. It truly is the most perfect ass I've ever seen.

I wrap a hand around to the front of her waist, working down and around to the apex of her thighs. Of course, she's already soaked. The thought of her sitting at the table tonight like this, drives me wild.

I slide my finger around her wetness, rubbing her lips then moving my finger up, swirling a figure eight around her clit. "Feels like you're all ready to go."

She moans as I stroke my erection, making quick work of pulling the condom on. Immediately, I feel myself start to leak into the rubber. Guess I'm ready too.

Adjusting her abdomen, I get her in the right position. Then grabbing both of her hips, I seat myself fully inside of her, making her gasp at the sudden fullness. "Fuck, Diego." She pants, adjusting to my size. "You always feel so goddamn good."

"Sweetheart, I'll never tire of hearing your dirty mouth praise me." I move my fingers back to her clit, while keeping my other hand on her waist, rubbing my thumb in slow circles right above her ass. And speaking of her fine ass, I love how it bounces in perfect rhythm to my thrusts.

God, I am not going to last long in this position. Thankfully, I think she's thinking the same thing because I feel her walls tightening around my cock. I do everything in my power to not finish with the new sensation.

"Fuck!" I bite my lip, trying to trick my brain to focus on something other than coming inside Emma's perfect pussy. "You're so fucking tight, Sweetheart."

I pick up my pace, bringing my hand up and running my fingers up in her hair, giving her a little tug. She lets out a loud moan and I lean close to her ear. "Oh, you like that, huh?"

"Yes." But it comes out all breathy.

"What was that?" I add a little more pressure on her clit with my thumb and tug a little more on her hair. She moans again. "I couldn't quite hear you."

She responds by shoving her ass even farther into me. I'm so fucking deep inside of her, there's no way I'll last two more thrusts.

"I'm going to make you come with me, Sweetheart." I pick up the speed of my thumb, as I slowly pull out, leaving just the tip in.

I use my grip in her hair to pull her head to the side, and bite her neck.

"Fuck!" She shouts out. "Baby, I'm so close."

Hearing her call me baby for the first time while she grinds her ass up against me, pushes me over. I try to thrust through the sensation, attempting to bring her along with me. Just when I think I came too fast, I feel her tightening around me while she curses my name.

When I finally catch my breath, I kiss down her spine before pulling out, ensuring her dress stays above her waist. "Don't move, Sweetheart. I'll be right back."

I walk over to the small sink in the cellar and grab a few things to clean us up. Making a mental note to remember to throw away the small trash bag where I threw away my used condom.

Bending down, I clean between her legs, tossing the wet paper towel in the bin when I finish.

We stand there staring at each other. Her strap hanging off her shoulder and hair pulled in all directions, looking freshly fucked, and me, well I'm sure I'm not too far of, standing in nothing but an unbuttoned dress shirt and socks.

Without much thought, I reach out to kiss her again. I don't think I want to leave this moment.

Emma breaks our kiss and rests her head on my chest. "Diego," she breathes out, "I think I'm falling for you."

She states her confession into my chest, just soft enough that I think she may have not known she even said it outloud.

Stroking her hair, I kiss the crown of her head. It's like a tick of mine. I'm not sure if it's the height thing or just the tenderness of the kiss, but I find myself kissing the top of her head more than

I think is normal. Then I realize I haven't responded to what she just said.

"Emma, I fell for you when you walked into Lorenzo's that very first night. And it was confirmed after you accused me of finishing your potatoes." She gives my chest a little nip and I chuckle into her hair.

She mumbles something under her breath that sounds a lot like, "Jury's still out on who ate the potatoes."

I rub my hands up and down her back once more.

"Think we can return to the others before anyone notices?"

Reaching for my pants, "I'm sure the whole party knows *exactly* what we were doing, Sweetheart."

She chuckles as she straightens out her dress, but it does nothing to hide the sex hair that both of us have.

"Do you have a hair clip or rubber band on you?" I ask, eyeing the bird's nest I created.

"No." Emma reaches up and attempts to straighten her hair. "Does it look bad?"

"I mean, I'm pretty proud of it," I say, grinning cheekily at her, but by the look on her face, I'd say she was less than impressed with my joke. "Maybe just bend over—" She smacks my arm. "Hey!" Rubbing my arm dramatically, I continue, "What I was *trying* to say was, why don't you try bending over and flipping your hair. Maybe fluffing it will help."

She does just that, only it doesn't help one bit. In fact, it makes things worse. "You know what, you look great. I'm sure no one will even notice."

Yeah, they'll definitely notice. And I'm sure I'll get an earful from each member of my family. Maybe even more from Lorenzo, if he's still here.

"Plus, it's dark, so it'll be hard to spot the ruffled up areas," I add as we walk up the steps out of the cellar. She attempts to straighten her hair out again as we rejoin the party.

We must have taken longer than I thought, because the party seems to have shrunk by half. As we approach the remaining group, I get an eye-roll from Mia while she mouths "you couldn't wait?"

Dad and Mom walk up to ask something, both giving us a once over before clearly fighting back the urge to say something on our appearance.

"Emma," Mom starts, "we can't thank you enough for everything you've done. Tonight was beautiful. You did a great job at bringing life into a space I would have never thought about using. Thank you for all of the work you've put into our business. It really means a lot." Mom's tearing up, but Dad's quick to comfort her by rubbing her back.

"We really are so grateful for you, Emma. We're going to retire for the night, but you kids enjoy." He gives my back a stern pat as they leave. Though I'm in the clear tonight, I'm sure Dad will have some words for me come tomorrow.

I spot the rest of the group, and can't help but notice Lorenzo dancing with Mia. My sister, Mia. Surely there's nothing there, right? I mean Lorenzo's older than I am. He might even be closer to Dad's age than hers.

"Hey, Diego?" Emma calls out and I turn toward her. "My driver just texted. He'll be here in a little over thirty minutes." Driver? When did she have time to call a car? "Do you want to start cleaning up a little with me before I have to leave?"

"You aren't staying overnight?"

"Oh . . ."

By her face, it looks like the thought didn't even cross her mind. I won't lie, that stings a little bit, but I also never asked. I just assumed she was going to stay over.

"I just guessed you wouldn't want me staying at your family's home. But I really don't mind going home anyways."

"Just cancel the driver. If you don't want to stay the night, that's fine. I'll drive you myself."

"Oh, no. That's really not nec—"

"Emma." I hook her with my arm and pull her close. "You

really think we're going to have a night like tonight, and then I'd let some other man take you home?"

She scoffs and shakes her head, but ultimately wraps her arms around my waist, pressing her forehead into my chest.

"How about this, we round up the remaining guests. Say our goodbyes. Perhaps gather up everything that isn't getting picked up tomorrow, and then I'll take you home, yeah?"

I feel the warmth from her exhale on my chest before she answers.

"Fine. But please, promise me you'll be super focused on the road. I already don't like being in cars, but add the danger of night . . . it just really gives me anxiety."

Rubbing her back, I reassure her of just that.

"Of course, I, Diego Sánchez, vow to be the safest driver I have ever been. After all, I have precious cargo." She gives me a quick pinch before I kiss her head and we start cleaning up for the night.

CHAPTER THIRTY-ONE

EMMA

My phone dings while we clean up for the night. Thankfully, there wasn't too much to do after everyone left. The tables and chairs are getting picked up in the morning. We told everyone who wanted one to take home a centerpiece, leaving only a couple lone vases that Diego's mom will enjoy, and Lorenzo took the serving containers with him when he left. So that just left the linens and plates. Mia helped bag up the linens, while Diego and I rinsed off the plates and glasses, stacking them in their crates as we went.

Drying my hands, I reach over to my phone and see a text from the sisters' group chat, but that's not what makes me freeze.

Under the text alert, a notification shows an email arrived earlier today; must've been while we were preparing for the party. It's an email with Royal Cruises in the address. I take a deep breath before hitting open. Doing a quick once over, I quickly realize the phenomenal news.

"We got it!" I squeal, my smile big and bright. I look from my phone to Diego, it's clear he has no idea what I'm talking about. "The cruise line! They chose your tasting room to be one of their excursions, Diego!"

"Are you serious?" Diego's not doing anything to hide the shock painted across his face.

I nod and hear Mia shout "Holy shit!" behind us.

"That's . . . that's . . . " Diego's at a loss for words, mouth wide open, scrubbing his chin. "That's incredible news, Emma!"

"Are we done here?" Mia drops the bag of linens by the crates. "Because I have to go tell Mom and Dad about this."

I giggle in disbelief at the news we just got. "Yeah, we're good. I'll see you later, Mia. Tell your parents congratulations from me."

Before she leaves, she surprises me with a hug, squeezing me tight before she lets go. "Thank you. You sure rode into our lives at the right time and saved the day." My eyes start to tear up as she leaves. I hoped everything would work out in the end, and here we are.

"That really is amazing news." Diego reaches out, and grabs my hand, pulling me away from the packed crates. He kisses me earnestly while we both soak in the news. "Now let's get you home so I can thank you properly."

"Mmm. I like the sound of that." He smacks my ass and we gather our stuff to leave.

It takes about fifteen minutes in the car for my anxiety to finally calm down.

The roads by the winery aren't lit well, but thankfully, there aren't many cars on the road. Music is playing but at a low level, just loud enough for a little bit of ambient noise, not making it a distraction for Diego while he's driving.

I slowly become distracted by talking about what the future of the winery could look like now that it got its second chance.

Manifesting all the weddings and happy memories that will be made there.

Diego talks about his dreams of traveling.

"I've always felt bad talking about it in front of my family. I never want to give the impression that I'm ungrateful for all the sacrifices they made. Plus, it's sort of a sore subject with Mia."

"Because she didn't get the same opportunity as you?"

"Yeah. I've tried to bring up traveling in the past but it always ends with some passive aggressive reply. Something like 'at least you got the chance to leave the country.'"

"But that's not fair to you. If you want to travel, you should travel," I add.

I know from prior conversations that Diego feels a strong sense of responsibility about finding a way to give Mia an opportunity to travel as well, but he shouldn't put his life on hold over the fear that Mia *might* not approve.

"I feel guilty for even saying this," Diego pauses, taking a deep breath, "but when I heard there was a chance the winery was going to close or be sold, there was a quick second where part of me was excited for what that could mean for the family."

"What do you mean?"

"For generations, our family has always focused on the business. Never leaving the surrounding area. I think I was the first person in our family to actually leave Spain. When I came back, I talked the family into opening the shop in Barcelona, hoping to expand our brand's reach.

"I had some money saved up from my time working in the States, and after a couple more years, I saved enough to get the apartment I'm in now. As time passed, and as my sister got older, she got more vocal about not having the same opportunities as me.

"I felt guilty for getting the chance to leave while she didn't. Hell, I still do. But that's when I decided to take a step back, slowly pulling away in order to give her more freedom. I know it's not the same as leaving the country, but it was a start." He clears his throat, and I can see he's grasping the steering wheel a little harder now.

I'm sure I'm the first person he's confessed this to, so I give him the time he needs before continuing.

"At the time, I made some excuse about not liking city life, which is partially true. I don't like always being surrounded by people. In the end, I provided the perfect opportunity for my sister to have a little more freedom. I told her she'd be better off running the shop, while I stayed up at the house."

"And let me guess, that's where the dragon nickname came in?" I ask.

"Correct. For her, it's a cute nickname. For me, it's a reminder of what I chose to give up." He rubs his hand over his mouth.

"That house is all my family has ever known. If the winery was sold, my family would be given the chance to go wherever they chose. Mia and I would have the option to travel wherever we wanted to without feeling like we're being selfish, or disappointing our family."

He looks over to me then shakes his head.

"God, I feel so awful for even thinking it. Obviously, I know my parents wouldn't choose to do anything other than run the winery. That's their whole life, and they love it. But I just can't help thinking . . . what if?"

"I get it. I really do. I never left my home town until this job. When I was a kid, all the girls in the family were in a car accident, so after that, the only places I went were school, the ranch Dad worked at, and back home. Occasionally, I'd go to the doctor's office. Tory did most of the grocery shopping and errands in town, while either Taylor or Lindsay stayed home with me.

"I was so afraid of cars after the crash. I even lived on campus for college so I could cut down on my time in a car. The only time I regularly get in a car is when one of my sisters picks me up for the thirty minute drive to my parents' house for Sunday brunch. But that's basically the only time I ride in a car." I take a deep breath, composing my thoughts before continuing.

"When I heard about the position in Barcelona, I jumped at

it. It was a great opportunity for me to travel. I'd get to stay in a popular city, known for its walkability. And it was temporary." I sigh, not being able to fight the sting of knowing my time is almost up.

"If I didn't like the city, that would be okay because I was only staying for six weeks. And after that, I'd go back home and return to my routine. But at least I got out, even if it was too short."

Diego reaches his hand over to my thigh. "The night we went to dinner with your sister, she mentioned something about you two being in a car accident. It didn't feel like the right time to ask about it." He strokes his thumb in soothing circles, causing the silk fabric to bunch up. "Do you mind telling me about it? If you want, that is."

I nestle into the seat a little more, attempting to find a more comfortable position. Unfortunately, my discomfort isn't from the seat, so it does absolutely nothing to calm the building storm inside of me.

"I guess now's as good a time as any." I sigh and lean my head back. I close my eyes and prepare to tell the story of that day.

"Mom was driving us home from school one day when we got run off the road. Some jackass was driving too fast and swerved in front of us, causing our car to crash into the ditch that was running along the side of the road, which resulted in knocking my mom out cold. The other car didn't even bother stopping." I scoff at the last part. We were probably just a blip in that person's life, but that day altered our family forever.

"Luckily, my sisters and I weren't hurt too badly. Just a few bruises and cuts. Since it was a country road, it was rare to see cars traveling by. Tory ended up having to walk to the nearest house to call for help while we waited, since there weren't any cell phones yet.

"My memory's a little fuzzy with how long the wait was, but the ambulance came sometime later. Dad wasn't too far behind. He took us all to the hospital while we waited for news on Mom."

The road in front of Diego and me is getting a little busier as we enter the city. More cars zooming by. Their headlights look blurry with the tears filling up my eyes.

"Turns out mom had three ribs that broke. One punctured her lung, giving her internal bleeding. She was in the hospital for a while recovering after that. And even when she came home, she still required a bunch of help."

Diego grips my hand tighter, noticing the emotion taking over.

"Mom's completely fine now, and you would never have known something like that ever happened by looking at her. But everybody in my family has their own memory of that day and the months that followed after, not to mention the unique trauma we carry around. Mine's just more obvious with my fear of cars, but each one of us struggles with something that can be tied back to that day."

This has been the first car ride where I've felt somewhat relaxed. Okay, maybe relaxed is the wrong word; more at ease is a better description. Sure, Diego is a great driver and that's definitely part of it, but he also has this way of making me feel safe whenever I'm around him.

I haven't opened up about the car crash in . . . well, almost a decade. I mean sure, it gets brought up from time to time, but I try not to share my feelings on what happened that day, and how it shaped our lives after.

On the rare occasion it does get brought up with my sisters, they always say I was too young for it to make a lasting impression. Which is clearly bullshit, evidence being my fear of cars. But it feels different, good even, to finally be able to talk about this. Diego's giving me a safe space. Free of judgement. Free of interruptions. He didn't tell me how to feel or try to fix it. He just let me talk and feel the emotions as they came.

As we pull up to my apartment, Diego moves his hand to my face, brushing his thumb over the river of tears coming down my cheek. "Thank you for sharing, Emma. I can't imagine having to go through that." I lean into his touch as he parks.

He turns off the car and leans over, swiping the other cheek dry before giving me a soft kiss. "Come on, Sweetheart. Let's go to bed."

198

CHAPTER THIRTY-TWO

DIEGO

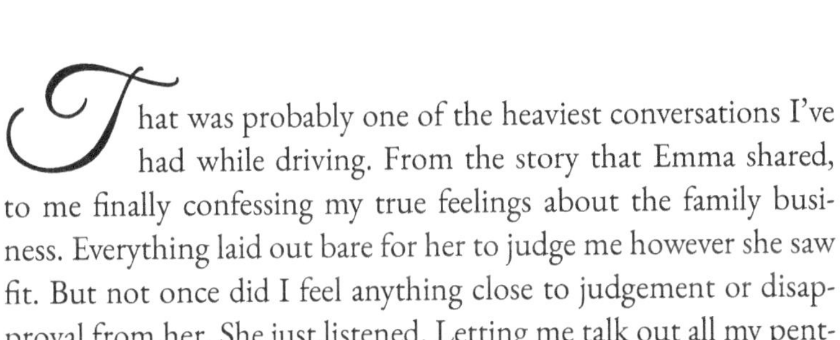

That was probably one of the heaviest conversations I've had while driving. From the story that Emma shared, to me finally confessing my true feelings about the family business. Everything laid out bare for her to judge me however she saw fit. But not once did I feel anything close to judgement or disapproval from her. She just listened. Letting me talk out all my pent-up emotions. Confessing all the things I've been holding on to for the last decade.

We walk hand-in-hand up the steps to her apartment. After the conversation we just had, the last thing I want to do is leave. An unspoken conversation happens between us as she slips off her shoes and motions me to follow her back to her room.

Our movements aren't rushed. Touches soft and gentle. Enjoying the feeling of being with each other. Stealing kisses between shedding the layers we're wearing. Before long, she stands beautifully naked in front of me. I can't help but feel like I'm in a dream, one I'll blink and wake up from.

Finding it hard to believe I'm with someone as breathtaking as Emma. That I'm the one she's choosing to spend her time with while in this beautiful city. That I'm the one she's choosing to trust with all she just shared.

She grabs my hands and pulls me on-top of her after falling back on her bed. I kiss the column of her neck, roaming my hands over her body. Taking my time to memorize every one of her curves as she explores the planes of my back with her delicate hands.

I reach over to grab the little foil square when Emma grabs my wrist. "I don't want anything between us tonight." Fuuuck.

She takes my pause as a sign of hesitation. "If that's okay with you, that is. I was just tested before I flew over here, and all is clear. And the only person I've been with since has been you."

"I'm clear too, Emma. But I don't want to pressure you. There were a lot of emotions tonight." She shuts me up with a kiss.

"Please, Diego." She pleads softly, like an angel come down to rescue me.

"You know I could never say no to your begging." Our bodies move in sync with one another, her wetness making it easy to slip inside her. Both groaning when I fully seat myself inside.

God, I will never tire of this feeling with her.

I pull her up to my chest, changing our position so I'm on my knees, keeping her wrapped around my hips and me still seated inside of her. My hands roam up and down her back as I pepper kisses along her chin, down her neck, and across her collarbone. Our movements become more frantic as we both get closer to finishing.

"Are you sure?" I ask once more and she nods. "Say it, Sweetheart."

"Finish inside me, Diego. *Please.*" And with one more thrust, I do, with her following immediately after. Both of us collapse onto the bed when we finish, tired from the physical and emotional toll of this evening's activities.

I wake to the sun creeping in from the window; it's still hazy outside so it can't be too late in the morning. My arms are wrapped around a sleeping Emma. She's tucked in close, using my body as a blanket, while one of my legs is weaved between both of hers. I sneak a kiss, not intending for her to wake up, but she does anyway.

She twists around so she's facing me. Her sleepy smile, wide on her face, and hair looking more red with the sun peeking in. "Hi," she whispers, her voice hoarse from sleep.

"Hi, Sweetheart. Sleep good?"

She walks her fingers up my exposed chest, playing with the hair as she goes. "Best sleep of my life. You?"

"Same." I lean in and kiss her, helpless to resist. "I don't have any reservations until this afternoon. So if you want . . . " I trace the curve of her spine with my fingers, causing her to shiver. "We could go get breakfast together before I open up."

"How about we make breakfast here?" Emma offers, but there's a mischievous glint to her eyes as she draws designs on my chest with her fingers. "That way we can still enjoy breakfast together" —she looks down in between us, then returns her icy blue eyes to mine—"only naked."

"Well, when you put it like that . . . " I squeeze her close, showering kisses on any part of her exposed body I can get my lips on. "How about I make some porras?"

Emma cocks her head to the side. "Porras?"

"Like churros, just a little bigger and softer." She seems to agree with the idea. "Plus if I remember correctly"—my lips graze her neck—"I still owe you some chocolate sauce."

She giggles and I can't help but turn her over on her back, caging her under me. I continue kissing her all over her beautiful body, enjoying the feel of her skin under my lips. God, she is perfect.

"I could pour some here . . . " I kiss the junction between her neck and shoulder.

"Or maybe here," I say, licking between her breasts.

"Or on both of these . . . " I give a teasing lick to each of her hardened nipples.

"Maybe pour a little here." I trail kisses down her stomach.

"And I can't forget to put some here." I use my mouth to suck on her clit as my hands grab hold of her hips, pulling her with me to the edge of the bed, only I hop up after a few sucks. "But breakfast first."

"You fucking tease!" She throws a pillow at me, one that I easily dodge. "I won't forget that."

"Is that a promise, Sweetheart?" I chuckle as I step out into the hall. Still completely naked. After all, she said she wanted breakfast naked. "I'll get breakfast started."

She comes out about ten minutes later, gloriously nude. "Sorry, my sisters texted me last night and I realized I never replied. Then I opened an email that was sent from Roger, my contact at Royal Cruises."

She walks over to the kitchen and plops herself down on the counter next to me. I'm pretty sure she just left an ass print in the flour I spilled on the counter. She seems disappointed, but I can't tell why.

"He sent the contracts over for you and your family to look through." Her tone is off. What am I missing here?

"Okay . . . that sounds like it's a good thing," I ask, confused. I stop my mixing as she continues.

"It would be. Only the contract start date is for *next* year." She sighs and puts down her phone.

"Apparently, all the contracts have already been signed for this summer and fall. They wouldn't start using the shop for excursions until next spring."

She folds her arms under her chest, and I won't lie, they make the perfect distraction right now. I almost get the feeling she's doing that on purpose. Almost like a pity peep show.

"Well that sucks," I say, starting to mix the batter again.

"My thoughts exactly." She lets out a frustrated sigh. "I

thought everything was figured out. This was going to be the best bet for saving your family's winery."

"Hey." I put a hand on her thigh. "We still have the new event space that we're launching next week. And if we get a decent amount of reservations for it this summer, we'll probably have enough money to cover expenses until next year."

"I just feel like I failed." She brings her hands up to cover her face, exposing those amazing tits of hers. Probably not the thing I should be focusing on, but I can't help but gawk at them in all their glory.

"Sweetheart, I'm going to say something and I don't want you to get upset."

"What?" She peeks out from behind her hands.

"It's really hard to feel anything but turned-on with you completely naked on the counter. With those perfect tits staring right at me." I make my way up her thigh, fingers inching closer to her center. "Knowing that I just need to spread your legs and I would have easy access to your pussy. It's probably still wet right now."

"Diego." She laughs, attempting to swat my wandering hands away. "I'm trying to be serious."

"I *am* being serious. I don't think I can wait for that chocolate sauce to be done." I step between her legs and lower my body down to my knees.

Just as I'm about to taste her, she blocks my face from her entrance. "Oh no, no, no. You could've had me in the bed but chose to be a little tease." God, I really hate that word. "You'll have to eat your breakfast first before you have dessert." I bite her on the inside of her thigh causing her to gasp while I pull away.

"Fine, fine. But do you have an apron? As much as I enjoy being naked in the kitchen with you, I would rather not have boiling oil splash on my dick." She laughs again while pointing to a drawer near the stove. "But back to the other thing, it'll all work out. You've already done so much for my family. And you completely overlooked the fact that you secured a contract with Royal Cruises. Even if it's for next year, that's still a huge win. You should be proud of that." I kiss her on her lips and whisper close to her lips, "I know I am."

And I kiss her again before I start frying the dough.

"Now get your perfect ass over here, and stir this chocolate. But put an apron on first. Don't want any of my favorite parts getting burned."

CHAPTER THIRTY-THREE

EMMA

It's been a week since dinner at the winery. We got the photos that weekend and it took no time for us to post them on the company's website and social media accounts. We had everything up and ready to start taking inquiries Monday morning.

We've already gotten quite a few interest forms back, but all have a date for next spring or summer. There are a few couples who are interested in some fall dates, but no contracts have been signed.

Normally, I'm so positive about this kind of stuff, having the whole "it'll all work out in the end" mentality hasn't steered me wrong, well up until this point.

We delayed the reprint of the rest of the bottle's labels, opting to save the family a little bit of money until their future is secured. I'm thankful I wasn't the one to break the news to Elena and Alejandro. Thankfully, Diego said his parents took the news better than expected.

They also signed the contract with Royal over the weekend, ensuring if they *do* make it to next year, they'll have that as a steady stream of income.

I walk into the glass conference room where I see Javier waiting for me. From what I'm told, it's customary to have a meeting with the branch manager when your time is almost finished. It's sort of like an evaluation, sometimes they invite you to stay longer, but with how things are looking with the Sánchez family, I highly doubt that will be the case today.

"*Bona tarda.* Please, have a seat, Emma."

I pull out the nearest chair and take my seat. This is the first time I'm walking into a meeting with a sense of impending doom. I actually have never had a bad performance review.

On the bright side, I'm scheduled to only have a week left in Spain, so what's the worst that could happen, right?

God, where's Lindsay's defensive pessimism when you need it? My sister is the best at planning for the worst, or really, any outcome for that matter. She'd already have a list of potential actions I could take if this meeting goes badly.

"I wanted to talk to you about your time here. How do you think your strategy went with the Sánchez winery?" He has a folder open in front of him, probably filled with the progress reports I've been emailing him during my time here.

"I won't lie, I was hoping for a different outcome, sir." I answer truthfully, determined not to beat around the bush.

"Is that so? From what I can gather, the Sánchez family's fate hasn't been set in stone yet. Unless you know something I don't." He raises his eyebrow, making his face even more serious. Which is weird, because up until now, I've seen nothing but smiles and relaxed expressions on his face.

"Oh no, sir. There's still a chance that they could survive another year, slim, but a chance nonetheless."

"Where did the optimistic Emma go?"

What the hell does that mean?

"Excuse me, sir?"

"I mean, up until this week, you have been very hopeful for the potential of what the winery could be. You did everything right, I hope you know that." His tone changes to something more sincere.

"Emma, if they are forced to sell, it's not for your lack of trying. I've been very impressed with the ideas you've come up with for this business' rebranding. You seem to really care for this business, and it shows." Maybe I care a little too much. "You've come up with some very creative solutions, all have the potential to be successful. But sometimes, we can't save a business no matter how hard we try in the end."

I'm not really sure what to say. I walked in here thinking I might be asked to leave early, but instead, Javier is sitting here, praising me for a job that I felt has completely derailed. I failed to achieve the family's overall goal, but here he sits, showering me with compliments I feel so undeserving of.

"Which leads me to my next topic," Javier adjusts his positioning, pulling out two pieces of paper from the stack in front of him. At this point, I have no idea what's to come. Is that the exit interview paperwork? Are those termination papers?

"We'd like to extend the offer to you of staying here, in the Barcelona office. Indefinitely." I must be hearing things because there is absolutely no way I just heard those words come out of his mouth.

"You fit well with the rest of the team, and the firm loves your creative problem solving. You seem to get along with the clients nicely." Helps when you're sleeping with them.

God, now I'm just thinking about sex with Diego. So not the time, Emma.

"Even if this project didn't end the way you wanted it to, you still did an amazing job with rebranding the business. We can't always save them, Emma."

He's right. I know he's right. It's just not that simple for me. I couldn't possibly stay in Barcelona, knowing I could've done more to save Diego's winery.

"There's another thing, I regretfully have to inform you about." Here it is. Here comes the bad news.

"You seem to be quite in-demand, Emma. One of my colleagues has been listening a little too intently whenever I deliver our branch's monthly reports, and has been impressed with your ideas as much as I have. The London office has also put in a request for you to join their team." *Two* offers? I thought for sure I was finished here.

"Wow. I . . . I don't know what to say." I attempt to clear my throat, buying myself time to form some semblance of a professional response, but Javier saves me from further embarrassment, gently holding up his hand, motioning me to stop.

"You don't need to decide now. Take until your original contract ends, so a week from today."

He stands up and sets both offers down in front of me. And that's when I see it, another contract. "The Raleigh office asked to have you back, as well. But what's Raleigh when you have London and Barcelona, am I right?" He adds the last part like a funny joke. I'd normally give a pity laugh, but I'm completely frozen in shock.

"Think it over, okay? And enjoy your weekend, Emma." And with that, he leaves me to sit alone in the glass fish bowl.

What the fuck am I going to do? On one hand, it would be nice to go back home. Maybe apply to a position similar to this when the opportunity presents itself. But who knows what that will be? It could be another year, or longer. And, what if it's to a place I don't even want to go?

But on the other hand . . . London. Fucking *London*! And they asked for me specifically. That's unbelievable.

And to make things even more confusing, I have Barcelona. And how could I say no to more time here? That would be like saying no to a future with Diego. And if I'm honest with myself, I'm not sure I would be able to do that.

But I also can't choose my future around a man I met less than two months ago. God, I never thought I'd say this, but I have too many options.

Three contracts. I can't believe it.

CHAPTER THIRTY-FOUR

DIEGO

The only thing on my mind all day is that tonight, I get to see Emma.

I've been staying at the family house the last few nights so Mia could get a break from being cooped up at the house. I drove her down earlier this week, staying for the day but leaving early in the afternoon. Mia ran the shop for most of the week, staying in my apartment while I stayed at the winery, and now I'm back to run it over the weekend.

Luckily, Mia had a friend who was in town and volunteered to drive her back to the winery, saving me the trip. God, I can't wait for her to get her license back.

Me being back in town also means time with Emma. We were inseparable the weekend following the dinner but haven't seen each other since. We've texted and called on several occasions but it's not the same.

I don't even want to think about what it's going to be like when she has to move back home to North Carolina. Video calls will definitely have to be the bread and butter of our relationship, at least until we can figure out a visiting schedule.

And don't even get me started on the time change. Thankfully, she's on the East Coast, so depending on Daylight Savings, it's only five to six hours behind, instead of the eight to nine it was when I lived in California and would try to call home.

Fuck. Why am I already married to the concept of her moving back? Maybe she doesn't have to. Maybe she could find a job here? She could even move in with me, it would be perfect with it being in the city. No sense in having two apartments when we're always sleeping over at each other's anyways.

No, I couldn't ask that of her. Hell, I don't even know if *I'll* be staying in Barcelona. The business' fate is still up in the air, so what happens if she gives up everything for me, only for me to end up having to move anyways? What would we do then?

No, she has to come first. She's crazy smart and deserves to put herself first, even if that means moving back to the States. Away from me.

I hear the door open and it dawns on me that I forgot to lock it during our mid-day break. I look up from the counter to see the goddess herself.

"What a pleasant surprise. What are you doing here so early?" It's around three in the afternoon, earlier than we agreed on meeting when we texted this morning, which reminds me, "I thought *I* was supposed to come pick *you* up. Not the other way around."

I walk toward her, but she has a strange look on her face. "Emma?" I bring my hand up to the side of her face, "Emma, what's wrong?"

"I've been walking around for the past hour, and I'm more confused than when I started." She sits down in the nearest chair, avoiding me completely.

It's like she's on autopilot, almost in a trace-like state, as she zones out. "I have no idea what to do." She whispers under her breath, almost to herself more than to me.

"Do about *what*?" Confusion clear in my voice as I go and lock the shop's door. Something I should've done earlier, plus I don't think this is a conversation we want interrupted.

I walk over to the table she's at, grabbing one of the open bottles and a pair of glasses on the way over. "Talk to me, Sweetheart."

She takes a drink before explaining. "I had a meeting today with Javier, the branch manager." By her attitude, I'm guessing it was not a good meeting. "He said not only does he want me to stay," oh hell yes, wait, this is bad news? "But my home office wants me back as well."

"Okay . . . this all sounds like great news. What am I missing?" She takes another sip and I do the same, preparing for the bomb that's going to drop.

"And he also informed me that the London office has extended an offer to me as well."

Well fuck me. Three offers in one day. I'm so proud of her, though I can't say I'm surprised; Emma is a treasure and anyone would be a fool to not see that.

"I have a week to make my decision, but I feel so over-whelmed. I have no idea what I'm going to do. There are positives to each location." She takes another sip. "North Carolina is my home. I'm comfortable there. All my family is there." She props her elbow on the table, leaning her head on her raised fist. "I'm just not sure I belong there now."

I take a deep breath, one down. Now it's just between Barcelona and London.

Fucking London. Of course, she's going to pick London. It's fucking *London*.

I pour us more wine, because we definitely need more alcohol for this conversation.

"And London . . . I mean it's *London*." She says by way of answer, taking a sip before adding, "It's a great opportunity to spend time in a city I've only dreamed about visiting. And their walkability is great over there, too."

She takes another sip as she jabs a finger into her chest. "And I know because I double checked while I was walking." Shit, she's already started researching it.

She takes an exhausted breath before continuing. "But then there's Barcelona." She finally looks at me. She's been avoiding eye contact up until this point. "Staying here, with you. And how could I pass on that?"

I'm silent, not wanting to say anything to sway her in one way or another.

"Plus . . . " She throws back the rest of her wine. I fill it back up without thought as soon as she puts the glass back on the table. "I didn't mention this before, but all three of these are permanent offers. That means no performance reviews after a few weeks. I could really settle in if I wanted to. I could find an apartment and actually put down some roots."

"Wow."

That three letter word is all I can muster up. I'm so blown away by this news. I'm overjoyed for her, but I would be lying if I said I wasn't a little sick at the possibility of her leaving.

I clear my throat and take a sip of wine to wet my mouth. "That's amazing news, Emma. You've worked hard for an offer, sorry, *offers* like these. I'm so proud of you and the work you've put in to get here."

I don't ask what option she's going to pick because that wouldn't be fair to either of us.

"I'm normally not an indecisive person. It's killing me that I'm in limbo right now. Seriously . . . I have no idea what option to pick." She runs her hands through her hair as she adds, "I feel like I can write Raleigh off, but every time I do, I'm reminded of how nice it is to be around family."

"I know how much family matters to you." And look at that, both of our glasses are empty again.

I get up to grab another bottle, sneaking some crackers and meats because I need some food to soak up the copious amounts of wine I will most definitely be drinking today, and through the rest of tonight if this conversation is any indicator.

"You have time to think about it though. Maybe make a list

about the benefits of each and then compare." I slide a plate of food in front of her.

"Yeah." She sighs before taking a bite out of one of the crackers. "Yeah, you're right. I should do that." She has this glazed look on her face. Her glacier blue eyes are staring off into the distance, not focusing on anything in particular.

"Emma?" I reach over and rest my hand on her wrist, causing her to jump a little out of her seat.

"Hmm? Sorry . . . what did you say?"

"Why don't I walk you to your apartment, okay? Maybe you should call one of your sisters. Maybe talk it out with them?"

As much as I'd like to be the one she talks to about this, I can't in good faith continue down this road. I'm barely able to hold back my opinion right now. And if she keeps going, I don't think I'll be able to restrain myself from asking her to stay here with me.

"Oh, yeah. O—okay. That sounds good." I pull her up out of her chair, walking her out of the shop before I lock up. We cross the street and I guide her up the four flights of stairs to her apartment.

She opens the door and I pull her close to me, kissing her before she enters the space.

"I'll see you in a couple of hours for dinner, okay? If you need anything, just text or call. I'm literally across the street."

"Thanks, Diego. I appreciate it." It's her turn to steal a kiss, but it's too short, and she's out of my arms too fast. "Bye."

I give a small wave as she closes her apartment door. I hear the lock fall into place and can't help wondering, did I just seal our fate by not asking her to stay? Fuck.

CHAPTER THIRTY-FIVE

EMMA

I close the door after saying goodbye to Diego and just stand frozen in my apartment. Not sure what my next move should be, in every sense of the phrase.

Coming out of my daze, I march down to my room, deciding to strip down and put on something cozy, trading my work attire for an oversized tee and shorts. A bath sounds like a step in the right direction in calming my racing mind, so as I wait for it to fill, I text my sisters.

It's mid-morning in North Carolina, so they should all be up, but I'm not sure if anyone will be available. There's a good chance they are already busy doing their normal morning activities.

I get my answer when I see my phone light up with a video call notification from Lindsay. Not my initial guess on who would call me first, but it works all the same.

I hit the green "accept" button and am shocked to find all

three of my sisters all on my screen, each one in their own little box.

Just thinking that they all dropped everything . . . for me . . . well, it just reminds me that even though we may fight, when shit hits the fan, we're always there for each other.

"Okay so spill," Taylor greets.

"Hold on," Tory injects. "Is that my Foo Fighters tee?"

I look down and inspect the tee. Oh shit, I completely forgot I stole this from her a couple years back.

"Who are you talking to, Tory?" I go with the playing dumb routine, which normally works. Though I'm not feeling so confident about it today, especially since I'm the only one currently wearing a T-shirt.

"You, Emma. I'm talking to you." She rolls her eyes. "Oh my god! It fucking is! It has the same grease stain on the shoulder where I spilled nacho cheese. God, Emma! I've been looking for that shirt for years!"

"Well, I figured since it had a stain on it, you didn't want it anymore." It's a bullshit response, but it holds some merit.

"Are you kidd—" Tory starts up, but Lindsay interrupts.

"Ladies, let's get to the point of this call. I'm not sure when I'll get pulled away."

"Please continue, Emma," Taylor adds.

Forty minutes later, I find myself in the tub, phone propped on the porcelain edge.

After filling them in on everything, and I truly mean *everything*, that happened during these last five weeks in Barcelona, I'm ready to hear their thoughts.

My sisters each take their own turn explaining what they think I should do while I sit in the bath, adding little bits of hot water every now and then to keep it warm.

Tory is team Raleigh, no surprise there. "I just love having everyone so close."

"And while that's nice, Tory, I think London is the better pick for Emma. It could do wonders for her future with the firm." Lindsay's always thinking of the long game.

"And I think Emma should stay in Barcelona." Not going to lie, I'm a little caught off guard at hearing those words come out of Taylor's mouth.

"What?!" Both Tory and Lindsay shout in unison.

"I'm just saying," Taylor adds, "y'all didn't see them together. Even though I only visited for a couple of days, there was definitely something special between the two of them. It might be nothing, but wouldn't you rather stick around and find out, rather than asking yourself 'what if' the rest of your life?"

She does make a good point. A point I've asked myself a lot in the past few hours.

"Well who says you have to choose?' Lindsay adds.

I sit up in the tub. "Explain please."

Lindsay proceeds to explain an option I didn't even think of. And honestly, after she lays out the details, I think it's the only option.

All my sisters agree to the plan before we drift off topic, catching up with each other and swapping recent life events. It's nice, feeling like we're all here together. It makes me miss our time together back home.

"Ladies, I just got called to go into a meeting, but I'll text soon. Love you all!" Lindsay quickly leaves the call, with Tory following soon after.

Taylor lingers on the call with me. "Feeling any better after all that?"

"Actually, I am. That was some great problem solving and I couldn't have done it without y'all."

I put my phone down on the nearby counter before lifting myself out of the tub. Wrapping the fluffy white towel around my body before picking the phone back up.

"Speaking of problem solving, while I have you on the phone—"

"Nope. We're not talking about Lindsay's and my relationship. I have no idea how you always find a way to turn the topic back to this, but we're not doing it today. I love you, Em. Now go get your man."

I sigh, "Fine. I love you too, Taylor. Talk to you later." She smiles with her goodbye and then ends the call.

After grabbing a snack to settle my stomach, I draft an email to Javier, proposing the idea the girls and I came up with. Feeling confident with how I presented my plan, I send off the email. Hopefully with that problem semi-resolved, I can focus on getting ready and really enjoy my night with Diego.

CHAPTER THIRTY-SIX

DIEGO

*I*f I wasn't certain before, this past weekend solidified it for me.

I'm in love with Emma Hartman.

I actually don't think I've ever been in love before. Nor did I ever believe in something like love at first sight. Lust at first sight, sure. Attraction at first sight, absolutely. But with Emma, it was all of that and more. And ever since meeting that first night, the flame for her has been continuously burning.

After dinner on Thursday, I realize I don't want to miss out on any of the time we have left. Just because I want to give Emma space to make her decision, doesn't mean I can't spend time with her. I just won't bring the topic up unless she does first.

I sleep over at her apartment that night, and before leaving on Friday morning, I ask her if she wants to do a repeat of the previous night. She nods in agreement, and says she'll come to the shop after doing a few things for work.

In the afternoon, I lock the shop up to retrieve some essentials from the market for my apartment, hoping that I'll be able to coax Emma into staying with me all weekend long if I had a pantry full of food.

Emma comes by around five and keeps me company until closing. I bribe her with a round of what I'm calling "naked chef" and walk her up to my apartment for a homemade dinner.

We're sitting down, enjoying the dinner I've just made for us, both utterly naked. "So for dessert . . . " I lead, waiting to catch her gaze with mine.

"Oh, please do say we're finally breaking out the chocolate syrup?" She begs. And god, do I love it. "Because you still owe me from the other day when we got interrupted by your mom calling."

That was unfortunate timing. I had just pulled the chocolate sauce off of the range top when my mom called claiming there was something she needed done urgently at the shop. It ended up being nothing important but it still derailed our morning.

"My phone's already on silent." I take my last bite, then clean my face off with my napkin. I motion to grab her plate when I stand up. "Are you finished?"

"Yes, but I can wash these. You cooked."

I grab her plate and walk them over to the kitchen. "How about this? I'll take care of these dishes, if you warm up the syrup."

She taps her finger to her mouth, eyeing me up and down. "Deal. But only if you wear the rubber gloves."

I eye her suspiciously. "Really? Rubber gloves?" That's a new one, for me at least.

"What?" She shrugs. "Got to try it before you know if you like it. Plus, you have that whole domesticated vibe going on right now. It's kinda hot." She bites down on her lip again before shaking her head. "Syrup. I'm supposed to be getting syrup."

I chuckle as I pull the gloves out from under the sink, making sure I snap them both when they're fully on. I grab a dish and start rubbing the suds all over it.

"I take it back. That's *really* hot." Emma says from her spot near the stove.

"Well, in about two minutes, I'll be able to taste how hot this really makes you," I tease as I finish loading the dishwasher.

"Longest two minutes of my life." She huffs out while testing the temperature of the chocolate, dipping a finger into the decadent liquid then sucking it clean. Fuck me, I think I just came at the sight. "Chocolate is good to go. Not too cold that it'll clump, but not too hot that it will burn."

"Perfect!" I close the dishwasher, hitting the start button after it latches. "I'm starving."

I throw her over my shoulder with one hand, while grabbing the small pot in the other, marching us both back to the dining table.

"Not the bed?" She questions.

"A feast like you deserves to be eaten where it can be displayed."

I place the pot down before doing the same with her, laying her down, spine to wood, with her knees hanging off the edge.

Stepping between her legs, I lift the handle of the pot and drizzle some of the chocolate over her body, making sure to pour a little extra in my favorite areas.

I stand back and admire my work as Emma swipes a finger through the delicious liquid coating her stomach, then trails it up between her breasts, exposing the skin underneath.

In the most seductive way possible, she slowly licks the chocolate off each of her fingers. "You should really try this," she teases.

"Oh I intend to." I bend down and lick alongside the trail she just left with her finger, making sure to spend extra time on her already hard breasts. I'm thorough with my tasting, making sure I get every drop of chocolate that's painting her chest. "You were right, perfect temperature."

I kiss each breast one more time before working my way down her body with my mouth, savoring the sticky mess while her moans fill the apartment.

I stop before I reach her pussy, needing to pull my chair over in order to enjoy her the way she deserves. As I spread her legs farther apart, I see her clear arousal.

Lifting the handle of the pot, I pour a little more at the apex of her thighs, right above her bundle of nerves. I decide to tease her even more, swirling the velvety liquid around her swollen clit and puffy lips as her back arches off the hard wood.

After I'm satisfied with the artwork in front of me, I dive in to indulge in the mouthwatering meal before me, starting with long swipes of my tongue.

"Fuck, Sweetheart, you taste so good."

After a few licks from opening to clit, I spread her legs even wider, allowing me to work my tongue inside. Ensuring I get every last drop of chocolate, as my thumb works above my mouth, moving together in rhythm.

"Don't stop! Don't stop!" she chants, grinding her pussy against my mouth. I keep the pace for a bit longer, all while she moans my name during her release. "Diego, yes! Fuck yes, Diego!"

I ease her down from her climax, slowing my thumb and moving my face reluctantly away from her open legs. But not before I lick her once more, making her jolt and gasp from being so sensitive.

Thumbing my chin, I realize I have chocolate all over my mustache and beard. Nothing a wet towel can't fix, and if the end result is Emma coming on my mouth while her shaking legs are wrapped around my head, I'll happily get chocolate anywhere and everywhere for her.

"I think you've," she pauses to catch her breath, "forever ruined chocolate sauce for me."

I chuckle and shake my head. "I don't think I want chocolate any other way now, Sweetheart."

We only leave the apartment for a few hours on Saturday to open the shop.

As much as I wished we could spend all day playing human pretzels in bed, it's a Saturday, the shop's busiest day. We can't afford not to open the shop on days like these, especially now that we don't have the cruise customers coming until next summer. We could use all the business we can get.

Emma vows to keep me company in the shop all day thankfully. With most of the work done for our business, she gets a much needed weekend off.

During her time in the shop, she gets to read, not one but two, of the books we got back on Saint George's Day. Emma's a surprisingly fast reader. She sits and reads, enjoying some wine and a little charcuterie board I craft for her during my down time, while I tend to the customers that walk in throughout the day.

There are more than a few times where I get called out by some customers for being too distracted. Some in a teasing tone, but a few are not as nice, mad at me for losing focus and not answering the question they ask.

You'd think I'd be embarrassed being caught staring at the ray of sunshine sitting in the corner, but I'm not in the slightest. I've completely fallen for her.

After locking up for the night, Emma and I agree to grab a quick bite at Lorenzo's.

"What are you doing down there?" I whisper in her ear as I feel her hand wrap around my thigh, coming dangerously close to my crotch.

"Just enjoying my time with you, of course."

I force a cough to cover my groan when she moves her hand over my dick. I place my hand on hers. "Something tells me I'm going to be enjoying my time with you a little too much if you keep that up."

"I'm just having a bit of fun." I feel myself harden under her palm and that's when I use my other hand to motion for the check.

Thankfully, our waiter is quick with bringing the bill, allowing us to pay then make a quick exit. We laugh as we run all the way back to my apartment for the night, enjoying the rest of the night tangled in each others' legs and my sheets.

The following morning, we do a repeat of the naked chef, only eggs are on the menu, so no need for an apron to block rogue oil burns.

"No apron this morning?" Emma asks from her perch on the counter.

"No apron," I repeat. "Why, enjoying the view?" I wink at her before lowering the heat on the eggs, stirring them while I do so, allowing them to get nice and fluffy.

She slides off the counter, wedging her naked body between me and the range. "What are you—" but before I can finish, she's on her knees, wrapping her mouth around my cock. Since I already had a semi due to her naked body being on display, it takes no time for her to get me hard.

"Fuck, Sweetheart." She relaxes her jaw, allowing her to take me even deeper into her mouth.

I scramble to turn off the heat, not wanting to burn any of her hair while I enjoy the gift she's giving me. I rake my fingers through her hair, guiding her head with my hands as she works her mouth.

She pulls her head away, allowing her tongue to swirl around my tip before taking me whole again. She moans and it's just then I see where her hand is at. She's riding her goddamn hand while I'm fucking her mouth. The image is glorious and enough to bring me close to the edge.

"That's my girl. Fuck your hand while you swallow my cock like a good girl."

With my praise, she sucks even harder. I have to brace one hand on the ledge to keep my balance as the other stays in her hair, pulling tight at her roots.

"Sweetheart . . . " I try to pull her off but she fights back. "I'm go—" I try again but she swats my hand. "Emma! I'm goin—

fuck!" She gags as I come down her throat and it's only after I'm spent that I see the hurried movements from her coming around her own hand.

She looks up at me with a devilish grin while she wipes her mouth clean. I can't help but pull her up to me and kiss her.

As she pulls away, she stares pointedly at the ruined eggs. Chewing her finger, she bats her lashes. "Oops."

Looking at the sad eggs on the stove, I chuckle as I grab the handle. "I'll make us some new ones." I toss the eggs into the trash and start on a fresh batch.

As of Sunday evening, she still hasn't told me if she has made a decision on where she'll be moving in a week. Or not moving if she chooses to stay. It's driving me crazy not asking, but I'm not about to put any more pressure on her.

I still have no clue on where she'll choose, but for now, I'll just try to enjoy the time left with her, without worrying about what location she'll choose next week.

It's Monday morning and by ten, my phone is already blowing up with calls, voicemails, and emails.

Apparently, a local winery just sold to an international company, which is great for the family, but sucks for all the people who booked a wedding or other events at their winery. The new company doesn't have any interests in hosting events so they refunded all of the reservations, leaving hundreds of weddings and parties stranded without a location.

It's really shitty on the company's part, but amazing for my family. Most of these couples reached out to us since we were the only nearby winery with a completely available calendar.

By Monday afternoon, we potentially have a booked-out

summer. Nearly every Friday, Saturday, and Sunday is booked out until the end of September! I'm working with Mia to get all the contracts signed and deposits paid fast, but in an organized way.

It's the news my family really needed. I've been calling Emma whenever I can to share the news, but the few times I've had a break from the madness, she doesn't pick up. The plan was to see her tonight, but I'm so busy trying to straighten out these contracts, and our now very full calendar, I had to send a text letting her know I'd be a little late getting to her apartment tonight.

Staying after closing gives me the chance to focus fully on the new deposits for the remainder of the afternoon. Thankfully, I only have a little more to do until I reach a stopping point with all of the new contracts.

Mia calls me just as I am finishing up, wanting to recount all the work we did throughout the day. It's unreal to think that just yesterday, we were preparing for this to be our last summer at the winery.

I'm beyond thankful for Emma's organization; if we hadn't had the brochures and contracts ready to go, we would've been drowning in even more work today. And who knows, maybe if we didn't have all that paperwork readily available, some couples may have gone in another direction entirely.

Lorenzo almost shit himself when I called about the news. With the location he'll be using for catering being fairly new, he said it's nice to have reliable income for the foreseeable future.

If this amount of interest keeps up, we might need to hire someone to help with all the events. With Mom and Dad handling the day-to-day activities at the winery, Mia and I will have a busy couple of weeks adjusting to the new work load between the shop and the increase in interest for our new event space. It's a lot, but I'm excited for this new season for my family.

And through this whole chaos of a day, I keep going back to how we couldn't have done it without Emma.

She's the one who made all of this happen. Things between us may have started with me saving the day, but she's the real knight in shining armor in our story. I'm so lucky to have met her, and the more I think about it, there's no way I'll be okay with only having her in my life for a few more days. I need to tell her that I want her to stay.

Looking up at the clock, it's around eight at night, but there still hasn't been any word from Emma. Earlier in the day, I tried not getting worked up over it, but now . . . after not hearing from her the whole day?

I'm sure she's fine. After all, I only have to walk across the street and I'm sure I'll find her waiting in her apartment. Maybe something came up at work? Or maybe she's sick with food poisoning?

I greet Manuel once I'm inside. He smiles and asks about my day before I head up. I don't want to be rude, so I return the question even though I'm anxious to see my girl. I've gotten to know him a little better since I've been coming around a lot more.

Rounding the last of the four flights of stairs—fuck, why haven't they fixed that elevator yet—I finally reach Emma's door.

She opens it a minute or so after my knocking, a smile painted on her face when she does. I grab her by the back of her head and kiss her with all the passion I can muster, pushing her inside the apartment while doing so.

She breaks our kiss and locks the door. "Well hello to you, too! Is this you asking for my forgiveness for standing me up?"

"Standing you up? I texted you earlier today to let you know I'd be late."

"I didn't get that text. In fact, I haven't received any texts or calls today from . . . well, anyone." She walks towards the kitchen and grabs her phone off the charger. "Oh shit, my phone was on airplane mode. Must've accidentally switched it on earlier in the day and that's why none of my texts were going through either."

The phone lights up her face as she sees all the missed calls and texts from today. Not just from me, but from her sisters, too.

She puts her phone up to her ear, I assume to listen to one of the few voicemails I left earlier. But her face is one of confusion. Then shock. Then joy.

God, what in the world did I say to her over voicemail? I can't even remember. I know I didn't talk about all of the new bookings because I wanted to tell her in person.

Emma puts the phone down and she's beaming. Her smile is spread from ear to ear, tears lining her eyes. What the hell was on that voicemail? She wipes her nose and sniffs a little.

"Emma, you're kind of scaring me. What just happened?"

Clearing her throat, she walks back over to me and holds my hands in hers.

"That was a message from Roger, the guy from Royal." She grips my hands tighter as she continues. "He said a winery they were using for excursions this summer just sold to a huge company, so now, they're in need of another winery to fill its space for the remainder of the season."

My mind is slow to comprehend what she's saying.

"Diego, they're asking for you! They called to ask if your family is willing to bring up your start date. He said people could start coming as early as next week, assuming all the paperwork gets finished on time."

Holy shit! Holy fucking shit!

"Are you serious right now?" I can't hide the shock clearly in my tone, and I'm sure, it's written all over my face.

I don't know how, but she smiles even bigger, nodding frantically. "Yes! Isn't that amazing news? I can't believe it!"

As the news sinks in, I realize she doesn't know about the other good news that rocked our world this morning. "I bet it's the same business that kept me working late tonight."

She rears her head back in my arms. "What do you mean?"

"This morning, our website got an insane amount of inquiry forms submitted for weddings and other reservations, most inquiring about dates for this summer." Emma's mouth gapes open as I explain more.

"After calling a few of the couples, it seemed like they all had the same story. All of them were scrambling to find a new place for their weddings after another winery canceled and refunded their deposits."

"Oh my god. That's fantastic!" she exclaims but scrunches her face immediately after. "I mean awful for them, but great for us." We kiss again, but she's quick to pull back. "Wait, do you think it's the same winery that sold?"

I shrug. "Probably."

"God, what are the chances?"

"Pretty fucking good, I guess." Laughing, she pulls me over to the couch where I take a seat and pull her onto my lap.

"I can't believe it." She's still in shock, and frankly, so am I. "So that's why you were so busy today. How many inquiries did you get?"

"Enough that I can proudly say our weekends are booked all summer long and even a little into fall. There's no way we're closing our doors now."

"That's incredible news, Diego!"

"We wouldn't have been able to do it without all the hard work you put in. Not just in advertising, but in drawing up the contracts and writing up all the brochures."

She blushes as she rests her hands on my chest.

"It was crazy helpful to already have paperwork ready to give those that were willing and ready to give their deposits." I run my hands up her arm, fingers tangling in the hair at the nape of her neck. "Words cannot describe how thankful I am having you in my life, Emma."

We kiss again and enjoy the night together celebrating this incredible win.

CHAPTER THIRTY-SEVEN

EMMA

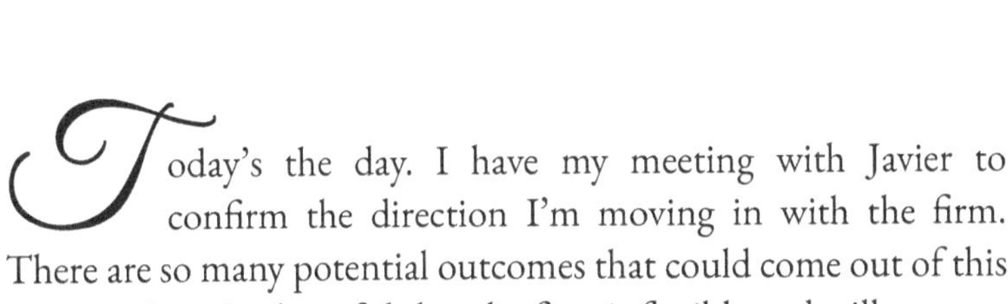

Today's the day. I have my meeting with Javier to confirm the direction I'm moving in with the firm. There are so many potential outcomes that could come out of this meeting, but I'm hopeful that the firm is flexible and will agree to my solution.

I wake up surrounded by the scent of Diego, smoky oak with a hint of dark berries. His arms are wrapped around my waist while my legs are wedged between his.

My head rises and falls as he breathes deeply in his sleep. As much as I don't want to leave the warmth of his embrace, checking the clock on my nightstand, I'm already running late. I left my phone out in the kitchen last night after we celebrated the amazing news, not remembering to set my alarm.

While Diego's family knows all about the mass influx of inquiries causing their events calendar to be booked, since they were so busy accommodating everyone yesterday, I'm excited to hear how they take the news Diego and I received last night.

Of course, they'll need to make a few last minute changes to make sure the shop is ready for cruisers, but all the legal forms have already been completed and filed from when we thought the contract was starting this year and not next.

"Good morning, Sweetheart." Diego kisses my bare shoulder. His voice comes out smoky, still hoarse from sleep.

"Hi, baby." I give him a quick peck as I try to wiggle out of his arms, but he's not budging. "As much as I hate to say this, it's almost eight-thirty and I have to go into the office this morning."

"Why?" he whines in between more kisses on my shoulder and up my neck. "You just saved our business. " The breath from his words, hot against my skin. "Let's celebrate," he adds with a flirty chuckle. Something tells me that the celebration he has in mind is going to be hard to turn down.

"*Diego . . .* " I draw out, trying to stay focused. My nipples harden when he starts to suck on my neck, his hand wandering down my stomach, inching closer to between my legs.

"Mmm . . . I won't ever tire of hearing my name on your lips."

I part my legs for him and he's quick to move, fingers swirling in the wetness that has gathered there.

"Especially when you're lying naked in bed with me."

God, his touch is bewitching. I'm finding myself questioning why, in fact, I have to go to this meeting, when I could stay here . . . in this room . . . with him.

Then it hits me. That's exactly why I *need* to leave. I clamp my legs shut, trapping his hand between my legs.

"Feisty this morning, are we?" he teases. "Normally, I don't get your brat out until after lunch."

I extract myself from his hold on me, hopping out of bed and grabbing an acceptable outfit for the meeting. "I'm really sorry, but I have a meeting with my manager about my next move." The playfulness immediately evaporates off his face.

Yup, I just ruined the sweet and cozy morning we were enjoying.

"I'll be back afterwards. Like you said, I've accomplished my goal for your business, so there's not much else I need to do in the office. But there are a few things I need to double check at the shop before the cruise line can start sending the cruisers your way. Why don't I meet you there after I'm done with Javier?"

"Yeah, sure." He pulls himself out of bed, grabbing his discarded clothes off the floor by the foot of the bed. "I'll head out. I've got to get the shop open soon anyway."

He slips on his pants, and walks over to me. Shirt in hand, he gives me a goodbye kiss, and though it's quick, I can still feel the emotion behind it. He's hurt, but clearly not ready to talk about it.

"Okay," I'm still naked, holding my outfit in one hand, but I don't want to let him go. I hold on to him a little longer, trying to convey . . . Well, I don't even know what. I just know I don't like this feeling. "I'll see you a little later then. Have a good morning."

"You too. Good luck with your meeting, Sweetheart." And with that, he walks out the room and leaves my apartment. Well, that's one way to start my morning.

I haven't told him about the decision I've made yet because I'm still not certain the firm will approve of it. My hope is to get all the details ironed out before informing him of my decision.

With that in mind, I refocus on the meeting that's set to start in . . . Wait, what time is it? I look over to my clock—*fuck*.

Only ten minutes until I have to leave.

Messy bun it is. Growing up with three older sisters, I was lucky enough to learn the art of a messy bun earlier in life. With over a decade of practice, I feel like I've mastered the art. Adding a few pins to tuck in any wild strands, I successfully create a look professional enough for the meeting I'm about to walk into. I'm normally a hair-down kind of girl, but when I'm low on time or have greasy hair, it's my go-to style.

As I button my shirt, I hear my front door open again.

I finish up the last button before rushing to my bedroom doorframe.

"*Hello*?" I call out cautiously. When I get a peek of the hallway, I see Diego rushing toward me.

And like a scene straight out of *The Notebook*, he lifts me up in his arms, and kisses me with all the fire in the world. The action tells me everything I need to know about the man I've already fallen in love with.

He gently sets me back down and rests his forehead on mine. "I'm sorry," he breathes out. "I'm sorry for being an ass. I've been trying so hard not to think about the idea of you moving away because I know if I do, I'm going to ask you if you've made your mind up yet. And Emma, I don't want to pressure you in any way. I truly do want you to pick the choice that's right for you. And that's why I've been holding back sharing what I think, but I don't think I can anymore."

He brings his hands up from my waist to my face. Rubbing his thumbs on my temples as he stares deeply into my eye. "Emma, I want you to stay. I want you to choose Barcelona. But I also don't want to be the reason you miss out on an opportunity like London."

He pauses and takes a breath before adding, "So what I'm saying is I'm choosing you. If you want to stay in Barcelona, stay in Barcelona with me. And if you want to go to London or back to Raleigh, let's go to London or Raleigh *together*."

I can't help but smile as he continues.

"I know it's selfish, and I know it's not fair of me to ask that of you, but here I am. And I'd be a fool to let you go into the meeting without you knowing how I truly feel." He brings me close to his lips, hovering there ever so slightly. "I love you, Emma Hartman." He seals his proclamation with a kiss unmatched by any before.

We break apart after a minute, leaning our foreheads together. "Yeah?" I say, looking up to him with a cheeky smile.

"Yeah. So don't think moving to Raleigh or London will get rid of me. If you *do* choose one of those instead of Barcelona, I'll find some way to be with you." He kisses me again. "Now let's get you to that meeting."

We leave the apartment, hand-in-hand, walking to my office. He gives me a quick peck on the lips and wishes me good luck before I step inside for the meeting that will determine my future.

"I won't lie, I'm a little disappointed with your decision. Are you sure this is what you want? We haven't signed anything to make it permanent yet." Javier asks from across the conference table.

"I'm certain about it, now more than ever." I smile thinking about the conversation I had with Diego before walking into this meeting. "I think it's the right path for me. I hope the firm knows how thankful I am for all three of the offers, and I'm sorry I didn't choose one."

"Hey, I understand, I really do. A change of scenery can be good for everyone. You'll keep me updated if things change in the fall, correct?" He looks up from the almost complete paperwork spread across the table in front of him. The only thing left is for me to sign on the dotted line.

"Absolutely."

"Well, that settles it then. Friday will be your last day with the Sánchez family as your client. Just sign here and the decision will be final." He slides the document over to me, and I sign my name without any hesitation.

"Emma, I want to let you know how proud I am with the work you've done on with that account. You really made a difference in that family's future. Hopefully, you know how talented you are and I am lucky to have whatever time I can with you working at my branch. Thank you for all the hard work you've done." He stands, and I take that as my cue to stand as well.

He walks over to me to grab the contract while reaching out to shake my hand. "It's been a real treasure working with you these last few weeks. You have a bright future ahead of you, and I can't wait to see what you do with it."

I wipe under my eye and my finger comes away wet. I suppose with words like that, it's hard not to get emotional.

"Words cannot describe how thankful I am for this opportunity. Thank you, Javier for welcoming me with arms wide open and helping me along the way. These have been some of the best weeks of my life."

He smiles and ushers me out of the conference room. I walk alone over to my cubicle to gather a couple notes I need to help me prepare the tasting room for the upcoming increase in visitors.

Stacia's not at her desk, so I guess I'll have to text her about the meeting later.

I hurry back down, anxious to get to Diego's shop, not wanting to wait another second to tell Diego of my decision. Only when I walk outside the building, I realize I don't have to wait at all.

He's standing there, waiting for me, holding a book with a single red rose tucked inside. Seeing his face light up when his eyes meet mine makes me all the more confident I've made the right choice.

CHAPTER THIRTY-EIGHT

DIEGO

*A*s soon as I see Emma, I wrap my arms around her and kiss her cheek.

"So?" I pull back, looking at her joyous face. "How'd it go?" She's beaming. Like pure sunshine in my arms.

"It went perfectly!" she cheers as she holds my waist tight, her other hand rubbing up and down my chest. "The firm accepted my counter-offer. I've already signed all the paperwork and I'm officially starting next Monday."

"And that decision was . . . " She's killing me, and by the bratty look in her eyes, she's enjoying torturing me.

"Well, pretty early on, I wrote off Raleigh. As much as it's comfortable being there, I still want to see the world. And I feel like I'd be silly to take that opportunity." I nod in agreement before she continues. "And London . . . I mean it's London. How could I say no to an opportunity like that?"

"So London?" I ask hesitantly.

"Diego, these past weeks have been more special than you will ever know." Fuck, here comes the but. "I've grown so much as a person, and I've been so lucky to have you here beside me the whole time. Spain was such an amazing opportunity, and I'll never regret my time here. But, I'm really interested in all the possibilities London could bring. "

I turn my head to look anywhere. Anywhere but her big, ice blue eyes, knowing I'm about to get my heart broken by this angel.

But she guides my head back to her with her delicate touch before continuing, staring right at me for this next part. "So that's why I asked for both."

My brain must've short circuited for a second because did she just say both? How would that even work?

"I accepted the position in Barcelona, but with the stipulation that in the fall, I'll move to the London office." I'm shocked. I didn't even *think* this was an option. "Or hopefully, *we'll* move to London," she adds under her breath.

"Wait, repeat that last part again."

She clears her throat, readjusting her position so she's standing tall. "I said, hopefully *we* will move to London. Like you and me, Diego."

Fuck. I love this woman.

I shower her in kisses, on her face, hair, and neck all while swinging her around in my arms. She giggles all through my attempts at kissing any part of her, desperately trying to convey my love for this woman.

"Oh, and one more *little* thing." She holds up her index finger and thumb, making a pinching motion with them. "Since I'm no longer here on a short-term contract with the firm, I need to move out of the firm's apartment."

"Okay, well that's easy enough."

"Like this weekend." She smiles sheepishly before adding, "I know it's a big ask, but I was thinking a move across the street wouldn't be so bad. You know, like maybe into *your* apartment."

"Sweetheart, I would love nothing more," I say with a smirk. "So London in the fall? Together?"

"Yeah, together." She smiles before reaching up to kiss me again. "It'll probably be late September. I'm ending my position with the Barcelona office at the end of August. That way I can fly home for all of Taylor's wedding stuff. I'm sure you'll be invited to that." She bites her lip, then smiles. "But yeah, London."

"I'll follow wherever you let me." I kiss her again, squeezing her close to me. Reality finally catches up, and I realize I won't ever have to say goodbye to her. And the time we have left in Barcelona allows me time to get creative with how I can still help the family business after we move.

"I love you, Diego." She says it so softly, I can barely hear it. But she said it all the same.

"I love you, Emma." After giving her a kiss on her forehead, I pull out of our embrace, but keep hold of her hand. "Alright, now if you're available, I'd love your help with a few things at the shop today."

It's just then I realize I'm still holding the rose and book I picked up across the street.

"Oh, and this . . . " I hand over the book, with the single red rose tucked inside, over to her. " . . . is for you. I figured it was fitting."

She grabs it and reads the colorful cover out loud. "'Stuck in the Middle'? Oh my god!" Gasping, she stops and faces me. "You got me a book with a double penetration trope?!"

"That I did." Grinning, I try to recount the weirdly in-depth conversation I had with the book store owner. "Apparently, this is part of a ten book series. According to the book store owner, every book is worth a read, but sadly, not all have the double penetration trope I know you enjoy so much."

"Aw, that's too bad. But good to know." She turns the book over and starts reading the back. "Oh, it seems like this one's about a woman who gets lost in the woods and stumbles upon a cabin where two step-brothers live."

"Sounds like it's going to be a good one. Maybe you can read a little to me." We continue talking while walking to the shop.

"Yeah?" She's got that look in her eye, knowing exactly what she's doing.

"Yeah. A little *naked* reading." I turn and wink to her.

"So it's okay when *you* say little but not me?"

Of course she'd bring that up again. "That's because when *you* use the word, you're just being a brat."

Emma laughs, and bumps into me. "But I'm *your* brat."

I smack her ass. "You got that fucking right, Sweetheart."

CHAPTER THIRTY-NINE

EMMA

The next day, Diego's dad drives Mia into the city so they can both help get the shop ready for the influx of people the upcoming week. As much as I want to help, Diego insists I spend the day packing up all my things from my apartment.

"I just think you're better off packing now before the busy weekend. Plus, I've got Mia helping me out, so take your time packing this place up."

"Alright, I guess I might as well get it done as soon as possible, that way it's one less thing to worry about," I concede.

Thankfully, I only have a few bags to pack, mostly clothes and shoes.

I move the food I have in the fridge and pantry over to Diego's first because it's the easiest. Before moving any of the books that Diego bought me during my stay, I emptied one of the packed suitcases at Diego's apartment before bringing it back over to fill up with books. I figure moving the books would be easier with wheels instead of a box. Work smarter, not harder.

And as luck would have it, the elevator finally got fixed last night. So at least I'm able to take advantage of the small rectangular box, using it to help bring my suitcases down, one by one to ensure I don't put too much stress on the newly fixed elevator.

After doing one final sweep of the apartment, ensuring nothing's left behind, I do a quick clean and lock-up. I brought over a couple bottles from the winery earlier so I could give them as a "thank you" gift to Manuel when I leave for the last time.

Dropping my keys off with him, I thank him for all his help and welcoming smiles during the last six weeks.

"Your smile always made my day brighter. Drop in any time." He tells me, making me tear up before he gives me a goodbye hug. God, my luteal phase is wreaking havoc on my emotions.

After an hour or so unpacking, it's about time for the shop to close. I change into some fresh clothes and head down. When I open the door, I'm greeted by what seems to be a very heated discussion between Mia, Diego, and their dad. So heated, they don't even hear me walk in. I'm not sure if I should say something to let them know I'm here, or go back out and text Diego that I'm on my way down.

Alejandro is talking so fast, so it's hard to keep up with him while doing the translation in my head. Over the last few weeks, I've vastly improved on my Catalan, but it's still far from perfect. I'm not certain about my translation, but given his tone, it seems like he's yelling at Mia. Maybe something about not being responsible, but I'm not familiar with some of the words he's using.

He says a few more sentences and then I hear something else about driving. I step inside the shop a little more, making my footsteps extra loud so it's obvious they are no longer alone. Diego's head turns my way almost immediately. His face shifts from worry to relief in an instant.

"Hey, Sweetheart."

Mia turns to me, I don't think it's anger on her face but she's definitely not happy.

"Hey, Emma. Congrats on the job offers. I'm glad you're

sticking around for a bit. Seems to me like the dragon finally found his princess." She chuckles a bit with her last comment.

By the time she finishes, Diego's in front of me, giving me the biggest hug. Clearly, something else happened here.

"I'd like to think he's more like the knight in our story." I rub Diego's chest as I add, "I hope you don't mind me stealing him away in the fall." I peek over Diego's shoulder and find both Mia and their father staring intensely at each other.

"Actually, we were just talking about that, but I'll leave that conversation for you, son. Mia," Alejandro calls out, "let's get going. It's already late enough without staying any longer."

"You know what, Dad? I think I'm just going to stay over, that way I can help Diego a little more before things start picking up next week."

She sends a pleading look our way. I guess it's more for Diego's sake than mine.

"Yeah," Diego looks down to me then back to his dad. "We could really use all the help we can get at this point. Dad, you could stay too, if you didn't want to drive in the dark."

"No, I'll leave you kids to it." He points at Mia and says something in Catalan. From the look on their faces, it's not a good thing.

"Alright, Dad, I think it's time to go. Best be heading out before it gets too dark." Diego's stern tone silences his dad.

"Bye, Dad." she adds with mock sweetness and he leaves without another word. "God, you'd think after you helped save the only thing he's ever been proud of, he'd be a little happier." She claps her hands together and a real smile appears on her face. "So, Lorenzo's?"

"Lorenzo's sounds perfect." I agree as we walk out of the shop. I'm craving some fried potatoes.

Diego pulls me under his arm on one side while leaning over to Mia on his other. Cupping his mouth in her direction, he pretends to whisper, but his voice is loud, clearly wanting me to hear.

"Just make sure to order your own plates because Emma isn't the best at sharing."

"Oh my god, that was *one* time!" I hip check him while we cross the street.

He leans back over to me and kisses the top of my head, speaking into my hair. "Yeah, but it made a lasting impression, Sweetheart." He raises his head again to be at full height before adding, "Don't worry, we'll get you all the fried potatoes you want." God, is it possible to love this man even more.

I moan playfully. "I like the sound of that." But then remember that Mia is *right* there. "Oops, sorry Mia!"

"You know what? Why don't I get a seat at the bar while the two of you do . . . Well, whatever this is." She teases as we enter the tapas bar.

"No, please." I grab her hand and tug her towards our table. "Don't leave me alone with your brother." She laughs with me at my plea.

"Okay, well when you put it that way, how can I say no?"

We take our seats and all smile when we see Lorenzo head over.

"Hey, everybody."

He pats Diego on the shoulder then goes and stands by Mia's chair. Am I seeing things or is his palm resting on her back? Interesting. I mean, I guess, with this angle, his hand could be on the back of the chair. But they did seem sort of cozy when we had that dinner at the winery.

We chat for a bit and then he grabs our orders. But before he leaves us, there was definitely a shared look between him and Mia. Very interesting, indeed.

"So, you don't mind me stealing your brother away to London?"

"Hey," she holds up her hands and shrugs, "as long as I can visit whenever I want, you could take him to Australia for all I care." The waiter comes with our beverages, passing them out as

Mia finishes. "Even a dragon has to spread their wings, just be sure to think of me when you fly."

Shit, and now I'm crying.

I wipe my eyes as Diego squeezes my thigh. "Thanks, sis. We'll work on getting you out there for a visit." Mia gives Diego a sweet smile before giving a toast.

"Here's to a bright future for you both!" Mia cheers, raising her glass.

"And to Emma, for you have been a ray of sunshine in one of our darkest times. I can't wait for this next adventure to begin!" Diego raises his glass to join Mia, and I follow suit while wiping the tears running down my face.

"*Salut!*" We all say in unison.

CHAPTER FORTY

DIEGO

After dinner, the three of us walk straight back to the apartment. We all exchange our goodnights before heading to our rooms. Naturally, Emma follows me into mine. Or *our* room now. It's going to take a minute to get used to the change, but it's a change I'm excited about.

"So what was your dad talking about when I walked in? It didn't look good." Emma asks as we settle into bed.

"He wasn't the happiest when I told him the news about London, but we ended on good terms. Him agreeing my job could shift to one I can do from my laptop, after a few changes. Unfortunately," I sigh, "Mia got the bulk of his anger when we told him she'd be staying in the apartment after we move. When he asked why she couldn't just commute like she did before, or like I did before we started our relationship, she blurted out that it would be impossible since she won't have her license until at least October."

"And let me guess, your dad didn't know she'd lost her license?" Emma assumes. We're both lying on our sides at this point, facing each other, bodies naked under the covers with only the soft light from the lamp illuminating each other's faces.

"You'd be correct. Both of my parents didn't have a clue. But I'm sure Dad has already told Mom by this point."

I bring my hand up and start playing with the ends of her wavy hair that have fallen over her shoulder.

"Anyways, Dad gave her the whole 'you're not taking life seriously' speech which is when I interjected, but he just shot back with 'at least she's not abandoning the family business.'"

I move my hand down to her hip and pull her closer to me.

"He's just riled up. Mom will calm him down. She always does. But I should probably call her first thing tomorrow and see how the rest of the night went."

"Well," Emma starts as she walks her fingers down the planes of my chest, "I'm sorry about your dad," then stomach, "and I hope your mom isn't too disappointed in Mia," then lower, fingers teasing me so close to where I need her "And I—"

I silence her with a kiss, then back my head away, just enough to look her in the eye. "As much as I appreciate your care for my family, I'd rather not talk about them when your fingers are inches away from my very hard dick." Emma tilts her head back laughing. "Especially when all I can think about is flipping you on your back and pushing deep inside your pussy, which I'm sure is soaked right now."

I move my palm to her ass, giving her a tight squeeze on her cheek before turning her on her back. Leaning down over her, I whisper in her ear, "Tell me I'm wrong?" before kissing down her neck.

She moans, "You're not, but your sister's in the next room over. Just like you don't appreciate talking about her while you have a hard-on, I'm sure she doesn't want to hear what you do *with* said hard-on."

"Well, that just means we'll need to be extra quiet," I taunt between kisses. "Can you do that for me, Sweetheart? Or do I need to find something to keep your mouth busy?"

"It depends . . . " she says, that cheeky smirk of hers showing. "On?"

"On what you plan on stuffing my mouth with. You know, it's got to be something pretty big to shut me up." God, this woman. "Otherwise, the sound will still be there, only muffled a little."

"I've got something big for you alright." I drag my erection up her thigh proving my point. "But the question is, can you handle all of it, Sweetheart?"

"You know I can," she chirps back.

"Prove it. Sit on my face while I stuff that bratty mouth of yours." Shifting positions, she rotates herself so she's straddling my face, her opening hovering over my mouth.

"Sweetheart, I said *sit*, not hover." I grab her hips on both sides and pull her down so her pussy is pushed up against my mouth, her thighs clamped around my head. Already, I can tell my earlier assumption was correct. She's a dripping mess.

I start to work my mouth and tongue before she's even gotten her mouth on my cock. She lets a moan slip out and I pause.

"Better stuff that mouth, Sweetheart. We wouldn't want me to stop, now would we?" The feel of her warm mouth around my cock is answer enough.

Both of my arms are wrapped around her legs, ensuring she stays pressed, as close as humanly possible, to my mouth. She uses one hand to keep a steady rhythm with her mouth, fist working up and down my shaft, while the other is playing with my balls.

Wanting to make her come first, I bring a hand down and use my fingers in tandem with my tongue, making sure her clit is always stimulated.

She pops her mouth off my dick. "Fuck Diego!" I lick around her opening, while keeping the same pace with my fingers on her swollen clit. "I'm coming! I'm coming!" She chants as she rides my face through her climax.

She's attempting to keep her hand moving on my dick while she comes, but the movements are frantic. Lucky for me, it turns out feeling her come on my tongue is all I need to finish alongside her.

Emma adjusts her position, so she's putting her weight on her hands and knees, still caging me underneath her. She bends her head down to the mess between my thighs and proceeds to lick it clean, not letting a single inch of it go to waste.

After finishing, she raises her body up on her knees, bringing one over my head while twisting the rest of her body, making it so she's facing me as she sits her ass on the bed.

She sighs out an exhausted breath while running her fingers through her hair, pulling it out of her face in the process. "Well, that was something for the books." She chuckles under her breath.

"Indeed it was," I agree as I fold one arm under my head, positioning the other around her hip, fitting her in the space between my arm and side.

"Though I'm pretty sure I'm going to need to apologize to your sister in the morning." Emma looks down at me, hair falling back in front of her face.

Brushing the wild strands behind her ear, I say, "You *were* pretty enthusiastic there at one point." She pinches my exposed nipple. "Oh Sweetheart, that's not the punishment you think it is." Smirking, I grab her ass again as she tries to wiggle free of my hold.

"Guess I'll need to keep that in mind for next time." She winks, then wiggles again. "Okay, but seriously, I need to pee. So can you please let me go now?"

Releasing my hold on her, she scrambles off the bed and into the connecting bathroom. I hear a stream of what I'm assuming is pee before I realize, she didn't even bother closing the door. I smile at myself, knowing she wouldn't do that unless she really had to go or she's just that comfortable. I choose to believe it's the latter of the two.

I hear a flush, then water running from the sink, letting me know it's clear for me to go in and clean myself off. Only when I approach the door, I hear another faucet running, followed by a splash and Emma sing-songing under her breath, "Shit! Shit. Shit. Shit."

I'd probably not be able to hear her if I wasn't already so close to the bathroom, and if the door wasn't left open.

"Everything okay in there, Emma?"

"Um . . . yeah! I'm fine, but your bathroom floor isn't." She sounds a bit shrill. " . . . But it's nothing a few towels can't fix."

"Let me grab some and I'll be right there to help." I chuckle as I grab a few extra towels in the hallway, returning only to find Emma standing by the bidet, drying her chest and stomach off with a small hand towel.

I look from her to the floor, and then back up to her, trying to hold back my smile. "So you want to tell me how this happened?"

"Don't look at me that way! My curiosity got the best of me, and I finally decided to use the bidet. Or at least, I *attempted* to use the bidet." I walk over to her and kneel on the wet floor, drying it as she continues. "I didn't realize the pressure on those things was so . . . aggressive."

I fail at holding back my laughter while I continue to soak up the wet mess.

"Well, you probably turned the thing on full blast. Here," I stand back up, "you see these two side nobs? One is for hot water and the other for cold, but the knob in the center, that's the one that controls the pressure. The more you turn, the more pressure will be applied to the jet. But not every bidet has a jet or dual temperature control."

Emma crosses her arms over her bare tits, popping her hip out. I'd be a bit more intimidated if she wasn't deliciously naked.

"So what you're saying is you have a *fancy* bidet."

Rolling my eyes, I pick up the sopping wet towels. "I wouldn't go *that* far, but mine does have a little more of a learning curve." I wring the towels out in the tub and hang them over the edge before I clean myself off. "But now you know for next time."

"Oh no. There will be no next time."

"Why not? I'm sure it would actually be good to start using it.

Especially with all the sex we're going to be having now that you're living with me."

Did I think tonight was going to end in a talk about how to use the bidet? Definitely not. But there's something to be said about how no topic is off limits or taboo for us.

After washing my hands, I follow her back out to the bed, and we both get into our respective positions.

"I'll think about it," she promises as she snuggles into me under the comforter, her ass grinding up against me as I drape an arm around her, tucking her deeper into my embrace. She wraps her hands around mine and whispers, "Goodnight, Diego."

Squeezing her tight against me, I give her a kiss on her head before murmuring, "Goodnight, love."

"Mmm. I like that," she adds sleepily.

"What's that?" I ask, settling in behind her for the night.

"Knowing you love me." She shifts her hips, tucking herself even further into my body, and we both fall asleep.

CHAPTER FORTY-ONE

DIEGO

"Okay, the first group should be here in," I check my phone for the current time, "ten minutes. Tables look great. Bottles seem to be ready to go. You good, Mia?"

She gives an exaggerated smile and two thumbs up, nodding her head a little too much.

"Okay, okay. Dial it down a bit. We don't want to scare them off on the first day."

"I know this is exciting for you, really for all of us, but it's basically like any other scheduled tasting." Mia sighs and there's definitely some truth to what she says.

After receiving the schedule from the reps at Royal, we found out that we'd be having four groups of people each day, three days a week. Mondays, Tuesdays, and Fridays.

The plan for now is to have Mia come to the apartment and stay the night before on those days. That way she's in the city and able to give me a helpful hand in the shop, ensuring someone is always with the group, if the other is needed to help with other customers.

We all agreed that we wanted to *attempt* to keep the shop operational while we do the tastings, at least for now. We're testing it out for the first few weeks, but I have a feeling we're going to need to hire a few new employees to help with all the new traffic in both the shop and winery.

After talking to both my parents this weekend, I can tell that Dad calmed down after his initial reaction last week. He actually apologized to Mia for his behavior, which is a new development in their relationship.

It doesn't make his actions any better, but maybe it's a step in the right direction, hopefully finding a healthier way to deal with his anger and disappointment.

Mom was obviously sad when she heard I would be moving to London in a couple months, but she's excited to see what opportunities the move will bring for Emma and me.

She also said she's going to start asking some of her friends if they have any kids or grandkids that would like a summer job helping us set up for all the planned events. She's decided that with Mia helping me out in the city, she could try running the event side of things at the winery.

The shop door opens, and from the line of people coming in, I assume it's the first excursion group of the day.

"*Bon dia!* Welcome, everyone. Please," I wave around to the tables, "take a seat and we can get this tasting started."

Several bottles and even more bite-sized snacks later, we finish the last group of the day. I lock up as soon as they leave, and sigh.

"And we're done."

Mia comes up and gives me a high five. "That was such a rush! And did you see how many bottles they bought?"

I wasn't paying much attention to the counter, since Mia volunteered to check out the guests while I cleaned up after each tour, making sure we were ready for the next group.

"No. How many did we sell?"

"Over a hundred bottles, Diego! And that's just with the groups that were here. That doesn't include some of the customers that walked in throughout the day."

Fuck. That's even more than we sometimes sell in a week. Hell, even in two weeks if it's really slow.

Mia walks over to the almost bare shelves. "Something tells me we might need to start bringing more bottles over here." Can't disagree with her there.

"Let's see how the other two days go this week before doing that. We can bring some more bottles up from the cellar, and next time we go back home, I'll be sure to increase the amount of bottles we bring to the shop. But I think you're right, we're going to need to figure out a long-term solution if it continues like this."

As we finish cleaning up, I hear a knock on the glass of the door. I turn and see Emma waiting outside, a big smile painted across her face.

Walking over, I usher her in before locking back up. "So? How'd your first day go? Tell me everything!"

I give her a hug and brief kiss before answering, keeping her wrapped in my embrace while I do. "Today was a good day." I can't help but let the smile take over my face.

We did it and none of it could've been done without this incredible woman in my arms.

"Yeah?" Her voice creeps up with excitement as she peeks over to Mia for confirmation.

"Emma, it was amazing! You should've seen it. I've never seen the shop so full of energy. Plus the sales we made on top of the money we'll make from tours themselves . . . let's just say if this keeps up, the only issue we'll have is keeping bottles on the shelves."

"Ah!" Emma screeches out in glee as she squeezes me tight. "Oh I'm so happy for you all! This is such amazing news!"

"And how was *your* first day? How was your new client?"

"It was great. It's a local meat company who needs help expanding their brand in the city. Something I thought you might be able to help with."

"Oh yeah? How about we talk about it over some dinner?"

"Sounds good to me. Mia," Emma calls out, "you joining us?"

"No, I've got plans of my own tonight, but you two have fun! I'll finish up here. Enjoy dinner!" She waves us off and continues cleaning up.

"Thanks, Mia. Hope you have a great night." Emma says as I usher us out the front door. "And congrats on such a successful first day!"

"Thanks, Em!"

I can't help but notice the smile that creeps up Emma's face at Mia's use of the nickname as we walk out.

CHAPTER FORTY-TWO

EMMA

EMMA:

Just landed in Raleigh. I'll text you when I'm at my parents.

DIEGO:

Thanks for the text, Sweetheart. I'll talk to you soon. Love you.

EMMA:

Love you too.

*I*t's been a long travel day, but I'm finally back in North Carolina. After customs, I grab my bag, and take a seat on a nearby bench. There's no way I'm stepping outside until I get the call from Mom letting me know she's arrived.

It's July, so it's fucking hell outside. If I were to walk outside now, I'd have frizzy hair within a minute, sticking to my face from all the sweat I created from the awful humidity.

Don't get me wrong, the humidity in Barcelona can be just as bad, but nothing is worse than spending most of your day in a stuffy plane, surrounded by all the body heat from other passengers, then hauling all your baggage off of the carousel, all while your shirt is sticking to your back from all the sweat, only to feel like you've stepped out into the devil's armpit when you schlep everything outside. Humidity is one of the only things in life I have yet to find the bright side of.

Mom gives me a quick call saying she's rounding the corner, so I gather my things and make my way out. Feeling like I'm walking through soup, I quickly spot Dad's car and Mom's frantically waving arm outside the window. She's crazy for having that window rolled down in this weather.

"Hi, baby!" Mom greets and she hops out of the car.

"Hey, Mom." She gives a kiss on my check while squeezing me close, making me cringe at the contact with my drenched shirt. "Sorry for all the sweat. I've missed you."

"Not as much as we've missed you, Em!" Dad shouts as he walks around the car. "Sorry, it's so hot. A heat wave just rolled into town two nights ago. But, we're glad you're home. I'm sure you have some stories to tell."

"You bet." Not all of them for my parents' ears though.

"Well, let's get out of this swamp and get you back home. Want me to sit in the back with you?"

That was always Mom's helpful way of calming me down when I had to ride in the car. Whether it was when I was a child or just a couple months ago, she's never judged or teased me for it.

"That's sweet, but only if you want to." Dad helps me load the bags in the trunk. "Actually, my stress around cars has gotten a lot more manageable." I think fondly about the memories I made with Diego that helped make that happen.

"Wow. Good for you honey," Mom says before all of us take our seats in the car.

After pulling out of the loading zone, it's Dad who asks, "How'd that happen, Em?"

"Well, funny story . . . " I start laughing because really there are so many things I want to share with my family about all the amazing things I've done these past few months. And almost every one of them involves Diego.

Even though I'm only here for a few days, we decided it was best for Diego to stay back with how busy the winery and shop have been. They actually just contracted with three other local wineries, helping to add more labels to the shop in the city.

Originally, we had worked on scouting out a few worldwide retailers where the Sánchez brand could start selling their wines, but with the amount of wine the cruise line groups are buying, they couldn't produce enough for any additional bulk orders. The winery can hardly keep up with their current orders as is.

On one of the Sundays last month, Diego and I went walking around the vineyard and got to talking about my driving.

"I think you might find some empowerment if you took matters into your own hands."

"So what does that look like?" I say, uncertain where this conversation is going.

"I think . . . " He grabs my hands in his, causing me to stop in my tracks. ". . . we work on getting your license. I researched it a little further and found it can even transfer when we move to London. Maybe you'll feel more in control being in the literal *driver's seat."*

"Hmm . . . " I bite my lip and ponder the thought. "I can see the thought process behind that. But when would I have time to even start?"

"We could start today," he says with a grin on his face. "I think the roads around the winery would be a great place to start." He grabs my chin between his fingers, bringing his face down to mine. "And I'll be right next to you the whole way, cheering you on and making sure you stay safe."

We continue walking, while I think about what he's offering. It's so much more than just the ability to drive. It's the power over something that has controlled me almost my whole life. It's the freedom of releasing myself from those chains.

"Okay," I agree, "but only if you're there every step of the way." I send a smile his way and see he's already beaming, smiling ear to ear with a shimmer to his eyes.

"There's my girl."

"Diego actually taught me how to drive last month." I smile at the memory. "Got my license just last week."

"Oh my god, Emma! That's incredible." Mom praises as she turns around and reaches over to pat my thigh. If I'm not mistaken, her eyes are looking a little damp, but maybe it's just the humidity.

"Good for you, Em!" Dad joins in on the cheers.

"Thanks, Mom and Dad."

It's nice to be back at my parents, but I'd be lying if I said it felt like home.

So much has changed for me recently, and there's still so much change coming in the next few months. I'll be back here with Diego in September for a couple of weeks, helping Taylor with all her wedding festivities. Then we'll have to go back and pack up everything for our move to London.

Researching places to eat when we finally get to London has been a favorite pastime of ours. We have a shared folder of all the places we've promised to try.

Diego is going to try out remote working while we're away. There's still so much help needed to manage his family's business, but he's done his best at picking up the slack. He really has fallen into the role perfectly and I have full confidence that he'll do great working remotely. It may not be the role his father saw for him, but at least Diego's still with the family's business.

I'm on the couch in the living room with everyone when Lindsay finally arrives. Taylor had her doubts Lindsay would show when Mom announced she was coming by a little earlier this morning.

Mom's quick to greet her at the entry. From what I hear, Lindsay has been even more of a recluse than normal. Not going to brunch with Taylor and Tory. Barely making an appearance at Sunday lunches at Mom and Dad's. I feel lucky I've been able to get a hold of her on text.

"Hey, ladies.'" She waves as she walks over to us.

We all exchange our hi's and hellos as she takes a seat in Dad's chair, looking around the living room like she hasn't seen it in awhile. "How's everyone been?"

"Well, Haylee and I just booked our flights to Greece for her gap year." Mom filled me in on the trip Tory was planning last night. Apparently, an old friend of Mom's has an olive orchard in Crete with a ton of land. Mom worked it out so Tory and Haylee could spend some time in one of their guest houses on the property for a few weeks in November.

"Well that sounds like a fun time. I'm sure you'll eat a ton of great food and make some great memories with each other," Lindsay adds, but she's being kind of weird about it. I can't put my finger on why though.

"And a great tan," Taylor adds.

"Or even a man!" I smirk.

"*Emma*!" Tory bites out.

"What?" I shrug. "Men are just made different over there. Must be something in the water."

"Speaking of men . . . how are wedding plans coming along Taylor?" Really smooth segue, Mom.

"It's been going well. You know how Jess' mom is. She's handling everything. I just show up whenever and wherever she tells me. Less stress that way."

"Ladies, ribs are done." Dad shouts from the kitchen.

"Come on, let's get some food girls." Mom stands and we all follow her into the kitchen.

One thing I've really missed about being away from Mom and Dad, is their cooking. Don't get me wrong, the food in Barcelona is incredible. Seriously, I'm spoiled with all the delicious meals I get to enjoy; not only with the restaurants, but by the hands of my favorite naked chef. I'm graced with the view of his rock-hard ass working away at our stove *at least* once a week.

But the nostalgia I have with the meal in front of me, it makes me feel extra warm and special. The counter's lined with mashed potatoes, summer salad, and Dad's famous ribs.

After dishing up my plate, I join the rest of the family at the table.

"So it's been a minute, Linds. How's work going?" Happily surprised with Taylor for initiating the conversation with Lindsay.

"Funny you should ask,"

Oh, shit.

"I was put on a sabbatical starting, well . . . immediately." What the fuck?

"*What*?!" I think I hear Mom shriek while I drop my fork. Everyone at the table is frozen and staring at Lindsay.

"What happened Lindsay?" Dad asks with a concerned tone.

"Nothing *happened*. We have a new regional manager and she's big on making sure we don't over stress ourselves." Everyone, including me, is silent as she continues with her story. "She may have mentioned I haven't taken a sick day since I've been at this job. So she put me on leave in hopes I'll come back 'refreshed.'" She uses air quotes for the last part.

"Well, we know you love your job and take pride in it so that must've been hard to hear," I hear Dad say, but I'm still comprehending what Lindsay just said.

"How long's the sabbatical?" Tory questions.

"She said at least two weeks. Oh and get this." She chuckles but she definitely isn't finding any of this humorous. "They're sending me to some small boutique hotel in Provence for the first half. All expenses paid and everything."

"Provence? You mean France?"

Of course this would perk Mom's attention. She's always dreamed about traveling there. Visiting the lavender farms in that region is on her bucket list. From the pictures and videos I've seen, I wouldn't mind a trip over there myself.

"Yeah. I looked it up and the hotel looks nice and quiet. There seems to be a small lavender field surrounding one side of the property. Real pretty."

I look over to Mom and see her eyes go all dreamy.

"When do you leave?" I ask as I finally find my voice.

"In a few hours actually. My flight takes off around six tonight."

"Way to bury the lead, Linds." Taylor scoffs. It's not the best response if she's trying to repair her relationship with Lindsay, but they have to start somewhere.

"Sorry. I'm still adjusting to the news myself. Fran just told me Friday afternoon. I spent all day yesterday packing and making sure I have everything I need."

I've never seen Lindsay so . . . flustered? Maybe muddled? Is that the right word for what she is right now?

"Well, that will definitely be an adventure for you. Do you need anything else? How are you getting to the airport? You probably need to leave soon then." Mom asks while we all start clearing the table.

"Luckily Fran seems to have organized everything already for the trip, so I basically just needed to pack yesterday and show up at the airport later today."

"Oh, and make sure your eReader is stuffed with some good books," Haylee chirps before heading outside to help Dad finish cleaning up.

"Good idea, Haylee," Lindsay shouts out while handing me a dish to scrub. "And yes, I should leave soon, but not without stealing a plate of your blackberry pie, Mom."

"Oh, I guess I can wrap a piece up for you." Mom kisses Lindsay's cheek then gets some pie for her to take.

After finishing the dishes, Lindsay grabs her plate and heads out. "Love y'all. I'll send a text on the group chat when I've landed."

A bunch of 'love you's' and 'safe travels' get called out by all of us as she leaves, slamming the door shut behind herself.

"Well," Mom huffs out.

"That's going to be one *interesting* trip for her," Taylor says sitting back down on the couch. "I don't think she even knows what it means to relax."

I chuckle as I take my seat. "Guess she's about to get a crash course."

EPILOGUE

EMMA

After a month of traveling around Europe, visiting several family members and friends, we're back home in London. My first day back in the office was filled with client meetings and a meeting with the branch manager later in the afternoon. A meeting I've been nervous about since my manager left a voicemail while we were visiting with Diego's family last week.

It's July and humid as fuck. Thankfully, our flat has an air conditioning unit, but I still have to walk outside in order to get to said air conditioning. Even though our place has nice cold air blowing throughout it, the stairwell to get to it does not. Something we weren't aware of when we signed the lease papers last fall.

By the time I reach our door, I'm drenched in sweat. I open the door to find Diego standing in the kitchen, gloriously naked, which immediately brightens my mood.

"Oh, naked chef for the third night this week?" I ask, closing the door and unloading my things on the entryway table.

"Well, when there's record setting temperatures outside, it's bound to be hot inside." His mouth tips up on one side, and I can't help but giggle at his cheekiness while I slide my shoes off.

"But I regret to inform you, I am cooking sausage. So I will need to cover up eventually in order to protect your favorite part of me."

"Hate to break it to you, babe, but your ass is my favorite part." Slapping his exposed ass, I reach in the drawer beside him and grab the folded fabric inside, stealing a quick kiss on his check as I loop the neck strap around his head. "Here you go. The goods are now protected."

Every time I see him wearing it, I can't help but laugh at the inside joke. It's a simple black apron with white embroidery, reading "I cook better naked." I bought the apron for Diego as a funny Christmas present last year, but it's the joke that keeps giving.

"I poured you a glass already." He motions with the tongs to the glass on the bar. "Why don't you sit down and tell me about your meeting with Arthur?" Grabbing my glass, I do just that.

"He started the conversation with how happy he was with all the amazing work I've done over the last ten months, and he offered me some great incentives to stay in London."

"But you don't want to stay in London . . . do you?" And this is why I love Diego. I don't even have to say what I'm thinking for him to already know. "So who else made an offer?" He questions with a knowing look as he turns the meat.

The front of the apron barely covers his chest; he's giving me a little peepshow whenever he has to turn, nipples peeking out from where the fabric meets the thin strap wrapped around his neck. I follow the edge of the apron down lower, picturing what's hidden beneath.

"Emma?" I hear Diego call.

"Huh?" I wipe my mouth, finding a small amount of drool.

Diego chuckles, low and smoky. He points to me with his tongs. "Stop checking out my sausage and focus." I can't help laughing. "Now, who else made an offer?" he repeats.

I take a sip before answering. "So we have London, obviously."

"Obviously." He rolls his eyes, but with a smirk. How is it possible that I've found the man who's the perfect combination of cute and sexy?

"You know, it's pretty hard to have a serious conversation when you're in there looking like," I motion with the hand holding the wine glass to his general area, "*that.*"

"If the naked chef is too distracting, the naked chef can become the clothed chef."

"No, no. I promise to pay attention."

"Good girl, because I'd hate to punish you later for it." He threatens while flipping the sausage for the last time.

I bite my lip, thinking about whether those punishments would be worth it. I shake the mental image out of my head. Focus now, play *later*, Emma.

"Dallas and New York have both sent offers over for me. But there's one other office that is emailing their offer tomorrow, and I think it's the one I'm most excited for. Somewhere we can forget about this damn humidity."

Diego lets out a chuckle as he turns off the burner. "Which location is that?" After plating up our food, he grabs two forks and knives, along with our plates and joins me at the bar.

"Hopefully you like pierogies and kielbasa." Diego gives me a look conveying his interest. "How do you feel about Poland?"

"You know I'm always ready for an adventure with you, Sweetheart."

ACKNOWLEDGMENTS

I would first like to start by thanking my husband once again, because a dedication page isn't enough thanks for the level of support you have given me, not just through the ups and downs of writing, but through our time spent together.

My two amazing daughters, I love and cherish you more than words can describe. Without your reminder of how important it is to live a life filled with creativity, I'm not sure I would've embarked on this journey.

My sisters and parents, who I've spent countless hours talking about this series to. Thank you for always having a listening ear and encouraging me to keep writing.

A special thank you to my wonderful editor, Amy Pritt. You were the first person to read Rose-Tinted and were a crucial part in making it the book that it is today. I am forever grateful for your kind words of encouragement and helpful critiques.

I would also like to thank my Beta readers. Raquel, Bree, Dee, and Jennifer, you all are such rockstars. Your comments and feedback helped me create the best possible version of Rose-Tinted. Thank you for making it so easy to trust you with my first book baby.

Also, to my ARC readers. Thank you for giving me the opportunity to share Emma and Diego's story with you. With your help, you've spread the word about Rose-Tinted, allowing more people to fall in love with them as much as I have.

And finally, I would like to acknowledge my deepest appreciation to my readers. Thank you for loving this story as much as I do!

See you all in France!

-A